ILLUSION'S VEIL . . .

The forcefield stretched away on both sides into infinity.

"How do we get through?" Rheba asked.

"The field thins out here and illusions appear," her Yhelle shipmate replied. "To get where you want to go, just pick a destination's clan symbol and step through. Be fast, though. It's no fun getting caught between illusions."

Rheba looked uneasily at the kaleidoscopic forces of the veil, changing even as she watched. She was loathe to let her illusionist friends out of reach for fear of being forever lost in a shifting Yhelle fantasy.

Then, making her decision, she motioned the illusionists to get on with it. They joined hands and concentrated, riding the veil like an unruly beast. Finally, grudgingly, the field thinned, revealing cracked pavements and desolation.

The illusionists walked through and vanished. And, after an instant of hesitation, Rheba and Kirtn followed. The field broke over them like black water, drowning them. . . .

SIGNET Science Fiction You'll Enjoy

Dancer's Illusion

by
Ann Maxwell

A SIGNET BOOK
NEW AMERICAN LIBRARY
TIMES MIRROR

Copyright © 1983 by Ann Maxwell

SIGNET, SIGNET CLASSICS, MENTOR, PLUME, MERIDIAN AND NAL BOOKS
are published by The New American Library, Inc.,
1633 Broadway, New York, New York 10019

First Printing, August, 1983

1 2 3 4 5 6 7 8 9

PRINTED IN THE UNITED STATES OF AMERICA

I

The tension in the *Devalon*'s crowded control room was as unbearable as the air. The ship's life-support systems were overloaded. Passengers and crew were being kept alive, but not in comfort. Rheba wiped her forehead with the back of her arm. Both arm and face were sweaty, both pulsed with intricate gold lines that were visible manifestations of the power latent within her.

She looked at her Bre'n. Rivulets of sweat darkened Kirtn's suede-textured skin. The fine, very short copper fur that covered his powerful body made the control room's heat even more exhausting for him than it was for her.

"Ready?" she said, wiping her face again.

"Yesss," hissed Fssa, dangling his head out of her hair. His thin, infinitely flexible body was alive with metallic colors. He loved heat.

"Not you, snake," Rheba muttered. "Kirtn."

The Bre'n smiled, making his yellow eyes seem even more slanted in their mask of almost invisibly fine gold fur. "Ready. Maybe it will be an ice planet," he added hopefully.

Rheba looked around the control room at the sweaty races of Fourth People she had rescued from a lifetime of slavery on Loo. Some were furred, some not. They had as many colors as Rainbow, the Zaarain construct that was at the moment a necklace knocking against Kirtn's chest.

All of the passengers had two things in common: their past slavery on Loo and their present hope that it would be their planet's number that would be chosen by the *Devalon*'s computer in the lottery. The winner was given the best prize of all—a trip home.

The owners of the ship, Rheba and Kirtn, were not included in the lottery. Their home had died beneath the hot lash of an unstable sun, sending the young Bre'n and his even younger Senyas fire dancer fleeing for their lives. They had survived, and they had managed to find two others who had survived. One was Ilfn, a woman of Kirtn's race. The other was her storm dancer, a blind boy called Lheket. Rheba had sworn to find more survivors, to comb the galaxy until she had found enough Bre'ns and Senyasi to ensure that neither race became extinct.

But first she had light-years to go and promises to keep. She had to deliver each one of the people on the ship to his, her, or *hir* home. The first such delivery—to a planet called Daemen—had nearly killed both her and Kirtn. Since then there had been several other planets, none dangerous. But each number the computer spat out could be another Daemen.

"You may be ready," Rheba sighed, "but I'm not sure I am."

She licked her lips, then whistled a phrase in the intricate, poetic Bre'n language. Instantly the computer displayed a number in the air just above her head.

311:Yhelle

Kirtn whistled in lyric relief. That was the most civilized planet in the Yhelle Equality. Certainly there could be no difficulty there. Besides, the Yhelle illusionists on board had more than earned their chance to go home. Without them, Kirtn certainly would have died on Daemen, and Rheba, too.

On the other hand, they would miss the illusionists. It was piquant not knowing who or what would appear in the crowded corridors of the *Devalon.*

Fssa keened softly into Rheba's ear. He, too, would miss the illusionists. When they were practicing their trade, they had a fey energy about them that could appeal only to a Fssireeme—or another illusionist.

"I know, snake," Rheba said, stroking him with a fingertip. She sent currents of energy through her hair to console the Fssireeme. "But it wouldn't be fair to ask them to wait just because we like their company."

Fssa subsided. With a final soft sound he vanished into her seething gold hair.

Rheba stood on tiptoe to see over the heads of the people crowding the control room. "Where are they?"

Kirtn, taller than anyone else, spotted the illusionists. "By the hall."

"Are they happy?"

"With an illusionist, who can tell?" he said dryly. Then he relented and lifted Rheba so that she could see.

"They don't look happy," she said.

Kirtn whistled a phrase from the "Autumn Song," one of Deva's most famous poems, variations on the theme of parting.

"Yes, but they still should be happy," whistled Rheba. "They're going *home*."

All of her longing for the home she had lost was in her Bre'n whistle. Kirtn's arms tightened around her. She had been so young; she had so few memories to comfort her.

And she was right. The illusionists did not look happy.

With a silent sigh, Kirtn put her back on her own feet. He tried to imagine why anyone would be reluctant to go back home after years of slavery. What he imagined did not comfort him. At best, they might simply dislike their planet. At worst, they might have been exiled and therefore did not expect to be welcomed back.

He pushed through the disappointed people who were slowly leaving the control room. Rheba followed, unobtrusively protected by two J/taals. On Loo, the mercenaries had chosen her as their J/taaleri, the focus of their devotion. They continued to protect her whenever she permitted it—and even when she did not.

"Congratulations," said Kirtn, smiling at the illusionists. "The ship is computing *replacements* from here to Yhelle. Are there any defenses we should know about?"

F'lTiri tried to smile. "Probably not. No one has fought with Yhelle for thousands of years. The last people who did conquered us. They retreated five years later, babbling." This time he managed a true smile. "Yhelle is hard on people who expect reality to be what it seems to be."

"Is that what you're doing?" said Rheba. "Practicing?"

I'sNara's confusion showed in her voice as well as her face. "What do you mean? We're appearing as ourselves right now. No illusions."

"Then why aren't you happy?" Rheba asked bluntly. "You're going home."

The two illusionists looked quickly at one another. At the same instant, both of them appeared to glow with pleasure. Rheba made an impatient gesture. She had been with them long enough to separate their illusions from their reality . . . some of the time.

"Forget it," she snapped. "Just tell me what's wrong."

"Nothing," they said in unison. "We're just overcome with surprise," added i'sNara. "We never expected to go home so soon."

Kirtn grunted. Their voices were as unhappy as their faces

had been a few moments ago. "Fssa, tell everyone to clear the control room and get ready for replacement."

The Fssireeme slid out of Rheba's hair into her hands. There he underwent a series of astonishing transformations as he made the necessary apparatus to speak a multitude of languages simultaneously. It was not difficult for the Fssireeme. The snakes had evolved on a hot, gigantic planet as sonic mimics, then had been genetically modified during one of the earlier Cycles. The result was a resilient, nearly indestructible translator who needed only a few phrases to learn any new language.

In response to the languages pouring out of the snake, people hurried out of the control room. When the illusionists turned to go, Kirtn stopped them. "Not you two."

He waited until only four plus Fssireeme were left in the room. He stretched with obvious pleasure, flexing his powerful body. The *Devalon* had been designed originally for twelve crew members and hurriedly rigged for the two who had survived Deva's solar flare. Even after dropping off people on five planets, the remainder of the refugees from Loo's slave pens seriously overloaded the ship's facilities. As a result, Kirtn spent most of his time trying not to crush smaller beings.

"Now," he said, focusing on i'sNara and f'lTiri, "what's the problem?"

The illusionists looked at each other, then at him, then at Rheba. "We're not sure we should go home," said i'sNara simply.

"Why?" asked Rheba, slipping Fssa back into her hair.

The illusionists looked at each other again. "We are appearing naked before you," said f'lTiri, his voice strained.

Rheba blinked and began to object that they were fully dressed as far as she could tell, then realized that they meant naked of illusions, not clothes. "That's rare in your culture, isn't it?"

"Yes," they said together. "Only with children, very close friends and sometimes with lovers. A sign of deep trust."

"I see." Rheba hesitated, knowing the illusionists were proud as only ex-slaves could be. "You didn't leave your planet voluntarily . . . ?"

"No."

Rheba and Kirtn exchanged a long look. She slid her fingers between his. They did not have the intraspecies telepathy of the J/taals or the interspecies telepathy of master mind dancers, yet they sometimes could catch each other's thoughts when they were in physical contact. Once, on Daemen, telepathy had come without contact; but Kirtn had been dying then, too high a price to pay for soundless speech. Now there was no urgency, just a long sigh and the word *trouble* shared between them.

"Tell us." Rheba's tone was more commanding than inviting, but her smile was sympathetic.

"It's a long story," began f'lTiri, "and rather complex."

Kirtn laughed shortly. "I'd expect nothing else from a culture based on pure illusions."

"Don't leave anything out," added Rheba. "If we'd known more about Daemen, we would have had less trouble there."

F'lTiri sighed. "I'd rather be invisible while I talk," he muttered. "Holding invisibility couldn't be much harder than telling you. . . ." He made a curt gesture. "As you said, our society is based on illusion. Nearly all Yhelles can project illusions. Some are better than others. There are different categories of illusion, as well."

Rheba remembered the young Yhelle illusionist she had seen on Loo. His gift was appearing to be the essence of everyone's individual sexual desire. The result had been compelling for the audience and confusing for her—she had seen the appearance of Kirtn on the young illusionist, yet Kirtn was her mentor, not her lover. The image still returned to disturb her. She banished it each time, telling herself that it was merely her knowledge of legendary Bre'n sensuality that had caused her to identify Yhelle illusion as Bre'n reality.

"The result is that while other societies have tangible means of rewarding their members, Yhelle doesn't," continued f'lTiri. "What good is a jeweled badge when even children can make the *appearance* of that badge on themselves? What good is a magnificent house when most Yhelles can project the appearance of a castle? What good is a famous face when almost anyone can duplicate the appearance of that face? What good is beauty? Even poetry can appear more exquisite than it is. One of my daughters could project a poem that would make you weep . . . but when anyone else read the words, they were merely ordinary."

The illusionist sighed, and i'sNara took up the explanation. "He doesn't mean that everything on Yhelle is illusory. Our money is real enough most of the time, because we need it for the framework of real food and cloth and shelter we build our illusions on. But the elaboration of necessity that is the foundation of most societies just doesn't exist on Yhelle. We have nearly everything we want—or at least the *appearance* of having it." She looked anxiously from Bre'n to Senyas. "Do you understand?"

"I doubt it," said Kirtn, "but I'm trying. Do you mean that a Yhelle could take mush and make it appear to be a feast?"

"Yes," said i'sNara eagerly. "A good illusionist can even make it *taste* like a feast."

"But can't you see through the illusions?" asked Rheba.

Both illusionists looked very uncomfortable. "That's a . . . difficult . . . subject for us. Like cowardice for the J/taals or reproduction for the Lerns."

"That may be," said Rheba neutrally, "but it's crucial. We won't be shocked."

F'lTiri almost smiled. Even so, his words were slow, his tone reluctant. "Some illusions are easier to penetrate than others. It depends on your skill, and the power of the creator. But it is unspeakably . . . crude . . . to comment on reality. And who would want to? Who prefers real mush to an apparent feast? Especially as they are equally nourishing. Do you understand?"

Bre'n and Senyas exchanged a long silence. "Keep going," said Rheba at last. "We're behind you, but we're not out of breath yet."

I'sNara's laughter was light and pleasing. Rheba realized that it was the first time she had heard either Yhelle really laugh.

"You'll catch up soon," said f'lTiri confidently. "After Loo and Daemen, I don't think anything can stay ahead of either of you."

Rheba smiled sourly and said nothing. They had been lucky to survive those planets.

"We don't have much government," continued f'lTiri. "It's difficult to tax illusions, and without taxes government isn't much more than an amusement for wellborn families. There's some structure, of course. We are Fourth People, and Fourth People seem doomed to hierarchy. We're organized into clans, or rather, *dis*organized into clans. Each clan specializes—traders or artists or carpenters, that sort of thing. I'sNara and I belong to the Liberation clan. We're master snatchers," he said proudly. "Thieves."

Rheba blinked. The illusionists treated reality as a dirty

word and thievery as a proud occupation. She sensed Kirtn's yellow eyes on her but did not return his look. She was afraid she would laugh, offending the Yhelles.

"And quite good at it," said Kirtn blandly, "if Onan is any proof of your skill. Without you two we'd still be stuck in Nontondondo, trying to scrape up the price of an Equality navtrix."

F'lTiri made a modest noise. "We were out of practice. The only thing we've stolen in five years worth mentioning is our freedom—and *you* stole that for us." He sighed. "Anyway, we weren't good enough on Yhelle. We were assigned to steal the Ecstasy Stones from the Redistribution clan. We were caught and sold to Loo."

"I'm out of breath," said Rheba flatly. "You spent a lot of time telling us about appearances being equal or superior to reality, then you tell us that you tried to steal something. Why? Couldn't you just make an illusion of the Ecstasy Stones?"

"That's the whole point. Oh, we could make something that looked like the Stones, but no illusionist in Yhelle history has been able to make anything that *felt* like the Stones. That's their value," said f'lTiri. "They make you feel loved. That's their illusion."

Rheba looked at Kirtn, silently asking if he understood. He smiled. "You're too pragmatic, fire dancer. It's your Senyas genes. Think of it this way. The Yhelles have, or *seem* to have, everything that Fourth People have pursued since the First of the Seventeen Cycles. Wealth, beauty, power over their environment—if there is a name for it, the Yhelles have someone able to make it appear. Or," he added dryly, "*appear* to appear. The illusion of love is the only exception."

He looked at the illusionists. They moved their hands in a gesture of agreement. "Exactly," said the Yhelles together.

F'lTiri continued, "We create illusions, but we aren't deluded by them. Illusionists who fool themselves are, by definition, fools. So when it comes to love, we're no better off than the rest of the Fourth People."

"Except for the Stones," put in i'sNara. "Their fabulous illusion—if it indeed *is* an illusion—is love. They love you totally. The more Stones you have, the more intense is the feeling of loving and being loved."

"That would make them valuable in any society," said Rheba.

"Perhaps," conceded f'lTiri. "But in Serriolia, the city-

state where we were born and the most accomplished illusionists live, the illusion of everything is available. Except love.
In Serriolia, the Ecstasy Stones are priceless. Most of our
history hinges on the masterful illusions that have gone into
stealing one or more of the Stones. Master snatchers of each
generation used to try their skills on whoever owned one or
more Stones."

"Used to?" asked Kirtn. "What happened?"

"The Redis—the Redistribution clan—snatched almost all
of Serriolia's Stones. You see, the Redis were formed out of
the discontented thieves of various clans. That was hundreds
of years ago. For generations, the clan trained and sent out
platoons of master snatchers. In the beginning, the clan's sole
reason for existence was to steal Ecstasy Stones from the
selfish few who had them. The Redis hoped to combine the
Stones into one Grand Illusion available to every citizen."

"That doesn't sound too bad," said Rheba hesitantly.

"It wasn't," agreed i'sNara. "But the Redis didn't share.
Only Redis were allowed into the Stones' presence. And only
a few Redis, at that. So another clan was formed out of
unhappy snatchers, the Liberation clan. Besides," she smiled,
"there were all those highly trained snatchers and nothing to
practice on but their own clan—unthinkable. Stealing from
your own clan is grounds for *disillusionment*."

"And you were caught stealing the Stones?" said Kirtn.
"Is that why you were exiled?"

"We're Libs," said f'lTiri proudly. "It was our duty to
snatch Stones from the Redis. But the Redis didn't have any
sense of humor. It wasn't just that we were snatchers—our
history is full of snatchers—but that our mere existence suggested that the Redis were not holding the Stones for the good
of *all* Serriolians. The Redis Charter is quite specific about
the Redis stealing Stones for high purposes rather than for
selfish pleasures. The Redis Charter is posted in every clan
hall. The fact that the Charter rather than the Stones circulates
among the clans is attributed to the Stones' extreme worth."

"Or the Charter's extreme worthlessness," added i'sNara
sarcastically.

Rheba rubbed her temples and wondered why she had
urged the Yhelles to tell her everything. She was totally confused.
Her hair crackled. Kirtn stroked the seething mass, gently
pulling out excess energy. After a moment her hair settled
into golden waves that covered her shoulders.

"What's the worst that can happen if you go back?" Rheba asked bluntly.

"That's just it," said i'sNara, her voice soft. "We don't know."

"Will your clan disown you?" asked Kirtn.

"No," answered f'lTiri. "Never."

"You haven't broken any local laws?" pressed Rheba.

"No."

"Then why are you reluctant to go home?"

"We may be sent after the Stones again, and caught again, and sold to Loo again. Or worse."

Rheba tried not to groan aloud. The more she heard of Yhelle and Serriolia, the less she liked it. She could, and should, just set down in Serriolia, sadly but firmly say goodbye to the illusionists, and then lift for deep space with all the power in the *Devalon*'s drive.

But without f'lTiri's masterful illusions, a fire dancer and a Bre'n would have died on Loo or Daemen.

"You don't know what will happen to you?" said Kirtn, his voice divided between statement and question.

"No, we don't."

Kirtn sighed. "Then we'd better go find out."

II

Rheba activated the privacy shield on her bunk, enclosing herself in darkness. She sat cross-legged, eyes unfocused, her breathing slow and even. Light bloomed from her hands, curling up from akhenet lines of power that were so dense her fingers seemed solid gold. Within the pool of light, like a leaf floating on a sunset pond, lay her Bre'n Face. She stared at it, letting her worry about the illusionists' future slide away with each breath.

The Face had been carved by Kirtn and given to his dancer when she was ten years old. Each Senyas dancer had a Bre'n carving; no Face was the same. Normally Rheba wore the carving as an earring, depending from the seven intricate fastenings that insured against accidental loss. It was more than a decoration, and more than a pledge of Kirtn's Choice of her as an akhenet partner. The Face was also a teaching device. Dancers, especially young ones, were supposed to meditate upon their individual Face every day. In time, the Face would teach them all they needed to know about the relationship between Senyas and Bre'n.

Rheba, however, had not spent enough time in meditation. The fact that she had spent most of her hours since Deva's burn-off in pursuit of bare survival did not excuse her. If her partnership with Kirtn went sour because she did not understand what was required of her, neither one of them would survive. Bre'ns whose akhenet partners thwarted them long enough went into a berserker state called *rez*. In that state they killed everything within reach—most especially their dancers—and ended by killing themselves.

No one knew precisely what drove a Bre'n to *rez*, or if anyone did, she had not been told. Kirtn had slid into *rez* once on Loo. Only a combination of her innate skill as a fire dancer and Fssa's incredible ability to withstand heat had saved them from burning to ash and gone. Afterward she had silently vowed to study the Face no matter what happened. Except for her time on Daemen, she had done just that.

She gathered her thoughts, focusing only on the Face. It looked back at her, benign and aloof, waiting. Then, as she inhaled, the Face changed into a Bre'n profile against a subtly seething field of dancer energy. In the next breath it was two faces, Bre'n and . . . was it Senyas? Was that bright shadow a young woman's face, eyes half closed, transported by an unknown emotion? Her smile was slow, mysterious, as inhumanly beautiful as Kirtn, but the woman was Senyas, not Bre'n. It looked like her own face, but she was not half so beautiful, had never felt an emotion so intense.

The Face shifted with each breath, each pulse of her blood. It was countless faces now, waves on an ocean stretching back into time, waves swelling toward future consummation on an unseen shore. Bre'ns and Senyasi intertwined, turning slowly, akhenet pairs focused in one another, touching and turning until they flowed together, inseparable.

Their faces were all familiar, all the same, Kirtn's face with yellow eyes hotter than dancer fire. He turned and saw her and she burned. He called her and she came, turning slowly, touching him passionately, and his eyes another kind of fire touching her. . . .

Rheba's hands shook, breaking the Face's hold on her mind. She realized that her akhenet lines were alight, burning in the closed compartment until the heat was stifling. Reflexively she damped her fire, sucking energy out of the air until it was a bearable temperature.

She did not look at the earring. She fastened the Face to her ear with fingers that still trembled. She was glad that Kirtn was not with her. What would he think of a dancer so undisciplined that she could not control her own thoughts? Instead of learning more about Bre'n and Senyas, her willful mind had combined her present worry about the illusionists with her past experience on Loo, when a young Yhelle illusionist had appeared as Kirtn, sensuality made flesh.

She did not know why that experience had gone so deep into her psyche, but it had. Bad enough that she had dreamed about it while asleep; to have it interfere with dancer meditation was intolerable.

She whistled a curt phrase. The shield retracted into the bunk. M/dere waited outside. The J/taal smiled and gestured for Rheba to follow. Rheba did, wondering who wanted her and for what. Without Fssa there was no way of knowing;

J/taals did not speak Universal, Senyas or Bre'n, and she did not speak J/taal.

Kirtn was in the control room arguing with the illusionists. Fssa, dangling from Kirtn's neck, let out a delighted hiss when he sensed Rheba's unique energy fields. Without pausing in his argument, Kirtn lofted the snake in Rheba's direction. She snatched him out of the air, bracing herself as his weight smacked into her hands.

No matter how many times she held him, she was always surprised. His dense flesh was unreasonably heavy. In her hair, however, he weighed almost nothing. He had once told her that he "translated" her dancer energy into his own private support system. She had questioned him further, only to be told in arch tones that she "lacked the vocabulary to understand."

"If you get any heavier I'll drop you," she muttered as she wove him into her long hair.

"You'll break your toe," whistled Fssa smugly. Whenever possible, he used the whistle language of Bre'n. It required the least amount of shape-changing to reproduce. In addition, Bre'n was lyric, multileveled and evocative, all of which made it irresistible to the linguistically inclined Fssireeme. "Don't take a snake's word for it," he encouraged. "Drop me."

Rheba made a flatulent sound, a Fssireeme way of expressing disgust. Fssa's hissing laughter tickled her neck.

Both illusionists began shouting. As they shouted they seemed to grow taller and wider with each word until they loomed threateningly over the control room.

"What's the problem with them?" Rheba said softly to Fssa.

"Fourth People." Fssa sighed like a human. "Sometimes I think you pay for having legs by lacking brains."

"Tell me something new, snake."

"The illusionists are trying to convince Kirtn that he should just drop them at Serriolia's spaceport and leave. He's trying to convince them that—"

Kirtn's roar drowned out Fssa's speech. The snake hummed in admiration. As far as he was concerned, Bre'ns made the best sounds of any Fourth People.

"—going with you! Now shut up and get ready for the landing!"

"But—"

"*Shut up!*"

Rheba winced. The illusionists slowly deflated until they were normal size. Kirtn took a deep breath and reached for his lunch—a cup of mush that nourished the body and left the palate to fend for itself. With the life-support systems overloaded, it was the best the ship could do. He tasted the mush, grimaced, and slammed the cup into its nook on the control console.

"Cold." It was just one word, but whistled in Bre'n it described a world of disgust.

Rheba walked over to the cup. She pointed at it with her finger. Energy flared for an instant. She handed the cup to her disgruntled Bre'n. "Don't burn yourself."

"The zoolipt would take care of it."

Rheba shuddered. She did not like to think about the turquoise alien that had entered their bodies on Daemen. Kirtn was more philosophical than she about the `zoolipt, perhaps because it had saved his life when the Seurs were doing their best to kill him. She did not deny that the turquoise soup had its uses. She was just uneasy knowing that a Zaarain hospital had taken up residence in her cells. Things Zaarain had a habit of being unpredictable.

The ship's lights flickered so briefly that only she and the energy-sensitive Fssireeme noticed it. A chime sounded twice, then twice again. Fssa's voice, via a memory cube, notified the inhabitants in thirty-three languages that landing was imminent.

I'sNara approached, a look of determination on her normally bland features. "We've decided that we want to be put down on Tivveriolia. It has a good spaceport with all the most modern downside connectors."

"What's the transportation like from there?" asked Rheba innocently.

"Very fast. F'lTiri and I won't have any problem at all getting to Serrio . . ." Her voice faded as she realized that Rheba had tricked her into admitting that Serriolia was still their ultimate destination. "You're worse than he is."

Rheba smiled. "I've been working on it."

I'sNara hesitated, then whispered, "Thank you," and hurriedly withdrew to stand next to her husband. Neither illusionist spoke again until the ship touched down and the downside connectors were in place.

"No formalities?" asked Kirtn when the call board remained dark.

"If you need anything more than the port supplies, you just

send out a call in Universal. If anyone is interested, you'll get
an answer. The port facilities are free, although it's custom-
ary to show yourselves on Reality Street as payment. You
two will be a sensation," added f'lTiri. "We've never seen
your kind before. You'll be the source of a thousand new
illusions."

"And after Reality Street?" asked Rheba.

"The Liberation clan hall. They'll tell us where our family
is, and"—he smiled grimly—"whether we have to spend the
rest of our lives projecting invisibility."

Rheba and Kirtn looked at the control board. A series of
numbers and colors moved in a continuous loop, describing
the environment around the ship. She sighed. Hardly an ice
planet. It was warm, even for Senyas tastes. Kirtn would
begin to shed after an hour out there.

The illusionists stood eagerly by the downside door. They
had no luggage, having escaped Loo with no more than their
lives. When the door retracted, they stepped eagerly onto the
ramp.

Kirtn and Rheba stood quietly for a moment, letting their
bodies respond to the alien planet. The gravity was slightly
heavier than Daemen's had been, but the difference was not
enough to be tedious. All of the Equality planets—indeed, all
of the planets inhabited by Fourth People—were functionally
identical in such gross characteristics as gravity and atmo-
spheric content. Where one Fourth People could survive, all
could survive.

The degree of comfort in which Fourth People could survive changed markedly from planet to planet, however. Loo
had been too cold for Senyas tastes, Daemen too barren, and
Onan too chaotic. Yhelle felt to Rheba as if it would be too
hot and far too humid.

Kirtn grunted as though agreeing with her unspoken thoughts.
Sweat sprang beneath his weapon harness and brief shorts.
Within moments, his whole body was wet. Even the gold
mask surrounding his eyes was dark.

"You won't need my robe to keep warm here," said Kirtn,
glancing down at his fire dancer. "And I don't need my fur."

"I could skin you," she suggested, lips straight in an effort
not to smile.

"Promises, promises. By the Inmost Fire," he sighed, "I
wonder what an illusion of coolness is worth here."

A thoughtful look crossed Rheba's face. She held her
hands near his face and concentrated. Her hands pulsed with

subdued gold, but no flames came. Instead, a cool sensation came to him as she sucked heat out of the air around him.

"How's that?" she asked.

He smiled and hugged her. "Nice."

She concentrated again, trying to keep the heat at bay. He blew gently on her lips, teasing and distracting her. "Don't tire yourself out keeping me cool. I'll survive."

"But you'll shed," she said flatly. She held up her hands. Tiny coppery hairs stuck to her moist skin. "You're shedding already!" She made a sound of mock disgust. Every spring on Deva, she had teased her mentor about his unsavory habits. "Senyasi never shed."

"Really?" whistled Kirtn, pulling a long gold hair off his shoulder harness. "What's this?"

"An illusion," she said serenely. "We're on Yhelle, remember?"

Kirtn looked around. The spaceport with its scarred apron and downside connectors looked like every other Equality spaceport he had seen. Cleaner, perhaps. Certainly cleaner than Daemen's had been. But for a planet of illusionists, the landscape was disappointingly mundane. Only later did he realize just how subtle Yhelle's first illusion really was.

"Let's get it over with," said Rheba, taking his sweaty hand in hers and pulling him down the ramp. " 'The sooner we begin, the sooner we end,' " she intoned, quoting an ancient Senyas engineering text.

The Bre'n gulped a chestful of the stifling air and followed, whistling minor-key curses.

As Kirtn and Rheba left the *Devalon*'s protective radius, the J/taals and their war dogs—clepts—flowed smoothly outward until Rheba was surrounded. She was their J/taaleri, and their job was to see that she came to no harm.

A clept ranged by i'sNara, its silver eyes smoldering in Yhelle's humid light. I'sNara made a startled sound and stopped.

"What's wrong?" said Rheba.

"The J/taals," said i'sNara. "They're forbidden."

"What?" said Kirtn.

"Forbidden," repeated i'sNara. "They're death, and death doesn't respect illusions."

Rheba stared at the illusionist's face. "But—"

I'sNara simply looked more stubborn. F'lTiri came and stood by her side. "It's true," he said. "If the J/taals are along, every Yhelle will be against us, even our own clan."

"Ice and ashes!" swore Rheba. "Fssa, tell the J/taals to take their clepts and wait in the ship." Then, remembering Daemen, where the J/taals had disobeyed and followed her, she added, "Make sure they know that I'll be worse off if they're with me than if they're in the ship."

Fssa shifted in her hair until he was the proper shape to emit the grunts, clicks and gratings that composed most of J/taal communication. Their language was very primitive, because intraspecies telepathy made speech useful only with outsiders and enemies.

The J/taals did not like one syllable of what they heard. That much was obvious from the ferocious expressions that settled on their faces. Equally obvious was the fact that they were not going to protest their orders.

"Why aren't they arguing?" asked Kirtn.

"They know it's useless," whistled Fssa. "Yhelle's phobia about J/taals is common knowledge in the Equality. But they weren't sure Rheba knew, since she isn't from the Equality."

Rheba frowned. "They won't try to follow me as they did on Daemen?"

"No." Fssa's whistle carried overtones of absolute confidence.

"Explain," she snapped in Senyas, the language of precision and directness.

Hastily, the snake shifted to create Senyas vocal apparatus. "It would be pointless for them to follow. Without Yhelle guides—and no illusionist would come near them—they would be hopelessly lost in Serriolia's streets."

"Why?"

"Illusions."

"That doesn't make sense," said Rheba, glancing around the spaceport, where everything looked normal to the point of boredom.

"It will," the snake hissed.

III

Reality Street led at an oblique angle away from the spaceport. The transition from port to city was ominous. An ebony arch loomed above the entrance to the street. The arch was filled with a sable nothingness that was like a curtain sealing off whatever was beyond.

When Rheba glanced around she saw nothing but the spaceport. There were no buildings rising beyond the aprons, no hills or mountains or clouds, nothing but downside connectors and the functional, asymmetrical machines that cared for spaceships. It was as though the spaceport were the whole of the island city-state of Serriolia.

The illusionists looked back to where their friends waited, gestured encouragingly, and vanished into the black emptiness beneath the arch. Kirtn and Rheba looked at each other. As one, they stopped.

"What's wrong?" whistled Fssa.

The snake's head rested on top of Rheba's. His twin multi-colored sensors wheeled, "seeing" his surroundings in a barrage of returning sound waves. His whole length was incandescent, burning beneath her rippling hair like very hot embers beneath flames. He was in a high state of excitement. He liked new planets almost as much as he liked new languages. Especially warm planets, although by Fssireeme standards Yhelle was only a few shades removed from frigid. It was, however, much better than Daemen had been.

"We don't like the look of that black arch," said Rheba. "Although the illusionists didn't seem to mind it."

"Arch? Where?"

Kirtn turned and stared from the snake to the enormous arch looming in front of them. "Right ahead of us."

Fssa's sensors focused into the area beyond his two friends. He moved his head restlessly from side to side like a clept questing for an elusive scent. He hissed and turned back to Kirtn. "I don't see anything but air."

"You don't *see* anything at all," muttered the Bre'n, referring to the fact that Fssireemes were blind to the wavelengths of light that were the visible spectrum for Fourth People.

"That's what I said," whistled Fssa, a musical confusion in his trill.

"No," said Rheba, touching Kirtn's arm. "Fssa is right. The arch must be an illusion that exists only in the visible wavelengths of light. Since Fssa uses other means of 'seeing,' he isn't fooled."

"Wait here," said Kirtn.

He strode toward the arch, stopping a hand's width away. He reached out . . . and his fingers vanished into darkness.

The illusionists reappeared beneath the arch, startling him. They were polite enough to conceal their smiles, although laughter rippled in their voices.

"It's only a simple illusion," said f'lTiri, dismissing the arch with a flip of his hand.

"It doesn't even have texture," added i'sNara, poking holes in the arch with her tiny white hands. "It never changes. Even our youngest son could do better."

"Fssa wasn't fooled," Rheba said, walking up behind Kirtn.

F'lTiri looked at the Fssireeme with new appreciation. "I'd like to see the planet you came from, snake."

"So would I," responded the Fssireeme in a sad tremolo.

Rheba touched him with a comforting fingertip. The snake had been born—if that was the proper term for Fssireeme reproduction—beyond the Equality's borders, on a planet so distant that no one knew its Equality name. In fact, neither the old Deva navtrix nor the new Equality navtrix had ever heard of a planet called Ssimmi. Fssa could not go home, because without a location on the navigation matrix, no one knew where in the galaxy his home was. And Fssa wanted very badly to go home.

"He uses sound waves to see," said Rheba. "That's why he saw through the arch's illusion."

I'sNara looked thoughtful. "That might help with some Yhelle illusions. But the most enduring illusions are based on reality. The best ones have feel and texture. The extraordinary ones precisely mimic reality in every way."

"Then how can you tell the difference?" asked Kirtn.

"When their creator gets bored or dies, his illusions vanish."

"You can tell the difference between normal illusions and reality?" asked Rheba.

"Of course."

"How?" she asked plaintively.

"How can you create fire?" asked f'lTiri.

She shrugged. "I'm a fire dancer. It's what I *do*."

"And we're illusionists. We can be fooled, though."

"And I can be burned," said Rheba wryly. She looked at the uninviting illusion ahead of her. "Why do you call it Reality Street?"

F'lTiri laughed. "Because most of the people who use the street are tourists, not illusionists. It's the only place a realist can go on Yhelle without a guide."

Kirtn sighed and turned to Rheba. "I'm ready if you are."

"You're a poet," she said accusingly. "You'd trade reality for a good illusion any day." But she followed him through the arch, for she was a dancer and he was her Bre'n.

Reality Street was a riot fit to boggle the sensory apparatus of any Fourth People worthy of the name. If a plant grew anywhere in the Equality, it grew along Reality Street. If an animal breathed anywhere in the Equality, it breathed on Reality Street. If anything was manufactured or imagined anywhere in the Equality, its counterpart thrived on Reality Street.

Or at least it appeared that way.

The city-state of Serriolia was the centerpiece of Yhelle's master illusionists. It also was the center of intra-Equality trade. Not everything on Reality Street was an illusion, but deciding what was and was not real would take a concatenation of First People . . . or perhaps a single Fssireeme.

It was early morning in Serriolia, but groups of people wandered Reality Street's straight line, stopping to marvel at various manifestations. The people were as mixed a group as Kirtn and Rheba had left behind on the *Devalon*. There were one or two races that they had not seen on Loo, though the Loo-chim had prided itself on owning two of every kind of living being known in the galaxy.

Kirtn thought that at least one of the strange races wandering Reality Street was an illusion. Even a Bre'n poet balked at accepting a tall, fluffy-tailed, rainbow-striped biped as a real Fourth People. Especially when it shook out flowered wings longer than it was tall. Its teeth, however, might have been real, so Kirtn was careful not to stare.

Nearby, a grove of Second People whispered between purple leaves. Laughter rustled and whiplike branches snapped in amusement. Kirtn remembered the carnivorous Second People he and Rheba had burned to stinking ash on Loo, though not in time to save the children who had stumbled into the grove's lethal embrace. He wondered if this grove, too, was insane.

He snarled soundlessly and looked away, not wanting to remember how the children had died. He hoped that the grove was only an illusion, and that Rheba would not see it at all. He glanced around and saw that she had stopped halfway down Reality Street. He walked back to her.

Rheba was entranced by a fern growing in lyric profusion among dark cobblestones. Long fronds rose in graceful curves. Each lacy frond was an iridescent blue, trembling with hidden life. A cool perfume pervaded the air near the fern. Hesitantly, she touched a frond. The fern bent down, enveloping her in scent.

"That's a beautiful illusion," she sighed. "I haven't touched or smelled anything that nice since the gold dust on Daemen."

I'sNara reached past Rheba and took a frond between her fingertips. She broke off a small piece and waited. The frond remained the same.

"That's either real or a class twelve," she said, sniffing the piece of plant appreciatively. "Probably real. Ghost ferns are difficult illusions. Not many get the scent just right."

"Where do they grow normally?"

"On Ghost."

Rheba turned to see if i'sNara was teasing her, but the illusionist seemed lost in her enjoyment of the fern's delicate scent. "I thought Ghost was just a myth."

"Oh no," said i'sNara, surprised. "It's not part of the Equality, but it's real enough."

"Have you ever seen a Fifth People?" asked Kirtn.

"They're rather hard to see," said i'sNara wryly. "I've never had the pleasure, but my mother's second grandfather saw a Ghost once."

"How did he know it wasn't an illusion?"

"Ghosts aren't illusions. Only a realist could confuse them."

Rheba was still trying to think of an answer when Kirtn distracted her.

"Look at that!" He pointed down the road, away from the spaceport.

A starsurfer was swooping down on them. Its vast, mirror-finish sail was belled out by an invisible wind. The sail worked as a huge lens, magnifying and reflecting their astonished faces, their mouths like black caves opening endlessly until sail and ship were swallowed up and nothing remained but a giggle drifting down from a nearby tree.

F'lTiri snickered. "I forgot to mention that Serriolia's children practice their trade on Reality Street. Only the young ones, though. Realists are such easy prey."

Kirtn turned toward the tree and bowed, adding a Bre'n whistle for good measure. The pink leaves shook. A small Yhelle leaped from a branch and hit the ground running.

"You scared him," said i'sNara, but there was no censure in her voice.

"I meant to compliment him," said Kirtn. "Being swallowed up by our own astonishment is a shrewd illusion for one so young."

"But he didn't know you were real. He'd never seen someone like you before, so he assumed you were an illusion," explained f'lTiri. "Then he tried to penetrate your illusion, and couldn't. Then he assumed you were at least a class eight teasing him by pretending to be a realist. So he fled, leaving you to tease tourists rather than one small Yhelle."

Rheba looked down the long, straight street. Colors she had no name for surged brightly on either side. In the distance, well back from the street, fantastic buildings grew, architecture representing every Cycle from First to Seventeenth, made up of every material from mud to force fields.

She sighed and rubbed her aching eyes. Itching eyes. They itched like new akhenet lines of power beneath her skin. She rubbed her shoulders where new lines had formed when she had been forced to tap a Zaarain core on Daemen. But it was not her shoulders that itched, it was the back of her eyes.

Kirtn bent over her and pulled her fingers away from her eyes. "Did you get something in them? Spores? Pollen?"

She blinked rapidly, but her eyes did not water. Nor did they feel as if anything foreign was in them. "They just itch in back. As if new lines are forming."

"I've never heard of a dancer getting lines back there." He looked carefully at her. Twin, cinnamon-colored eyes looked back at him, translucent pools with a hint of gold veining. The whites of her eyes were clear and glossy, visible sign of her health. "They look fine."

"They don't feel that way. The zoolipt must be asleep." She shook her head fiercely. "Wake up, you useless parasite. I *itch*!" Nothing happened. She whistled a Bre'n curse. "It did fine on my other akhenet lines. I only itched a little, even after wrestling with that Zaarain core."

Kirtn tilted back her chin. New lines lay gold beneath her tawny skin, thicker lines, deeply curved, line upon line sliding beneath the scarlet silk of her brief ship clothes. His whistle was a combination of disbelief and distress. "You're too young for so many lines, fire dancer. If you develop too quickly—"

He did not finish his sentence. He did not have to. Rheba knew that it was as dangerous to push a dancer's growth as it was to push a Bre'n balanced on the edge of *rez*. But there had been no choice, not on Daemen or Loo or Onan. They had done what they must to survive. If that forced her to develop too quickly, so be it. It was better than dying.

"Besides," said Rheba, as though she had been speaking aloud all the time, "I'm the first dancer to have a zoolipt inside. It will keep me healthy." She smiled sourly. "Until it gets tired of my taste, that is."

"At least you don't itch anymore."

"Except my eyes," she said, knuckling them in exasperation. "Oh well, nothing's perfect. Not even a Zaarain construct." She blinked rapidly and looked for the illusionists. They were gone. "Where are they?"

Kirtn looked around. All he saw was flowers, ferns, trees, and a cluster of First People humming softly among themselves. They must have stopped growing eons in the past, for their crystal faces were worn and dull. Their songs were still pure, though, as haunting as an autumn moonrise.

And then he realized that the stones were singing a Bre'n work song. The biggest stone laughed, shimmered, and became f'lTiri. Beside him was i'sNara, equally amused. The illusionists' pleasure was so transparent that Kirtn could not be angry. He smiled and made a gesture of defeat.

Fssa made a startled sound. "They fooled even me," he whistled. "Their sounds were real, and shaped just like First People."

"Did you bounce sound off us?" asked f'lTiri.

"No. I just listened."

"Try it."

The illusionists promptly became the image of First People. They chimed and quivered sweetly.

Fssa went through a series of transformations, then froze in an odd convolution of quills and cups. "Got you!"

The stones became furred quadrupeds sleeping in the sun, snoring deeply.

"Where did they go?" hissed Fssa, then answered his own question by changing shapes until he caught the illusionists again. "There!"

The furred animals became a carpet of flowers covered in silence. At least, to Rheba and Kirtn it was silence. To Fssa, it was a sound absorber. No matter which frequency he used to probe, no echo returned. The illusionists were effectively invisible to him. In desperation, he assumed the grotesque fungoid shape that he used to talk with Rainbow.

Rheba yelped and knocked Fssa out of her hair. "Forget it, snake! I'll take silent illusion to your sonic reality."

Fssa collapsed into a dark snake shape. "I didn't hurt you, did I? I barely whispered," he added meekly, turning black with chagrin.

She bent over and put him back into her hair. "Even a whisper on that wavelength gives me a headache."

I'sNara and f'lTiri reappeared, obviously delighted.

"You must be twelves," said Kirtn. He whistled in the sliding loops of Bre'n admiration.

"Alone, each of us is an eight," said i'sNara. "Together, we're nearly eleven. With our children or some of our friends, we're twelve." She laughed in exultation. "If you only knew how *good* it feels to stretch again! The Loo-chim never wanted anything more complex from us than an image of its own perfection staring out of its mirror."

"It's the first time we've really felt free," added f'lTiri in oblique apology. "But don't worry. We won't tease you or the snake anymore."

"Good," said the Bre'n. "Now, if you could just hold the rest of Serriolia to that promise . . ."

Fssa made a rude, fruity noise.

"You can say that again for me," muttered Rheba. She knew that Serriolia would be exactly what it was, an endless joke on nonillusionists.

With a final, flatulent mutter, Fssa buried himself up to his sensors in Rheba's consoling hair.

IV

By the time they reached the end of Reality Street, Rheba and Kirtn were in a state of sensory surfeit. They stood and stared at the force field that divided them from the rest of Yhelle. The field was even more daunting than the ominous arch had been.

Rheba allowed a filament of her energy to brush the outer edges of the field. There was a crackle and a sense of dissonant power in the instant before she disengaged. Kirtn looked at her, a question in his yellow eyes.

"If it isn't real, it's so close that it makes no difference," she said.

Kirtn asked no more questions. If a fire dancer said an energy field was real, then it was real in every way that mattered. "Can you penetrate it?"

She hesitated. "If I had to, I probably could. It's not Zaarain, but it's more complex than the power Loo or Onan used." She looked around, but saw no one other than Kirtn. She sighed. "Where or what are the illusionists now?"

He did not even bother to look. The illusionists had gone giddy with laughter and mutual transformations before they were two-thirds of the way down Reality Street. When last he had seen them they were a thunderhead stitched with lightning that looked suspiciously like a mass of Fssireemes.

"F'lTiri?" called Rheba. "I'sNara?"

There was no answer, unless a snicker from the pavement beneath their feet could be counted.

Her hair stirred, whispering strand over strand in murmur of gathering power. "Enough is too much," she muttered.

"What are you going to do?" asked Kirtn.

"See if illusions burn."

Kirtn's lips fought not to smile. "I should stop you, dancer."

"But you won't."

His lips lifted in a predatory smile. "What poet could resist finding out the colors of a burning illusion?"

She waited, but the illusionists did not appear. Her hair fanned out, hiding Fssa in a seething cloud of gold. He hissed ecstatically, reveling in the energy she drew into herself from her surroundings. He floated in a chaos of energy, supported by hot strands of dancer hair. It was as close to his Guardian-induced memories of home as he had come in the Equality.

Akhenet lines lighted beneath Rheba's skin. Whorls and curves and racing lines of gold shimmered as she rechanneled the energy she was drawing into herself. Her lines remained cool, however; this was only a minor dance. She would not even need the partnership of her Bre'n. She glanced up at him with a sidelong smile and a question. "Any favorites?"

He pointed to some small bushes that grew along the margins of the force field. The bushes bore gnarled, spotted fruit that gave off an unpleasant odor. A similar plant had grown in the Loo slave compound. The fleshy fruit was not poisonous, but it tasted as vile as it looked.

She half closed her eyes as she reached out to the plant with her dancer senses. Gold pooled in the palm of her hand, viscous energy waiting to be used. She tipped her hand and let the fluid drip down.

The plant stank and died.

"Must have been real," observed Kirtn.

Her hand moved on to the next plant. Gold dripped. The outline of the fruit glowed oddly, then vanished rather than burned. A tiny skeleton of a real plant remained, withered and obviously dead. She recalled her fire before it could touch the skeleton.

Kirtn squatted and examined the brittle remains. "Feels real," he said, sniffing and cautiously tasting a fragment of withered fruit. He spat it out immediately. "Tastes real."

"It was," said f'lTiri's voice. "A long time ago."

Kirtn and Rheba turned. The illusionists were back, appearing as bright-blue fish swimming in an invisible sea.

"The most enduring illusions are based on reality," said i'sNara's voice, issuing from a wide fish mouth. "An illusion of ripe fruit based on a withered reality is easy to make and very hard to see through."

Rheba eyed the row of ugly bushes. She gathered energy until her hair whipped wildly. She pointed to each bush in turn, and each bush shimmered into flame. She concentrated, building a tiny bridge from individual bushes to the force field. As long as the field was on, the fires would continue to burn.

"That's a rather nice effect," said one of the fish, swimming up and down the row of burning bushes. Then, "Ouch!" F'lTiri appeared suddenly, sucking on a scorched fingertip. He looked reproachfully at Rheba. "You could have warned me."

"What did you expect?" said Kirtn. "We're on Reality Street, remember?"

F'lTiri smiled ruefully. "You win. We'll behave."

I'sNara seemed to condense out of the air beside him. "But we have to have *some* illusions," she said plaintively.

"You don't have to play hide-and-seek," pointed out Rheba, her voice crisp.

I'sNara blushed, or appeared to. Her outline shimmered. She became a blue-skinned Loo, naked but for a slaveholder's arrogance. "Now you'll know who I am whenever you see me. A real Loo would wear a robe."

Rheba shuddered. She had hoped never again to see any Loo. "I prefer you as yourself."

"But I can't appear naked at home!" said i'sNara, shocked.

Rheba looked at the unclothed illusion, opened her mouth to protest, then gave up. She had a feeling that she would be a long time understanding the niceties of illusory conduct. She blinked rapidly and knuckled her eyes. It did not stop the itching, but it made her feel better.

"Which way do we go to get to your clan?" she said, dropping her hands to her side. "And if you try to tell me that way," she said, jerking her chin toward the force field, "I'll roast your teeth."

F'lTiri smiled, but as he was now in the guise of a Stelsan scout, complete with fangs and feathers, the gesture was not reassuring. "No more tricks, fire dancer. You have our word . . . but," he added wistfully, "it was lovely to play again."

Rheba knuckled her itching eyes and said nothing.

F'lTiri led them parallel to the force field that stretched across the width of Reality Street, terminating it in a sullen glimmer of energy. The field reminded Kirtn of the lid that had sealed slaves into the Loo-chim Fold.

Rheba's hair showed a distinct tendency to drift toward the field, drawn by its energetic promises. When she realized what was happening, she took her hair and knotted it at the nape of her neck. It would be dangerous to tap accidentally into the oddly shaped forces.

Fssa grumbled, but accommodated himself to his reduced

surroundings. He knew the danger of dissonant energies as well as she did.

Kirtn sighed and wished for less heat or less humidity. His copper skin-fur had become the color of rust. Darker trails of sweat divided over his body. His weapon harness clung where it did not chafe. The air was so dense that breathing was an effort. In all, he would just as soon have left Yhelle to its illusionists.

He wiped his shoulder where sweat had gathered beneath Rainbow's faceted weight. As he moved his hand, parts of Rainbow clicked together with sullen sounds that echoed his own irritation. When he lifted his hand, it was coated with tiny hairs. He grimaced. He knew he would feel cooler after he shed out, but the process was unaesthetic. There were no odes to shedding Bre'ns. Limericks, however, abounded.

He followed in disgruntled silence as the illusionists led them parallel to the force field. Rheba turned suddenly, looking over their backtrail with narrowed eyes.

"What's wrong?" whistled Kirtn.

"I feel as if we're being followed. It's like an itch behind my eyes that I can't scratch."

The Bre'n looked over his shoulder. Nothing was nearby, not even an illusion. "Fssa." Kirtn's whistle was curt, demanding.

The snake's sensors took in the area behind them. When that failed, he anchored his tail firmly in her hair and went through a series of transformations. When he was finished, he again became a simple snake in shades of metallic gray. "Nothing that I can detect is moving after us," he said in precise Senyas.

Rheba made a frustrated noise and clenched her hands at her side.

"Maybe you should go back to the ship," Kirtn suggested.

"It's only an irritation—as heat is for you."

"Are you sure?"

She did not bother answering, and he did not mention returning to the ship again. Neither of them relished being separated. It seemed that whenever they were apart unlucky things happened.

The illusionists stopped, faced the force field, and waited for the others to catch up. When they did, i'sNara said, "Look through the veil very carefully."

Kirtn and Rheba stared into the force field's twisting, shimmering surface. Gradually the surface changed, becom-

ing more similar to the veil i'sNara had called it. Vague
images condensed, like ghostly scenes viewed underwater.

"What do you see?"

Rheba's lips thinned into an impatient line. Even a Fssireeme
did not have enough words to describe what she was seeing. Or
almost seeing. "Is this another illusionist joke?" she snapped.

"Please," said i'sNara. "It's important. Can you see
anything?"

"Why?"

"If we told you, it might influence what you see."

"You have the advantage," said Rheba curtly. "You've
had it since we left the ship."

"I'm sorry we teased you," whispered i'sNara. "Please?"

Rheba relented and faced the screen again, but it was Kirtn
who spoke first.

"I don't see anything." He stared at the force field with
eyes that were a hard yellow. "Wait. I see . . . faces. Faces
and more faces. Countless faces . . . worshiping. Faces like
yours, i'sNara, f'lTiri. A sea of faces surrounding a glittering
island. Everything is pouring into the island . . . all human
colors, all human hopes, dreams, lives pouring in endlessly. . . .
The island is crystal, no, many crystals piled high. They . . .
slowly consume their worshipers, consuming ecstasy, all the
faces, dying slowly, ecstatically. . . ."

The last words were sung in a keening Bre'n whistle
translated by Fssa into flat Universal. Even so, the illusionists
were shaken. The emotive qualities of Bre'n transcended
simple words.

Rheba tried to see what Kirtn had seen, but the back of her
eyes itched so fiercely she could not see anything. She rubbed
her eyes impatiently. By the time the itch faded, whatever
Kirtn had seen was gone. But he had seen something very
disturbing. She had only to look at the illusionists' faces to
know that.

"That was the Redis clan symbol," f'lTiri said hollowly.
"But it's changed. So much stronger."

"And the Stones," murmured i'sNara. "So many more
than they had when we left. I didn't know there were that
many Stones."

"Stones?" said Rheba.

"The island," sighed i'sNara. "The island you saw was
made of Ecstasy Stones."

"Ice and ashes," cursed Rheba. "My eyes picked a fine
time to itch. I'd like to have seen that." She blinked and

stared at the veil as the illusionists were staring at it. She hoped that what Kirtn had seen would reappear.

The illusionists made a dismayed sound and joined hands. Their illusions faded, leaving behind two normal people whose faces were lined with concentration.

The veil changed.

Rheba stared, unconsciously speaking aloud as an image condensed behind the veil. "An empty hall, cracked walls and broken floor and no people. Hands reaching for something. Whatever it is, they can't get it. Empty hands reaching forever."

Like Kirtn, she used Bre'n to describe what she had seen. But even as she described it, the image vanished. She hoped it had been only an illusion. There was a desperation about the grasping hands that made her uneasy.

"Was that a clan symbol?" asked Rheba, her voice harsh.

"Yes," said f'lTiri.

"Whose clan?" Then, with a sinking feeling of reality, Rheba said, "Yours, right? That was the symbol of the Liberation clan."

The illusionists looked at each other and said nothing. Finally, f'lTiri shifted his feet and looked away from his wife's eyes. "It could have been a fake," he muttered.

"Maybe." I'sNara's hands clenched and opened, unconsciously echoing the grasping hands beyond the force field. "It doesn't matter. We have to find out, and to find out we have to go through the veil. I hope that symbol was only a sick illusion. But I'm not counting on it."

Kirtn looked from the rippling field to the illusionist dressed as a naked Loo. "What's wrong? I didn't see anything except a few hands holding nothing."

"Exactly," said i'sNara. "The symbols are the essence of the living clans. And there was nothing."

"I don't understand," said Kirtn, but he kept his voice gentle, because he saw pain beneath i'sNara's illusion.

"The room Rheba saw," said f'lTiri. "The empty hall."

"Yes?"

"That was our clan home. Now it seems to be deserted. There's no one waiting there. Not even our children." He made an impatient gesture. "This is one time that waiting won't improve the illusion. Let's go."

"Where?" said Rheba, looking at the force field stretching away on both sides into infinity.

"To the hall," snapped f'lTiri.

"This is where we go through," said i'sNara. When she

saw the look on Rheba's face she added quickly, "We're not teasing you, dancer. The field thins out here and illusions appear. To get where you want to go, you just pick your destination's clan symbol and step through. Be fast, though. It's no fun to get caught between illusions."

Kirtn stared. He thought he could see shapes wavering beyond the field, but was not sure. Then again, he had not been sure of anything since he had set foot on misnamed Reality Street. He looked toward his dancer.

Akhenet lines shimmered briefly as she tested the force field. "It's patchy," she admitted. "If you choose the right spot, all you'll get is a tingle."

If. But how could anyone be sure the right spot would stay in place long enough to be used?

"We'll try to hold the illusion for you," said f'lTiri, "but we may not be able to. If that happens, stay here until the empty-hall symbol repeats and jump through. We'll be on the other side, waiting for you."

Rheba looked uneasily at the kaleidoscopic forces of the veil, changing even as she watched. She understood now why f'lTiri had wanted to be sure they could see through the field before he let them off Reality Street. If you could not see your destination's illusion/symbol through the veil, you were helpless. Even seeing it, she was loathe to let the illusionists out of reach for fear of being forever lost in a shifting Yhelle fantasy.

Her eyes itched maddeningly, telling her that someone was behind her, turning as she turned, always just out of sight. With a sound of exasperation she motioned the illusionists to get on with it. "Go through. Maybe it's the force field that's making me itch."

The illusionists joined hands and concentrated. An image of an empty hall was superimposed over the force field. The veil buckled and writhed as though refusing their illusion. They rode it like an unruly animal. Grudgingly, the field thinned, revealing cracked pavements and desolation.

The illusionists walked through and vanished.

After an instant of hesitation, fire dancer and Bre'n followed. The field broke over them like black water, drowning them.

V

Rheba staggered, then supported herself against Kirtn until she shook off the effects of the force field. To the average Fourth People, when the field was attenuated it was only a "veil." To a dancer, it was a cataract barely held in check. Even as Kirtn helped her by draining off her conflicting energies, he was poised to defend against more mundane dangers than an asynchronous force field.

A quick glance told him that the illusionists were nearby. However, they were not in the place he had seen through the veil. They were outside, not inside, standing on the edge of a deserted street. In the distance the street curved around a huge, ruined building. On either side of the street slovenly wooden buildings leaned against each other. Where no such support was available, houses had collapsed on themselves.

The wreckage was sharp-cornered, suggesting that riot, rather than time, had pulled down the buildings. The few plants he could see were quite dead. There were neither fountains nor scented breezes. After the colorful illusions of Reality Street, the Liberation clan's territory was painfully ugly.

"Is this an illusion?" asked Kirtn bluntly.

The Yhelles' outlines trembled, showing that the illusionists were fighting for control. After a time, their appearance steadied.

"No illusion," said f'lTiri in a tight voice. "Not one."

I'sNara's Loo image blurred as she looked around. "Almost no territory left. No illusions left, not even a simple facade." Her image solidified. She was no longer Loo. She was i'sNara, but an i'sNara who looked so old she was almost another person entirely. "Nothing."

"You're sure it isn't an illusion?" asked Rheba, feeling Fssa stir underneath her hair, changing shapes as he tested the street's reality as best he could.

"Yes," sadly, "we're sure. Disillusioned places feel *different*."

"It's true," whistled Fssa. "Those ruins are real." Then he added sourly, "As real as anything on this treacherous planet."

Rheba shivered in spite of the oppressive heat. The Liberation clan's home territory looked and felt like desolation in four dimensions. "Is this what Serriolia is like beneath the illusions?" Then, realizing that might be a taboo subject, she said quickly, "I didn't mean that as an insult."

F'lTiri smiled, but Rheba sensed it was an illusion. "At one level, yes. All of Serriolia is built on a reality that isn't much prettier than this. Other races paint their homes or design stone facades or extrude elaborate materials to make their homes beautiful. But all we need are a few walls and a roof. From that bare reality we make castles a Loo would envy." He smiled, and this time it was real. "As long as the roof doesn't leak on the illusion. . . ."

"What happened here? Why aren't there any illusions? Did they just wear out?"

The Yhelles looked at one another and then at the ramshackle street that was the reality of their home. "No. The illusions were stripped away," said i'sNara. "A house illusion"—she gestured across the street, and a leaning shack was transformed into an inviting mansion—"is simple to create. They're stable and easy to maintain. In the clans, children do it."

"How long will that last?" asked Kirtn, gesturing to the newly created mansion.

"A week or two. Months, if I took longer with the initial creation. But sooner or later even the strongest illusion needs retouching. That's what the children do."

I'sNara made an abrupt gesture and looked away. The mansion thinned into invisibility. The shack remained.

The transition was unnerving to Rheba. The shack seemed even more melancholy than before. She took Kirtn's hand, drawing comfort from his presence as though she were a child again.

Down the street, a figure darted from a pile of rubble into a ruined house. The person was without illusion and moved like a wild animal that had been persistently hunted. When Kirtn started to call out, he was stopped by f'lTiri's grip on his arm.

"No," said the illusionist urgently. "You didn't see anything."

"But I did," protested Kirtn. "I saw a Yhelle—"

"You saw a creature bereft of illusions." F'lTiri's voice was rough. *"You saw nothing at all."*

Kirtn started to argue, then realized it was futile. "I would like to question what I didn't see," he said in a reasonable tone. "If what I didn't see lives here, it might be able to tell me what happened to the Liberation clan. Or," sarcastically, "am I supposed to believe that nothing happened and any evidence to the contrary is illusion?"

I'sNara and her husband argued briefly in Yhelle before she turned and spoke to Kirtn in Universal. "Even if you caught that poor creature, it wouldn't be able to tell you anything." She hesitated and then spoke in a strained voice, as though what she was saying was very difficult, very unpleasant, or both. "It doesn't really exist. It's been disillusioned."

Kirtn started to speak, thought better of it, and whistled instead. "Fssa, we seem to have a communications problem even though we're all speaking Universal. Can you give me a Bre'n translation of the Yhelle word *disillusioned*?"

Fssa whistled a sliding, minor-key word that ended on a shattered note. The word described akhenets who had lost their gifts through brain injury, becoming people caught between madness and nightmare for the rest of their lives.

With a grimace, Kirtn gave up the idea of questioning the person he was not supposed to have seen. He doubted if even Fssa could communicate with a madman. "Then who—or what—do you suggest we question? Because something *has* happened here, something that's worse than you expected. If this"—he waved his arm at the barren street—"is home, you're better off on the *Devalon* with us. I get the feeling this is a very unlucky place to be."

The Yhelles were silent for a long moment. F'lTiri sighed finally and touched his wife with a small, comforting illusion. "You're right," he said, turning to Kirtn. "We don't have a home anymore. The Liberation clan doesn't exist. We'll go with you as soon as we find our children and tell them we're no longer slaves on Loo."

"Good." Kirtn did not bother to hide his relief. The poet in him was set on edge by the whole atmosphere of the street. Destruction, not creation, was the pervasive image. "Where do we go to ask about your children?"

I'sNara's expression was so bland and untroubled that it had to be an illusion. "The Liberation clan hall."

Silently, the Yhelles turned and walked toward the grim building that was girdled by a decaying street. Kirtn and Rheba followed.

The closer Rheba walked to the hall, the more uneasy she became. Gutted of every illusion, the building sagged inward. Its timbers were dank and moldy. Its roof was in fragments. Long runners from an invading vine quested for new strangleholds on the walls. An ambience of foreboding and despair transformed sunlight into shades of gray.

All in all, Rheba had seen more comforting places.

Neither she nor Kirtn wanted to follow the illusionists. There was something hostile about the clan hall's appearance. Nor did they want their friends to enter the crumbling building alone. Reluctantly, dancer and Bre'n walked along the rutted, curving street until they saw the hall's main entrance.

I'sNara and f'lTiri waited on the steps. Their illusions were so thin that Rheba could see through to the frightened Yhelles beneath. She realized that if the building's aggressive ugliness oppressed her, it had all but destroyed her friends. Unbidden, a memory of Deva's last moments twisted through her, smoke and ashes and screams.

Because she was touching him, Kirtn caught the painful images. He brushed his hand across her cheek and buried his fingers deep in her restless hair. Comfort flowed from his touch. Memory faded, leaving only the echo of screams.

In silence, the four of them mounted the steps into the Liberation clan's headquarters. The interior of the building was no better than the exterior. Holes in the roof let sunlight trickle through. Connectors that joined the building to Serriolia's machinery had been ripped out. Ordinary fluorescent strips had been sprayed along the floor. The job was haphazard. Obviously it had been done in great haste when more conventional means of lighting were disrupted.

Whatever had happened to the clan had not taken place overnight. There had been enough time for patchwork repairs and hopes that had eventually curdled into defeat.

"This way," said i'sNara hollowly, leading them over the wreckage of something that could have been furniture. Without illusions, it was hard to tell pieces of a table from fragments of a cupboard. "Watch the yellow moss. It leaves blisters."

The illusionist spoke in a monotone, like a primitive machine.

Rheba wanted to help, because she knew how much it hurt to pick through the rubble of a dream. But there was nothing she could say to comfort the Yhelles, so she said nothing at all. Fssa keened softly in her ear, Bre'n laments in a minor key.

A ring of tables stood in what had once been the center of the building. Some were broken now, mirror tops smashed to bright fragments. Others were intact, but cracked and blurred by dust. On one of them was a group of crystals the color of greasy smoke.

I'sNara cried out. At the same instant, Rainbow brightened. Beneath her skin, Rheba's akhenet lines began to glow. She walked toward the crystals.

"No." F'lTiri pulled on Rheba's arm, then let go in surprise. The dancer's lines were hot. "Stay away."

Rheba's hair moved restlessly, loosening itself from the coils she had imposed on it and drifting in the direction of the crystals. When she spoke, her eyes stayed on the sullen stones. "What are they?"

"Worry stones. Ecstasy Stones gone bad."

Rheba looked at her Bre'n in silent question. She saw that Rainbow was brighter. "Don't get any closer," she said quickly. "Rainbow might steal some."

Kirtn looked down, saw Rainbow's quiet interior glow, and stared at the table where stones grew like warts on the mirrored surface. "They don't look like Rainbow's type. The ones it swiped on Onan and Daemen were beautiful."

"I don't trust Rainbow," said Rheba flatly. "It has a mania for collecting crystals."

Fssa whistled a soft disclaimer. "Rainbow is just trying to rebuild itself. Replacing lost or broken components isn't really stealing."

She frowned and glared at the Zaarain construct hanging around Kirtn's neck. She and Fssa disagreed on the desirability of having Rainbow around. Yet the Fssireeme defended it so eloquently she usually gave in. "Stealing or not, I don't want Rainbow near those crystals."

Her voice was hard, brooking no argument. Fssa knew the value of discretion. He murmured soothingly and vanished into her hair.

"Is this what you were looking for?" asked Kirtn, gesturing toward the worry stones.

"In a way, yes," said f'lTiri.

"In what way?" prompted the Bre'n impatiently. He was in no mood to play guessing games among the ruins.

With an effort, f'lTiri looked away from the stones. "If even one member of the clan were left—if there were a clan at all—the central illusion would have been intact." His glance went back to the circle of shattered mirrors. "But even our Ecstasy Stones have changed. Worry stones." He shuddered. "They bring only craziness. There's nothing here for us."

Rheba knuckled her eyes. The maddening itch had returned, making it impossible for her to follow the conversation. She moved restlessly until she was within reach of the stones. As her akhenet lines glowed, the itch faded. She bent closer to the stones, intrigued by their cool energies. Before she had time to think better of it, her hand closed over the biggest crystal.

Her lines heated, expanding until there was very little bare flesh left in her palm. The stone remained a dark, uneven crystal whose facets refused even to reflect the incandescent gold of her akhenet lines. Indeed, her hand seemed to dim, as though the stone sucked up light and warmth.

Vaguely, she heard i'sNara scream at her to drop the stone. But i'sNara's voice was far away, not nearly so urgent as the cold blackness in her hand . . . a crystal hole in reality into which everything would drain forever until . . .

Dancer.

Kirtn's voice spoke within her mind. The world returned in a bright rush of warmth, his hands on her shoulders, his breath stirring her hair, his strength dividing her from nightmare. Tendrils of her hair curled around his wrists in a dancer's intimate caress.

It's all right.

Her reassurance reduced the fear driving him. His grip lightened and their small mind dance ended.

"This stone is a power sink rather than a power source," said Rheba in Senyas, the language of precision and measurements. "It surprised me. I was expecting the opposite."

Kirtn eyed the stones with displeasure, particularly the one still in her palm. "Zaarain?"

"I don't think so. They're similar, but more . . . delicate. Zaarain cores always feel like a short course in damnation until you get them under control. *If* you can. The last one I tangled with nearly burned me to ash and gone." She peered at the stone, but failed to see herself reflected on its dark surfaces. "The crystal is powerful, though. No mistake about that."

He bent to look more closely. Rainbow swung out from his neck with a bright flash. Rheba leaped away.

"No you don't!" She closed her hand around the stone. "This one is mine, you thieving construct."

"Put it back," said f'lTiri tightly.

Rheba's eyes itched, distracting her from the urgency in the illusionist's voice. "Does the stone belong to someone?" she asked, oddly determined not to let go of the ugly crystal.

I'sNara made a strangled sound. "*No*. Who would want them? I don't even know how they got here in the first place. No master snatcher would bother with them."

Rheba looked from the stone in her palm to the stones on the cracked mirror. "No one owns these?"

"No one." F'lTiri's voice was clipped.

"Then I'll take them."

Kirtn looked from her to the stones. "Why?"

"Their energies are unique." Then, stubbornly, "I want them."

He hesitated, knowing that dancers' tastes were as unusual as their gifts.

I'sNara did not hesitate. "Unique? That's one way of saying it," she retorted. "Another way is to say that they'll drive you crazy."

"Can you shield them?" asked the Bre'n, his voice that of a mentor waiting to be convinced.

Rheba concentrated on the large stone in her palm. Gradually, tiny filaments of light curled up around the stone, lacing and interlacing until there was a delicate shell of golden light around the stone. When she was finished, she handed the crystal to her mentor. "Try it."

Kirtn took the crystal, rolled it around in his hand, then touched it to his forehead. He grunted. "I can't feel anything. I'sNara?"

The illusionist looked at the crystal as though it were a trap set to spring at the least touch. "If it were anyone but Rheba," she muttered, extending a cautious fingertip. When there was no reaction, she became more confident, finally even taking the crystal into her palm. "What did you do?"

"I—" Rheba realized that Universal had no words to describe what she had done. She suspected that Yhelle had no words either. "I caged it," she said, shrugging like a Bre'n.

"How long will it last?" asked i'sNara, returning the crystal to Rheba.

"As long as it's close to me," she said absently, sorting

through the stones remaining on the cracked mirror surface. "My energy field will feed it." Crystals clicked together. When she was finished, there were two piles. "Those are dead. No energy at all, positive, negative, or stasis/neutral."

She built a fragile, flexible cage of light around the living crystals. As the cage closed, the room appeared to brighten and the air seemed less oppressive. She felt an acute sense of relief and delight that was like nothing she had ever experienced.

The feeling was disconcerting because it was unexpected. The stones had never worried her to the point that she should feel any particular relief that they were no longer unshielded. Nor was it Kirtn's emotion. She knew the textures of his relief; they had been in and out of danger so often lately that his responses were as familiar as her own. Frowning, she sealed the odd crystals into a pocket of her scarlet shorts.

The illusionists drew a deep breath and stretched like people coming out of a long confinement. Apparently they were peculiarly susceptible to the worry stones' negative effects.

I'sNara and f'ITiri looked around the room. Empty of its last illusion, the Liberation clan hall was humid, crumbling, inhabited only by memories. The ambience of total despair was gone. It had vanished with the stones into Rheba's pocket. Even so, the hall was a melancholy place.

F'ITiri turned toward a rear exit. "All that's left to check is the message wall."

There was neither door nor illusion of one, only a rectangle of Yhelle's steamy sunlight. A rough board wall leaned askance but still upright. The wood was bare of illusions. A list of names spiraled in toward the center of the board, each letter burned in wood. In silence, the Yhelles read the names.

"What is it?" asked Rheba finally, sensing that something was wrong.

"Names," sighed i'sNara.

"People who have vowed to liberate Ecstasy Stones," f'ITiri said. "Our names." He pointed toward the beginning of the spiral. His finger cut toward the center where the last names were burned in. His voice roughened. "Our children's names."

"Where are they now?" asked Kirtn. "Loo?"

"We don't know," whispered i'sNara. "They might have succeeded."

F'ITiri made a strangled sound. The state of the Liberation hall spoke eloquently of failure, not success.

"Someone will know," said i'sNara, touching f'lTiri's arm. "Clan Tllella?"

For a moment his illusion slipped, revealing a man caught between rage and despair. "Do you really want to know? They're either dead or slaves—or worse!" Then his exterior became once again that of an alien scout as he hid behind illusion. "Clan Tllella," he said flatly.

Rheba watched them walk out into Yhelle's moist gray sunlight. "What could be worse than slavery on Loo?" she asked softly, looking sideways at her Bre'n.

"I'm afraid we're going to find out," said Kirtn.

Rheba's akhenet lines ignited in reflexive response to the danger implicit in his words.

He was comforted by her reaction. Not for the first time since their flight from Deva, he congratulated himself on Choosing a dancer whose gifts were dangerous as well as beautiful. "I just hope we don't find more trouble than you can burn," he said, giving her a fierce Bre'n smile.

VI

The illusionists left the hall more circumspectly than they had come. They were little more than blurred shadows sliding down the stairway and up the street. Kirtn and Rheba fidgeted at the top of the steps, having promised that they would not follow the Yhelles too closely.

"Wonder what kind of trouble they're expecting," said Rheba, measuring nearby shadows with cinnamon eyes.

"Wonder how they'd recognize it if it came," the Bre'n said sourly. "Fssa, do your Guardian memories have anything to say about Yhelle?"

The Fssireeme's sensors gleamed beneath a glossy wing of Rheba's hair. He spoke in Senyas. He usually did, when he had bad news. "Yhelle has changed since the Eighth Cycle."

"Eighth! Is that your most recent memory?" asked Rheba. She knew that each Fssireeme had a Guardian who imprinted his (her? *hir*?) memories on the young snake. The Guardian's memories also included that Guardian's Guardian's memories, and so on all the way back to the first Guardian. Thus Fssa's memories were much older than he was.

"The Eighth Cycle is my most recent *Guardian* memory of Yhelle. I myself have never been to Yhelle."

"Welcome to the Eighteenth Cycle," Kirtn muttered.

"Thank you," hissed Fssa.

Rheba said something under her breath that the snake chose not to hear. They set off after the illusionists.

"The Tllella clan members are mostly traders," offered Fssa in oblique apology. "At least, they were in the Eighth Cycle. They probably haven't changed. It's a tenacious profession."

"Maybe it would help if we knew how Yhelle has changed since the Eighth Cycle," suggested Kirtn.

The snake was unusually succinct. "More illusion. Less reality."

"No help at all."

"No help," agreed the Fssireeme. "Perhaps Rainbow knows something. A fragment of knowledge is better than nothing at all."

"No," snapped Rheba. "We're not that desperate yet."

Fssa, knowing the agony his communications with the fragmentary Zaarain library caused her, said no more on that subject.

"Can you see the illusionists?" asked Kirtn. "I lost them when I blinked."

Fssa said, "They're waiting at the veil."

"You're sure?"

"They're keeping their illusions simple so I can follow."

Rheba stepped up the pace. Even outside the Liberation hall the atmosphere was oppressive to her. She felt she was being watched by nameless shadows growing out of the ruins. "I'd hate to be here at night," she muttered.

Kirtn said nothing, but his repeated glances into the shadows told her that he was as uneasy as she was. "I've got a feeling we're being watched."

"Itch behind your eyes?" she suggested hopefully.

"No. Just a feeling. By the Inmost Fire, I wish I could see through illusions," he said in fervent Senyas.

"Hurry," said Fssa. "They're having trouble controlling the veil."

Kirtn and Rheba ran toward the veil. Before they could see the destination symbol, they were yanked through by invisible hands.

Rheba stood dizzily for a moment, then shook off the effects of passage through the force field. "Where are we?"

"Tllella clan boundary," murmured a glossy white cat striding alongside Kirtn.

Rheba blinked, then decided the cat must be i'sNara. "What was the problem with the veil?"

"It only wanted to take us to the Redis hall," answered a man who appeared in the cat's wake.

Rheba could not help staring at the tall, thin stranger who must be f'lTiri. His hair was hip length, the color of water, and thick. It took the place of the shirt he did not wear. His pants were as tight as snakeskin and made of interlocking silver links. His lavender skin was the same suede texture as Kirtn's. She ran her finger down the illusion's arm and made a sound of pleasure.

F'lTiri turned and smiled at Rheba's open-mouthed admiration. "A simple illusion," he whispered.

The silver links of his pants rubbed over each other musically, making a liar out of f'lTiri. It was a complex illusion, beautifully realized. As was i'sNara's; she even threw a small, cat-shaped shadow.

"I feel naked," said Rheba plaintively to Kirtn.

The Bre'n smiled but knew what she meant. Yhelle was a complex place to live. It was even worse to visit. He hoped they would not be here long.

Tllella's boundary streets were well populated . . . or at least appeared to be. On Yhelle, it was hard to be sure of anything. Rheba tried to see through various entities that might or might not be illusions. So did Fssa. After a few minutes, they just decided to enjoy the show without worrying about tangential concerns such as reality and illusion.

Kirtn, with a poet's special pragmatism, had already decided that the distinction between the two was artificial and unaesthetic. He simply watched and appreciated what he could.

"Is it far?" asked Rheba. Then, almost as an afterthought, "I'm hungry." As she spoke, she realized that the air was full of enticing scents.

"Not far," said the cat's husky voice. "Serriolia isn't very big. It just seems that way."

They were passing what seemed to be a marketplace. Laughter and wonderful food smells drifted out from fantastically decorated houses. The cat's very long whiskers twitched in the direction of a small café that seemed to be constructed of moonlight floating on water. The subtle play of light and aroma promised coolness, pleasure and peace. And food.

"Smells wonderful," said the cat.

"Reminds me of Meel's best work," murmured the man with a voice like water rippling, echoing his hair.

"That would be too much to hope for."

"Meel is her mother's cousin," said the man to Rheba. "She might know what happened to the Liberation clan."

Rheba sniffed deeply and could not help hoping that food came with the information. Working with the worry stones had drained her energy. Her stomach would not relent until she ate. She wished she had the ability to turn sunlight into food, but that was a trick known only to plants and a few now-dead master fire dancers. And, she suspected, Fssireemes.

She leaned toward the thin man with hair like water—she simply could not think of him as f'lTiri—and whispered, "What does Yhelle use for money?"

"Only clan accountants handle real money," said f'lTiri, shaking his head to make his hair flow smoothly. His tone told her that people who handled money were a necessary evil, not a topic of polite conversation.

"Then how do you buy food at the cafés?" she persisted.

"You trade illusions." Then, seeing she did not understand, he added, "You get a meal as good as the illusion you project."

The explanation explained nothing. She made a frustrated sound and her lines sparked. Hungry dancers were notoriously irritable. Kirtn whistled softly and stroked her arm. After a few moments, her lines glowed harmoniously. She rubbed her cheek against his shoulder.

"But I'm still hungry," she whistled, evoking a vast rumbling hollowness with a handful of Bre'n notes.

The cat looked over her sleek shoulder, revealing eyes the color of autumn wine, blue on blue with magenta turning at the core. "Your illusion should get you the finest meal in Serriolia."

"I'm not an illusion," said Rheba, exasperated again. She threw up her arms. Akhenet lines blazed. "I'm exactly what I appear to be!"

"Sometimes," said i'sNara with a tiny cat smile, "reality is the best illusion of all."

The cat leaped up and sat on f'lTiri's shoulder. Rheba saw that it was not quite a cat. Its paws were small hands and the tips of its fangs winked poisonously. The smile was decidedly cruel.

"We'll go first," said f'lTiri. "Don't speak Universal. Let the snake do your talking."

Rheba smiled wryly. Yhelle was the only place in the Equality where a multilingual shape-changing snake would cause no comment.

"Eat whatever is given to you," he continued. "If you don't like the flavor, don't show it. You'll only be insulting your own illusion."

They entered the café. Neither Kirtn nor Rheba would have been surprised if the room vanished before their eyes. It did not. It remained just as it was, a construct of moonlight and still waters, redolent of feasts.

Fssa made a startled sound.

"What's wrong?" whistled Rheba in Bre'n. She had no fear of being overheard in that language. So far as she knew, only five living beings in the Equality understood Bre'n, and the other two were waiting aboard the *Devalon*.

"I've lost them," whistled Fssa in rising notes of surprise and displeasure.

"Who?"

"The illusionists!"

Rheba blinked. The shiny white cat and the man dressed in chiming silver were still just ahead of her. "F'lTiri?"

He turned so quickly that his hair frothed. "Don't use my name aloud until we find out what's going on!"

"Tell him, Fssa," she muttered in Senyas, not knowing any more of the Yhelle language than the illusionists' names.

"I can't see you," said the snake in soft Yhelle, choosing the idiom of sighted Fourth People over precision. Being a Fssireeme, he never really *saw* anything at all.

F'lTiri smiled. "Sorry, snake. If we hope to get food or information out of the resident illusionist, we have to put on our best appearance. But we'll stay as man and cat so you won't lose us."

Rheba stared. She had thought the previous illusions were complete, but realized she was wrong. The man and cat were indefinably more *real* than they had been. The cat's long white fur stirred with each breath, each vague breeze, each movement of the sinuous neck. The man's hair rippled to his hips, clung to his muscular body, separated into transparent locks with each turn of his head. His silver clothing links were now bright and now dark, slinking and tinkling with each step.

Kirtn whistled Bre'n praise as intricate as their illusions. Though f'lTiri did not understand the language, the meaning was clear. He smiled fleetingly, revealing the hollow pointed fangs of a blood eater. Rheba shivered and looked away. The vampire races of the Fourth People made her uneasy, despite the fact that they abhorred and avoided the carnivorous or omnivorous races of Fourth People. Vampires simply could not understand how civilized beings could eat carrion.

Rheba followed the lavender-skinned vampire into the café, feeling less hungry than she had a moment ago. Kirtn smiled thinly, as though he knew exactly how she felt. Even Bre'ns were queasy on the subject of blood eaters. Fssa was impervious. He rested his head on top of her ear and whistled beautiful translations of the fragmentary conversations he overheard as Rheba followed man and cat through the crowded café.

"—through the veil three days ago and hasn't been back."

"Would you go back to that see-through illusionist if—"

"—deserve better than cold mush!"

"—tempted to try it. *Total love*. What an illusion! But I hear that no one—"

"Marvelous flavor, don't you think? Yours isn't? Oh—"

"—heard that the Redis have a truly Grand Illusion."

"Who told you?"

"Someone who heard it from—"

"—garble honk—"

Fssa hissed frustration. Too many conversations were almost as bad as silence for a Fssireeme. His sensors spun and focused, seeking the familiar voices of the illusionists.

Nascent fire smoldered beneath Rheba's skin, reflexive response to the strangeness around her. If she closed her eyes and just listened to Fssa's whistle she was all right—until she tripped over an illusion. So she was forced to go open-eyed through as unlikely a concatenation of beings as she had seen in the casinos of Onan and the slave yards of Loo combined.

The crowd thinned around a small, brightly lit area. In the center of the spotlight was a gorgeous butterfly spinning a brilliant green web. As it walked, the butterfly's feet plucked music out of the green strands. Wings fluttered, scattering fragrance. With a final rill of notes, the insect took flight. As it landed on a nearby table, food appeared.

"How can we compete with that?" muttered Rheba in Senyas.

Kirtn whistled sourly. "We'll be lucky to get cold mush."

Fssa hissed laughter. "Speak for yourself. I have more shapes than these dilettantes ever dreamed of."

F'lTiri sauntered into the spotlit area. On his shoulder rode the white cat. In the spotlight she turned the color of honey and melted into his mouth. All that remained were fangs shining. Cat laughter echoed as she reappeared in the center of a nearby diner's meal, white not honey, fangs intact. With a single fluid leap she regained her perch on f'lTiri's lavender shoulder.

As though he had noticed nothing, not even the spotlight, f'lTiri combed his water-gleaming hair. Music cascaded out. A chorus of tiny voices came from a shoal of lavender fish swimming the clear currents of his hair. He shook his head. Fish leaped out and flew in purple flurries toward the dark corners of the room. They vanished, leaving behind the smell and feel of raindrops.

Kirtn sighed. "At least some of us will eat."

Yellow light surged through Rheba's lines. She shook Fssa
out of her hair and put him into Kirtn's hands. "Voices and
shapes, snake," she whistled. "Lots of them."

As Kirtn stepped into the spotlight, the Fssireeme began to
change. One moment he was a simple glistening snake, the
next he was a blue-steel spiral shot through with a babble of
languages. The spiral became a pink crystal lattice trembling
with music, whole worlds of song. Shapes and colors changed
so quickly there was no time to name them. With each
shape/color came new songs, new sounds, painful and beautiful,
silly and sublime. The shapes came faster and faster until they
became a single glistening cataract of change, an eerie cacophony of voices.

Then Fssa settled smugly back into snake form curled in a
Bre'n's strong hands. A voice whispered in Kirtn's ear. Fssa
translated the Yhelle worlds. "First table on your right."

Rheba watched while Kirtn sat at an empty table next to the
man and cat illusion. Food appeared in front of him. Rheba
held her breath while he took a bite. Bre'ns had exquisite
palates. It would be hard for him to disguise his reaction to
bad food.

He chewed with every evidence of pleasure. Breathing a
silent prayer, Rheba stepped into the light. Power smoldered
in her akhenet lines. Her hair fanned out, catching and holding light until it was every color of fire. She crackled with
energy. Tiny tongues of lightning played over her akhenet
lines.

Patterns of intricate fire burned over her body while she
searched the air for emanations from a local power source. As
she had hoped, the café's lights were real, drawn from
Serriolia's power grid. She tapped into the lights, taking
visible streams of power from them until she was a focus of
fire in a room suddenly dark.

She pirouetted. Flames streamed out, separated, became
single tongues in the center of each darkened table. In all the
languages of the Equality, the flames sweetly inquired if the
food was equal to a decent illusion. The impertinent voices
were Fssa's, but the whiplash of impatience beneath the
words was pure hungry dancer.

She burned in the center of the stage and waited for her
answer.

A voice whispered meaningless Yhelle words in her ear.
Fssa realized the difficulty just in time. He whistled a fast
translation. Still burning fitfully, she walked toward Kirtn's

table. There were several empty chairs. She pulled one over to him and sat.

The food was exquisite, but before she finished it, the chair developed aggressively familiar hands.

Rheba leaped to her feet and set fire to the sniggering chair. It exploded into a fat, outraged Yhelle male beating his palms against his burning clothes. A burst of laughter from the diners told him he was naked of illusion. Instantly he took on the aspect of a bush and rustled through the crowd toward the exit.

Realizing what had happened, Kirtn started after the lewd bush. It took a gout of dancer fire to keep the Bre'n from stripping the crude illusion twig from branch.

The white cat smiled and called sweetly, "If you're going to seat a class twelve illusion, you'd better *be* a class twelve."

Fssa whistled a translation, complete down to the malicious pleasure in the cat's husky voice.

Rheba waited until Kirtn sat down again. She ignored his clinical—and rather shocking—Senyas description of the fat illusionist. She looked skeptically at the remaining empty chairs. She gave the nearest one a sizzling bolt of fire. Kirtn would not let her sit down until he smelled wood burning. Only then was he satisfied that a chair rather than a lecher waited for his dancer.

As Rheba sat gingerly, the cat leaped to the center of the table and began cleaning its hands with a pale-blue tongue. "Meel will be here soon," she purred almost too low for Rheba to catch. "Eat fast." She flexed her poisonous nails and leaped back to the other table.

"I wonder if those claws are as lethal as they look," muttered Rheba.

"Bet on it," said Kirtn. Then, in a metallic voice, "I trust you burned more than that cherf's clothes."

Rheba's lips twitched. "Yes."

He took her hand and kissed the inside of her wrist. "Good."

There was a predatory satisfaction in his voice that made her look closely at her mentor. His slanted eyes were hard and yellow, the eyes of an angry Bre'n, but that was not what made heat sweep through her. Her wrist burned where his mouth touched her, burned with a fire that would have scorched any Fourth Person but a Bre'n or Senyas. He drank her heat like a Fssireeme, leaving her dizzy, her lines blazing with a restless incandescence that wanted to consume . . . something.

She had felt like this before, when they had "shared enzymes" in a lover's kiss. They had fooled the Loo-chim into believing that Bre'n and Senyas had a complex symbiosis based on such sharing, and would die if separated. The kiss had shocked her, for she had never thought of her Bre'n mentor as a man. Since then the thought had occurred with uncomfortable regularity. She knew that Bre'n sensuality was the core of many Senyas legends, but she did not know if akhenet pairs were also supposed to be lovers.

She had been too young to ask or even speculate on such a question when she was on Deva. Now there was no one to ask but Kirtn . . . and she could not find the words. It was not just fear of being rejected by him if the answer was no. In a way less intimate and more complex than enzymes, they needed each other to survive. She could not jeopardize their lives by ignorantly probing areas of akhenet life that might be taboo.

Nor could she pretend that Kirtn was not a man. His simplest touch excited her more than the hours she had spent with boyish Senyasi lovers. It was not a comforting realization. If she allowed herself to think about the sensual possibilities latent in her and her Bre'n, she would be tempted to pursue them in defiance of any taboos that might exist. She must think of him only as her Bre'n, her mentor, her partner, never her lover. And yet . . .

Fssa's low whistle startled her. She realized that she had begun to build a cage of fire around herself and her Bre'n. She had done that once before and not understood why. Now she was afraid she did understand.

Kirtn was watching her with eyes that burned.

Fssa whistled again. She sucked energy back into her lines, but that was not what the snake was concerned about. She looked toward the illusionists' table. There were two cats where formerly there had been just one, yet f'lTiri still appeared to be a tall blood eater. Suddenly the white cat's lips drew back in a snarl. The other cat, darker and much less defined, vanished. From the table where it had been rose visible tendrils of odor. The stink made Rheba gag.

"Out!" shrilled Fssa urgently. "Get out!"

VII

Before Rheba could stand up, Kirtn had grabbed her and was racing through the crowd with a fine disregard for patrons illusory and real. She helped by scattering minor lightning. Within seconds, they had a clear path to the door.

"The illusionists?" asked Rheba, squirming in Kirtn's grasp until she could see over his shoulder.

"Invisible," whistled Fssa. "They'll probably beat us to the door."

"What happened?" snapped Kirtn.

Fssa's sensors wheeled through metallic colors and finally settled on incandescent green. He scanned the crowds behind them as he answered. "Meel came. The cat illusion is a recognition signal for Tllellas, and i'sNara was Tllella before she joined illusions with f'lTiri. When Meel found out who the white cat was— Hit that blue lizard with some lightning!" Fire poured past the snake's head. He hissed satisfaction. "She won't be hungry for a week."

Serriolia's hot, moist air wrapped around them as they gained the sidewalk in a long leap. Fssa's sensors changed again, more blue than green. "Yellow flower," he snapped in Senyas.

Hot fire rained on a flower growing out of the street. The flower squawked, shivered, and vanished.

"Any more?" asked Rheba, wondering if the puddle ahead was truly the product of Yhelle's daily rains.

"Not that I can scan. I'sNara is that tree growing behind the house illusion. Oh, you can't see through that one, can you? But I can't find f'lTiri."

"Here," murmured the air next to Kirtn's right ear. "No," urgently, "keep walking. I can only hold invisibility over us for a few more seconds. Once we're around that house illusion—"

With the "house" between them and the café, f'lTiri let go of invisibility. In the instant before he formed a new illusion, they saw his real face, pale and sweating. Invisibility was the most exhausting illusion of all.

"What happened?" asked Kirtn. "Fssa said the dark cat was Meel."

A nearby tree shivered and split. Half of it became i'sNara. A different i'sNara, though. Short and thick, skin as black as the expression on her face. "Meel is afraid of her own illusions," she spat.

F'lTiri's outline blurred and reformed as that of a bird. The bird flapped to i'sNara's shoulder and closed its eyes. She stroked feathers as she explained. "When I told Meel who I was she nearly lost her illusion. At first she was happy. Then she was afraid. When I asked about my children, she said to go to k'Masei. When I asked again—" I'sNara made a cutting gesture. "You smelled her answer."

"Who is k'Masei?" asked Kirtn.

"A Liberation clan traitor."

The bird nuzzled i'sNara's ear. She sighed. "I know, but it makes me sick even to hear his name." Her lips twisted as though she were eating something as bad as the smell in the café. "K'Masei was the Liberation clan's master snatcher. He said he was going to use our few good Ecstasy Stones to help him snatch the Redis' Stones. So he went into the Redis clan hall with all our Stones. He never came back. He gave our Ecstasy Stones to the Redis!"

"Maybe he was caught," suggested Rheba.

The illusionist laughed bitterly. "He was the one who sold us into slavery. He's the head of the Redis clan—a position he bought with Lib clan Stones."

Rheba sighed. "Then I suppose that's what Meel meant. K'Masei will know where your children are."

"You don't understand," said i'sNara, her voice strained. "Saying to Libs 'Go to k'Masei' is wishing death or slavery on them. You saw our clan hall. What chance do you think we'd have with k'Masei?"

Kirtn's whistle sliced through mere words. "Then who do we ask?" he demanded.

"Meel isn't the only Tllella I know."

I'sNara strode confidently down the street with the blue bird perched on her shoulder. Kirtn watched her for a moment, then shrugged and started after her.

"I hope the other Tllellas she knows smell better," muttered Rheba.

As though it had heard, the bird looked over its shoulder and winked. Simultaneously, Kirtn took on the appearance of green Fourth People wearing a barbaric jeweled necklace. Her own skin became the exact turquoise color of the zoolipt pool on Daemen. Magenta drifted in front of her face. She flinched in the instant before she realized that it was her own hair, transformed by Yhelle illusion.

"Just simple reversals," called the bird in a tired voice. "That's all we can manage for a while."

"It's enough," said Kirtn, looking at his own hands in disbelief.

"I'sNara doesn't think there's any danger," added the bird, "but it's better not to have any more misunderstandings."

Rheba suspected that what had happened at the café was no misunderstanding. She kept quiet, though. Short of abandoning the search for their children, the illusionists were doing all that they could to keep everyone safe.

I'sNara turned off the road and walked through a wall. Kirtn and Rheba stopped, stared at each other, and walked forward cautiously. They discovered that the open road was an illusion concealing the reality of a wall. If they had followed what their eyes saw, they would have bloodied their noses on the invisible wall. The visible wall, however, was an illusion concealing a turn in the road. Without the illusionists to lead the way, Bre'n and Senyas would have been utterly baffled.

"Fssa, did you see—*scan*—the fact that the wall wasn't where it seemed to be?"

"I wasn't scanning," admitted the snake. He poked his head out of her hair and focused over her shoulder. "What wall?"

Rheba turned to point. The wall was gone. Akhenet lines flared in fire dancer reflex to being startled. "Kirtn—"

He turned, looked. His eyes narrowed in slow search. No wall. Even more unsettling, the road behind them was totally unfamiliar, as though they had crossed through a veil without realizing it. He looked at his dancer in silent query.

"No," she said positively, "we didn't go through a veil. There is no way even a class twelve illusionist could hide energy from a fire dancer."

"Fssa?" asked the Bre'n:

The snake turned dark with embarrassment. "I wasn't scanning. I gave it up as useless. By the time I strip away one illusion, another takes its place. Useless."

"But why?" wondered Rheba. Then, quickly, "Not you, snake. The illusions. Why would they change so completely?"

"Why would they have them in the first place?" countered Fssa in a deliberately off-key whistle.

"Argue while you walk," snapped the Bre'n. "If we lose track of our guides, we'll have hell's own time finding our way back to Reality Street."

His advice came none too soon. They caught up with i'sNara, in time to see her climb some narrow steps, turn left and walk serenely on pure air into the second story of a circular tower. Kirtn and Rheba scrambled to follow before the illusion changed beyond recognition.

The tower illusion was either an actual structure or closely based on one. They followed interior curves up several levels without going through walls or walking on air. That suited Rheba. She was still queasy from looking between her feet and seeing nothing at all.

The bird flew swiftly back, perched on Kirtn's shoulder, and spoke in a very soft voice. "Hiri, I'sNara's first illusion, lives here. When we go in, stand quietly and don't say anything."

Rheba wondered what a first illusion might be, but the bird flew off before she could ask. The wall in front of i'sNara dissolved. All four of them moved into the opening as one. Kirtn, however, was careful to look over his shoulder and see the nature of the illusion that formed behind them. If they had to leave quickly, he would know which way to jump.

I'sNara's outline blurred and reformed into her own image. A graceful mirror gave a startled cry and shattered, leaving behind the reality of a dark-haired Yhelle. He swept i'sNara into his arms and spoke in torrents of nearly incoherent Yhelle.

Fssa did not translate, which told Rheba that the conversation was private rather than pertinent. The snake's delicate sense of what was and was not meant to be translated was one of the things she liked best about him. Eventually, however, he began translating. He duplicated each voice so exactly that it was like understanding the language itself rather than merely hearing a translation.

"Where are you staying?" asked Hiri, his quick frown

revealing that he knew the subject to be an unhappy one. As members of the Liberation clan, they would normally have stayed in the clan hall until they found quarters.

"We won't be here any longer than it takes to find out about our children," said i'sNara bluntly.

Hiri's outline flickered. "I don't know where they are," he said miserably. "After you were sent to Loo, I tracked your children down. It wasn't easy. They have your finesse and f'lTiri's stamina." He glanced quickly at the bird on i'sNara's shoulder. The bird winked. Hiri smiled. "They insisted on staying with the clan. They were sure they could steal the Stones and redeem their parents' illusions."

"What about my brothers, f'lTiri's sisters, their children? Where are they?"

Hiri blurred. "Your older brother died. A street brawl that was more real than apparent. F'lTiri's sisters . . . one joined the Redis."

The bird ballooned into a solid, enraged f'lTiri. "I don't believe it!"

"It's true," sighed Hiri.

"Which sister?"

"My wife."

F'lTiri made an agonized sound and then said nothing at all. He could not question the look on Hiri's face.

"What about the others?" asked i'sNara tightly. "My younger brother?"

"Joined the Redis."

"F'lTiri's other sisters?"

"One dead."

"The other?" said i'sNara stiffly, taking her husband's hand as though she knew what was coming.

"Don't—" whispered Hiri.

"We shared first illusion," i'sNara said, her voice as harsh as the image forming around her. "Tell me."

"Disillusioned," he said very softly. Then he cried aloud, "*Disillusioned!* Like all the others. I was afraid one of the disillusioned was you and then I knew if I kept looking I would be one of *them.* K'Masei is insatiable! More converts and then more and he wants still more until Serriolia will be nothing but his own illusion admiring itself endlessly." His voice broke. "I'm sorry. I wasn't good enough to save your children."

"Neither was I, old friend," sighed i'sNara. "Neither was

I." She kissed Hiri gently. "When was the last time you saw my children?"

"Just before my wife became a Redis. A year ago. Maybe more. They aren't Redis, though. At least, they weren't then. They were still planning to steal the Ecstasy Stones." He hesitated, then looked searchingly from i'sNara to f'lTiri and back. "Don't stay in Serriolia. None of your clan is alive in any way you would want to know. There's nothing left here for you."

"Our children."

"If k'Masei doesn't have them already, he will soon. I tell you he is insatiable. I—" He looked away from them. "I dream of the Stones," he whispered. "Ecstasy."

The longing in his voice made Rheba ache. She knew what it was to dream of the unattainable, only for her it was a planet called Deva alive beneath a stable sun. Her hair stirred in restless magenta curves. Kirtn touched her and for an instant he felt her pain as his own.

"Please," said Hiri. "Go while you can."

"Our children."

Hiri's image paled almost to transparency. "Do you know that just a few days ago I was grateful you were on Loo? Slaves, but *safe*. No dreams sucking at your will." He looked at i'sNara. She waited, obdurate, reality and illusion fused in single determination. "Your children," he sighed. When he spoke again, it was quickly, as though he would have it over with. "Nine days ago Ara came. Do you remember her?"

"My son's first illusion," said f'lTiri.

"She was going to clan Yaocoon. To hide."

"From what?"

"Her dreams," snarled Hiri. He touched i'sNara, apologizing. "I've tried not to sleep. Sometimes it works."

"Why clan Yaocoon?" pressed f'lTiri.

"I don't know. There are rumors . . ."

"Yes?"

"Rebellion," whispered Hiri.

The word was spoken so softly that even Fssa had trouble catching it.

"Against what? K'Masei? The Redis?" asked i'sNara, her voice unnaturally loud in the hot room.

Hiri gestured silent agreement, obviously afraid even to speak.

"How?" asked f'lTiri bluntly.

He was answered so softly that only Fssa heard. "A raid on the Ecstasy Stones," translated the snake in a firm voice that sounded just like Hiri's.

Hiri looked up, startled. He saw only a restless cloud of magenta hair. "Sssssss," he hissed. "Whisper. They're everywhere."

"Who?" asked Rheba.

"The Soldiers of Ecstasy."

She looked at the illusionists. Their expressions told her they knew no more than she did about Soldiers and Ecstasy. Their expressions hinted that they were afraid Hiri had lost his grasp on the interface between reality and illusion.

"You think I believe my own illusions, don't you?" said Hiri, his voice divided between bitterness and amusement. "I wish I did. Life is much simpler for a fool." His image thickened, becoming more solid, as though he drew strength from some last inner resource. "Haven't you seen the notice?" he asked in a hard voice.

"What notice?" asked the illusionists in the same voice.

"Beside the entrance," he said harshly. "I've tried to hide or disguise the vile thing, but its illusions are too strong. There's one like it in every house in Serriolia."

They walked the few steps back to the entrance of the room. On the left symbols glowed. I'sNara read aloud:

" 'The Liberation clan has been found in violation of Illusion and Reality. I hereby declare the clan disbanded, anathema. Anyone, illusory or real, who aids said clan members will be disillusioned. Signed, k'Masei the Tyrant.' "

"I thought you said you didn't have a government," commented Kirtn.

"We don't," snapped f'lTiri. "This is an obscene joke."

Hiri made a sound between a laugh and a sob. "It's obscene and it's a joke but it's *real*." He blurred and once again became a mirror reflecting a reality he abhorred. "Leave while you still have your illusions," said the mirror in a brittle voice.

I'sNara lifted her hand and touched the cool surface that had once been her friend. As her hand fell, she became thick and dark once more, a hard woman with a black bird on her shoulder. The woman and the bird were not reflected in Hiri's mirror; they no longer shared either illusions or contiguous realities. Woman and bird turned and walked out of the room.

Only Rheba saw the mirror change. For an instant a younger i'sNara lived within the silvered glass, held by a younger Hiri, echoes of laughter and innocence swirling around them.

Then the mirror shivered and reflected nothing at all.

Silently, Rheba retreated from the room. It was obvious that what had begun as a competition between master snatchers had become a deadly private war.

VIII

Outside, the illusions had changed again. The sky had gone from misty white to moldy gray-green. It was hotter, stickier, and no breeze moved. The weather, at least, was no illusion. The *Devalon*'s computer had warned them that Yhelle was hot, humid, and given to leaky skies.

Rheba and Kirtn walked out of the tower on the ground floor rather than air, but only they seemed to notice the difference. The dark woman and the darker bird seemed oblivious to reality and illusion alike.

There were people on the street—or there seemed to be. Things walked in twos and fives, changing from step to step in an array of illusory prowess that finally left nonillusionists numbed rather than bemused. Like Fssa, Rheba and Kirtn gave up caring whether they saw what they saw or only thought they saw what they might have seen.

Rheba rubbed her eyes. At first she thought that she had been staring too hard at i'sNara's illusion. Then she realized that the itch was back. With an inward curse at the lazy zoolipt that could not be bothered to heal her scratchy eyes, she rubbed vigorously. All that happened was that her eyes watered to the point that she could see only blurs. She tripped over a subtly disguised piece of reality and went sprawling into mounds of flowers that were only apparent. What she fell into was hard, sharp and painful.

Kirtn pulled her to her feet. Her hands were covered with cuts that bled freely. Even as he bent to examine the ragged cuts, they began to close. Within seconds little was left but random smears of blood.

"I guess the zoolipt isn't asleep after all," muttered Rheba, blinking furiously. "But my eyes still *itch*."

"Don't rub them," said Kirtn mildly.

What Rheba said was not mild. She finished with, "Why can't the icy little beast take care of my eyes?"

"It hasn't been in you long. Maybe it's only good for gross things."

"The way it put you back together again on Daemen was hardly gross," snapped Rheba, remembering her Bre'n with a long knife wound in his back, lying in a puddle of his own bright blood. She had held him, sure that he was dead . . . until the zoolipt slid into the gruesome wound and vanished and her Bre'n began to breathe again.

"Maybe the itching is in your mind," said Kirtn, pulling her along as he hurried to catch up with i'sNara. "You could be allergic to illusions."

Rheba made a sound that even Fssa could not translate. It was easy for her mentor to talk about mental itches; he did not have nettles behind his eyes. "Listen, itch," she muttered in her head, "you're just a figment."

The itch itched more fiercely.

"Go away," she muttered.

"What?" asked Fssa.

"Nothing," she snapped. Then, "Do you speak figment?"

Fssa's head snaked out of her hair until he confronted her sensors to eyes. "Are you all right?"

"No."

"Oh."

Fssa retreated, knowing he had lost but not knowing how. None of his languages had the words to cope with an irritated fire dancer.

"I think we're going out of the city," said Kirtn, looking at the sky.

"What I think is unspeakable," she muttered. Then she made a determined effort to ignore her eyes. It was hard. With every step farther out of Tllella territory, her eyes became worse. She had the unnerving feeling that something was following her, frantically yammering at her in a language she could not hear. Maybe Kirtn was right. Maybe she was allergic to illusions.

And maybe it was cold in Serriolia.

Rheba wiped sweat off her face and spoke dancer litanies in her mind. After a time it seemed to help. At least her thoughts were not so chaotic. Even the itch relented a bit.

"We're turning back toward the center of the city," said Kirtn.

Rheba glanced around. She did not have a Bre'n's innate sense of direction. It all looked the same to her—different from anything in her experience. "Do you know where we're going?"

"Farther from the *Devalon*."

"Is it time to call in yet?"

"No." Kirtn touched a broad stud on his belt. No current of energy tickled his finger. "No message yet, either. Everything must be under control."

"That would be a treat," Rheba said.

An apparition approached. It had no head, a formidable tail, and a snarl on what could have been a face. It belched as it passed. Fssa responded in kind. The eyeless body stopped, swung around in their direction, smiled and resumed its random drift up the street.

"I didn't see that," said Rheba.

"Neither did I," said Fssa.

"You never see anything."

"Accurate, but not true."

The sky drooled over them. Rheba's hair and clothes stuck to her. The squat, dark woman with the brooding bird on her shoulder turned to face the damp fire dancer.

"We're coming to a veil," said i'sNara. Her voice was the same as it had been on Loo, colorless, the voice of a slave who asked nothing.

Rheba's lines flared uneasily. "Are we going to the Yaocoon clan?"

"When you see Reality Street through the veil," continued i'sNara in a monotone, "go across."

"What about you?" said Kirtn.

"We'll come as soon as we can," said f'lTiri's voice.

"How long?"

"Not long."

"Then there's no reason to separate," Kirtn said in a bland voice, "is there?"

The bird blurred and became a man. "You heard what t'oHiri said. *Disillusionment*."

"We have no illusions as it is," cut in Rheba, shaking out her damp magenta hair. "Only the ones we borrowed from you. We'll lose them with pleasure."

"You don't understand." His voice was as harsh as his wife's was colorless. "If you help us, they'll take you and put you in a machine. You won't be able to move, not even to breathe. A lightknife will cut into your brain. When you wake up, you won't be able to project or see through illusions."

"We can't do that now," she said, but her voice was less

sure than her words. She would hate to be strapped to a machine while a laser rummaged in her brain looking for illusions to extirpate. "We have nothing to lose."

"You're not a fool. Don't try to sound like one. You don't know what form your disillusionment might take."

"I know that you risked your life on Daemen so that Kirtn could keep a promise that had nothing to do with you."

"But—"

"If there's danger, we're not making it any better by standing here arguing," pointed out Rheba. "You can't force us through the veil. If you go invisible on us and sneak away we'll be totally at the mercy of your enemies. Given those conditions, the safest place we can be is with you."

F'lTiri bowed to Senyas pragmatism. "Given those conditions, follow me." Then, softly, "Thank you."

The veil was a vague thickness across the street. Rheba stared over i'sNara's shoulders while the illusionists projected their destination on the veil.

Faces. A whirlpool of faces spinning around a brilliant center. Crystals shattering light into illusion. Whirlpool spinning around, sucking faces down and down, pulling at them relentlessly, spinning them until there was no direction but center where crystals waited with perfect illusions . . .

The veil shook. Destinations raced by too fast to see or choose. The illusionists hung on to each other and their goal. The veil bucked like a fish on a hook, but destinations slowed until a single view held.

Kirtn did not need i'sNara's signal to know it was time to cross. He spread his arms and swept everyone through, afraid that the least hesitation would separate them. They arrived in a breathless scramble, but together.

"Is the force field always that stubborn?" asked Kirtn as he set Rheba down and held her until her dizziness passed.

"No," panted f'lTiri, breathless from his struggle with the veil. "It keeps wanting to take us to the Redis clan house."

Kirtn looked around grimly. "Did we come to the right place?"

"Yes. Clan Yaocoon."

Rheba wondered how they could be so sure. The street they were on was just as hot and improbably populated as the last one. The illusions seemed to run to plant life here . . . eight-legged vines and ambulatory melons. She sighed and closed her eyes. At least the itch had abated.

When she opened her eyes a moment later she was a ripe

tomato swinging from a virile vine. Fssa was a thick green worm. A moment's frantic groping assured her that Kirtn was the vine. The vine chuckled and wrapped around her, lifting her off her feet.

"You like this," she said accusingly.

The vine tightened in agreement.

"Where are your ticklish ears?" she muttered, patting the area where his head should be. She found his ears beneath dark vine leaves. He relented and put her down, but kept a tendril curled around her wrist.

The illusionists were just ahead, appearing as exotic leafy plants, fragrant to the point of perfume. "Our scent won't change," said i'sNara. "Will you be able to recognize it?"

"Yes." Kirtn's voice was confident. A major portion of a Bre'n's fine palate was in the olfactory discrimination.

"Good. We'll try not to change too often, but we're going to go on random memory, keeping only the scent. It's a way of resting," explained f'lTiri. "Controlling the veil was hard work."

"Won't projecting our disguises tire you out?" asked Rheba.

"Hardly. Eyes only, no other senses involved. Elementary. Besides, Ara's house isn't far from the veil."

The two plants moved down the street. Their gait was erratic and their shadows tended to show legs instead of stems. The illusionists were too tired to worry about anything more complex than first appearances.

The house they stopped in front of looked like a jungle tree. F'lTiri edged forward, spoke to an orchid, and waited. After what seemed a long time the greenery shifted and revealed a cucumber lounging beneath a canopy of cool leaves.

"Ara?" said f'lTiri curtly.

The cucumber blurred and reformed. It was rotten now, oozing pestilence. "She's gone."

"Where."

The cucumber puddled and stank. "The only wall in Yaocoon, and the only gate."

The leaves bent down and mopped up cucumber residue. The tree closed on itself. F'lTiri did not talk until they were well away from the unfriendly house.

"What happened?" asked Kirtn.

"Ara doesn't live there anymore."

Kirtn's whistle was shrill enough to make nearby flowers shrivel. "I don't think that cucumber was glad to see you in any shape or form."

"No, but he would have been glad to see Ara rot. He was afraid."

"Why? Did he recognize you?"

"I doubt it. Ara must be involved in the rebellion." F'lTiri spoke in Universal, as though he feared eavesdroppers.

"Where do we go now?" asked Rheba.

"To the wall."

Rheba rubbed her eyes but could not reach the itch that was tormenting her again. The feeling of being followed, of being exhorted to *do something* in an unknown, unheard language was like a pressure squeezing her eyes. She turned around, knowing she would see nothing but unable to stop herself.

Far down the street, a grove of trees marched silently toward them.

"Kirtn!"

The Bre'n spun, hearing the warning in her voice. He felt her wrist burn with sudden power beneath his hand. "I see them," he said. "Illusion?"

"I wish. Fssa?"

Concave sensors whirled. Energy pulsed soundlessly, returned. "Men."

"Certain?"

The snake's head became a frilled cone, then a spiral, then a sunburst. "Men," he said again, in unambiguous Senyas.

Rheba and Kirtn hurried until they were right behind the illusionists. "We're being followed."

The plants did not seem to change, but Rheba clearly heard f'lTiri's gasp.

"They're all alike!" His tone made it clear that sameness was more astonishing than any possible manifestation of the illusionist's art. Then, "They might not be after us."

Fssa made a flatulent sound. Fourth People's capacity for wishful thinking was ridiculous when it was not dangerous.

"How far is the wall?" said Kirtn, lengthening his stride.

"How fast can you run?" retorted the Yhelle.

Exotic plants, vine, and tomato with green worm clinging sprinted down the street.

As she ran, Rheba wove sunlight into fire until she was incandescent. Kirtn's hand on her wrist soothed and steadied her, letting her take in more and more energy, giving her a depth and fineness of control that was impossible without him. Each member of an akhenet pair could stand alone, but together they were much more than two.

Fssa became eyes in the back of her head. His sensors

focused on the not-trees. "Confusion," he whistled. "They're bending around like grass in a wind. They're arguing whether to grab you here or wait for—*here they come!*"

The illusionists turned right, leaped an invisible barrier, and scrambled up a hill. Kirtn and Rheba duplicated the motions exactly, even when there seemed to be no reason for twisting, turning or leaping.

The trees followed.

"They're getting closer," said Fssa calmly.

"Are they carrying weapons?" panted Rheba.

"Clubs, mostly. A few metal fists."

"Lightguns?" she asked hopefully. She had discovered on Onan that she could take the output of a lightgun and reflect it back on its user. Learning that particular trick had burned and nearly blinded her, but it had wiped out the Equality Rangers who were pursuing them.

"No lightguns."

They ducked beneath a bridge, waded through a real stream and clawed their way up the opposite bank. Along the top of the bank ran a high steel wall. The illusionists sprinted parallel to the wall, trailing their fingers along it. Suddenly they stopped.

"Here!" called i'sNara, beating her palms in a staccato rhythm against the wall. F'lTiri joined her, leaves blurring into hands as he pounded on steel.

Kirtn and Rheba pressed their backs to the wall and turned to face their pursuers. Trees blurred and became men scrambling under the bridge and across the stream.

The pursuers were indeed all alike, even when they appeared as men. Gray clothes, gray gloves, gray clubs. Only their eyes were alive, pale as crystals in gaunt skulls. They came up the slope in a silent, ragged line. As one they began to close in on the four people trapped against the high wall.

The illusionists' beat on the steel dividing them from safety. They had managed to find "the only wall in Yaocoon."

But where was the gate?

IX

Rheba sent an exploratory current of energy through the metal wall. Akhenet lines glowed as she followed the energy's path. She sensed no circuits, no blank areas, nothing to indicate that the wall concealed or was powered by outside energy. There was a seamless sameness throughout its depth. No hint of a break, a gate. She would have to search more deeply, and much more deftly.

The illusionists beat their fists on the wall and called to their Yaocoon cousins.

"Mentor."

The word formed as much in Rheba's mind as on her lips. Kirtn stepped behind her, placing his hands on her shoulders. His long thumbs rested lightly just behind her ears. In that position he not only could help her balance the energies she used, he could also send her into unconsciousness if she called more than they could control. He had been forced to that extreme only a few times, when she was very young.

She spared a quick glance at the advancing men. They had slowed, sure of their prey. Or perhaps it was simply that they had never seen an apparition as arresting as a dancer fully charged, burning through her illusion from within.

"Snake," she murmured, "some sounds to go with fire."

Fssa burned beneath his green illusion until he became an eye-hurting incandescence that was a Fssireeme at near-normal body temperature. At normal, he was a mirror of punishing brightness, a perfect reflector, but he had been that way only a few times in his memory. Fourth People planets were much colder than the huge planet/proto-star that was home to Fssireemes.

His body shifted, expanding into baffles and chambers, membranes to create sound and bellows to give voice. A high, terrible keening issued from him.

The sound was a knife in her ears. She felt Kirtn's hands tighten on her shoulders and knew it was worse for him. Then

Fssa projected his voice over the men and she understood that sound could be a weapon. Men went to their knees with their hands pressed to their ears, mouths open in a protest that could not be heard over the sound tormenting them.

Yet still they advanced, knee-walking, faces contorted.

Deft Bre'n fingers closed over Rheba's ears, shutting out much of the sound. The pain was vicious for Kirtn, but Bre'ns were bred to withstand much worse before blacking out. If it were not so, young dancers would have no one capable of teaching them how to control the energies they could not help attracting.

Rheba set her teeth and concentrated on her own kind of weapon. She took more energy from the sunlight, braided it until it was hot enough to burn and sent it hissing across the lush grass separating them from the attackers. Flames leaped upward, bright and graceful, dancing hotly.

The attackers thought it was an illusion. The first man to stumble into the flames threw himself backward, scrambling and clawing at his clothes. Others hesitated but could not believe that they were not seeing an illusion. By twos and threes they struggled toward the twisting flames, only to be driven back by a heat they had to believe in.

Deliberately she wove more energy into fire, thickening the barrier that held the men at bay. There was little natural fuel to help her maintain it. The grass quickly burned to dirt. She could set fire to that if she had to. She could burn the whole area down to bedrock and beyond. It would be easier simply to burn the men, but in Deva's final, searing revolution she had seen too many die by fire. Her nightmares were full of them.

She turned toward the wall. Kirtn moved with her smoothly, knowing what she needed as soon as she did. She spread her hands and pressed them against the steel wall. The energy she sent into the metal was neither mild nor testing. She poured out power until currents raced through the wall's length, bending as the wall bent until wall and energy met on the far side.

There was a gate. It fitted so smoothly into the wall that it had not interrupted the flow of her first questing energy. She probed again, balanced by her Bre'n's enormous strength. Discontinuities much smaller than the interface between gate and wall became as plain to her as the sun at noon. She could sense minute changes in the alloy, stresses of weather and time, tiny crustal shifts that created greater tension in one wall section. There were weaknesses she could exploit if she had to.

But first there was the gate, the built-in weakness in every wall. The illusionists had located it correctly. It was beneath their flailing hands. And it was locked.

A bump in the energy outlining the other side of the wall told her what kind of lock she had to deal with. A slidebolt. Primitive and effective. She would have preferred a sophisticated energy lock. As it was, she would have to burn through the bolt without heating the wall-gate interface so much that the metal expanded, jamming irretrievably. Burning through to the bolt would require coherent light exquisitely focused.

And time. She hoped she had enough of that. *The men?*

The question was not so much words in her mind as an image of trees surging toward them, trees haunted by danger and held back by flames that thinned precariously.

Kirtn's answer was precise: *Dance*.

The command/invitation/exhortation went through her like a shockwave. Her hands were consumed by akhenet lines. Intricate swirls of gold ran up her arms, thinning into feathery curls across her shoulders. She was hot now, in full dance; only her Bre'n or a Fssireeme could touch her and not be burned. If she got much hotter she would risk burning herself and her Bre'n. If she got hotter than that she might kill them both. Dancers, like Bre'ns, could be dangerous to be around. There was no danger at the moment, though. She was dancing well within the abilities of herself and her Bre'n.

She stared at the wall with eyes veined with gold. She saw not steel but energy, pattern on pattern, currents swirling, dark line of interface, a bolt swelling out on the other side of the wall. Hot gold fingertips traced the line, seeing with a sight more penetrating than standard vision or touch.

Light gathered at her fingertip, startlingly green light that narrowed into a beam almost invisibly fine. The beam slid along the interface, warming it dangerously. Almost imperceptibly the interface shrank. She sensed the beam searing into the bolt, heating a thin slice of it. Before light could burn more than a tiny hole, wall and gate expanded very slightly, closing the interface.

Instantly she stopped, feeling the flash of her frustration echoed by Kirtn. To cut through the bolt and free the gate she must use more heat. Yet more heat would jam the gate against the wall before the bolt was cut apart.

Brackets.

The thought was hers, Senyas precision, picture of the brackets that inevitably must support the bolt mechanism.

She concentrated on the bolt-shape, sensing its location on either side of the cooling interface. Two brackets at least. No, four. Two on the gate and two on the wall. Strong, but thinner than the bolt—and far enough away from the interface to burn through without expanding wall and gate into an immovable mass. She hoped.

Light formed again at her fingertip, light more blue than green. It was wider than the previous beam yet still so narrow as to be more sensed than seen. The beam leaped out, bringing first red, then orange and finally white incandescence to the blank steel face of the wall. A tiny hole bored inward, a hole no wider than three hairs laid side by side.

By slow increments her fingertip moved, drawing coherent light through steel. The bottom of one bracket developed a molten line. The light moved on. Steel quickly cooled, but could not draw together again; some of its substance had been volatilized by dancer light.

One bracket was cut in two. The next bracket was closer to the interface. She had to burn less hotly. It was slow work, almost as delicate as burning through the interface had been.

Behind her, men were stirring. The Fssireeme's cry never stopped, but the men either were deafened now or too desperate to give in to pain. Fssa could step up the power of the cry, but he could not protect his friends from the result. He could only delay, not defeat, the attackers.

Clumps of dirt and rocks rained against her. Kirtn's body shielded Rheba from the worst of it. Even so, there was a moment of distraction, light flaring too hot, too hard, before she was in control again. A piece of the second bracket fell away. As though at a distance she heard i'sNara scream warnings, f'lTiri or an illusion roaring by, confusing the attackers.

The third bracket also was close to the interface, attached to wall rather than gate. Part of her, the part that was Senyas rather than dancer, knew that the illusionists were being overwhelmed by a ragged surge of men. Control shifted wholly to her, smoothly yet quickly. Their outnumbered friends needed Kirtn more than she did. They needed her, too. Three people, even when one was a Bre'n, were no match for what was coming up the slope.

Rheba felt impatience seething deep inside her, a reckless urge to vaporize everything within her reach, most particularly the stubborn gate.

Suddenly the gate swung inward, opened by someone on

the other side. It was so unexpected that Rheba nearly burned the Yaocoon clansmen on the other side. She stumbled through the opening, yanked out of her dance by surprise. She spun around inside the gate, still afire, and saw her Bre'n meet the first attackers. She heard their startled cries as he scooped up three men at once and flung them back on the gray uniforms charging up the slope.

I'sNara and f'lTiri rushed by Rheba, routed by a Bre'n snarl when they would have stayed to help him. Kirtn knew what his dancer would do when she saw him in danger. He wanted the illusionists out of the way of what was coming.

Rheba lifted her hands. Fire swept out from her, fire that was renewed as fast as it was spent, fire drawn from inexhaustible sunlight and condensed into flames. Her hair was all akhenet now, searing corona, sucking every available unit of energy into her.

Kirtn jumped for the gate in the instant before the firestorm broke. Fire sleeted harmlessly over his head, scorching the attackers but not killing them. There was no need to kill now. He was safe. Then she saw blood swelling over his fur and wished she had killed.

The moment of irrational rage passed; but like fire, it left its mark on her mind. It was some consolation to see how rapidly the zoolipt inside Kirtn healed his bruises and ragged cuts. It was not enough to neutralize her anger.

"Don't bite off more than the zoolipt can chew," she snapped as she leaned against the gate to swing it shut.

Kirtn looked at her in disbelief. "You dance with coherent light and then tell *me* to be careful?" He laughed the rich laugh of Bre'n amusement. "When you follow your advice, I will."

He put his shoulder to the gate. As always, his easy power surprised her. The gate moved quickly, smoothly on its massive hinges. It closed without a sound. He slid the bolt home.

It was none too soon. From the far side came hoarse cries. The gate vibrated with the force of pounding fists. They had not thought to bring a battering ram, so they used themselves.

"Will it hold?" asked Kirtn, bending over to see how badly she had damaged the bolt's brackets.

Rheba picked up the pieces she had cut off the two brackets. The hot pieces burned her. She could draw out the heat, but it would take more time than it was worth. Her akhenet lines offered some protection to her fingers. What the lines missed, the zoolipt would have to heal later.

Energy flared hotly as she welded the pieces into place. It was an easy job, requiring power but little finesse. When she was finished she stepped back to suck on her burned fingertips.

"It should hold as soon as the metal cools," she said.

Fssa stretched out of her hair. His head darted to each bracket, touched, and withdrew. He was brighter. The brackets were darker. Cold. Fssireemes were, after all, energy parasites. It was not a heritage they were proud of, but it had its uses.

"Next time you can cool off the pieces before I handle them," said Rheba.

Contrition moved in dark pulses over the snake's radiant head. "I should have thought of that sooner. Are you badly burned?"

"Doubt it," she answered, looking critically at her fingertips. As she had expected, they were whole again. "The zoolipt is no good on figment itches, but it's death on burns. See? Brighten up, snake."

Fssa took her advice literally. He let himself glow until he was a sinuous shape stitched through her still-wild hair. He enjoyed her dances almost as much as Kirtn did. With so much energy flying around, no one missed what he siphoned into himself. And it felt so good to be *warm*. Almost as good as his Guardian memory-dream of home, formations of Fssireemes soaring in the seething sky-seas of Ssimmi.

"Fssa," patiently, Rheba's voice, "what are they saying?"

Belatedly, the snake realized that the illusionists were talking and he was not translating. "Sorry," he hissed. "When you dance it reminds me of home."

She touched Fssa comfortingly and nearly burned her finger all over again. She had promised to find Ssimmi if she could. And she meant to. The snake had done more to earn it than any of the former slaves waiting impatiently aboard the *Devalon* for the captains to return.

"The Yaocoons aren't pleased," summarized the snake, boiling whatever three ranting vegetables and a fruit tree were saying into four words.

"How bad is it?" asked Kirtn. His yellow eyes searched the immediate area in useless reflex. He probably would not see trouble coming or would not recognize it if he saw it. How threatening was a kippi in bloom? Or a plateful of sliced fruit?

Fssa's sensors, darker now than his energy-rich body, gleamed like black opals as he scanned the group of gesticulating vegetables. "I'sNara is talking now." The snake listened, then hummed in admiration. "What diction! What clarity! What invective!"

"What meaning," prompted Kirtn.

"Irrelevant. Her suggestions are impossible for a Fourth People's inflexible body. To do what she proposes would challenge a Fssireeme."

Kirtn and Rheba waited, wishing they could understand Yhelle. Fssa hissed with Fssireeme laughter.

"Talk, snake, or I'll tie you in knots," snapped Kirtn.

Fssa waited until a Yaocoon outburst ended. "Without obscenities, the Yaocoons say they've never heard of Ara."

Bre'n lips thinned into a snarl. "Who's lying—the Yaocoons or that crazy cucumber?"

"I'sNara suspects the Yaocoons are lying. She's quite emphatic about it. I never would have expected such . . . color . . . from her."

Rheba waited and sweated and wondered if it was safe for her to let go of the excess fire she had gathered. The longer she held it, the more tired she would be when she let it go. It was one of the dancer ironies; the greater the energies employed in the dance, the greater the dancer's depletion afterward.

"F'lTiri has taken over now," offered Fssa. "He's less original, but louder. Between epithets, he's asking about the children."

"And?" demanded Rheba when Fssa fell silent.

The answer was a sharp descending whistle, forceful Bre'n negative. "Now he's asking about the—"

Suddenly the vegetables transformed into screaming, angry Yaocoons. As the appearance of planthood vanished, so did the appearance of sanctuary. Beneath their illusions the Yaocoon carried guns. The guns were real.

"—rebellion," finished Fssa. The snake sighed like a human. "At least we don't need to worry about being thrown back over the wall. They wouldn't let go of us now if I begged in nine languages."

X

"Not yet, dancer," whistled Kirtn, sensing that she was weaving her energy into potentially deadly patterns.

"I could cool them off," suggested Fssa in Senyas understatement. He could turn their bodies into blocks of flesh as frigid as rocks orbiting a dead sun.

Rheba waited, hair seething, bright as fine wires burning. The guns were mechanical, like the gate. She would not be able to deflect the bullets. She might be able to distort the plastic barrels enough to make the guns useless. She could burn the people holding the guns. It would take time, though, more time than bullets needed to reach them.

She moved closer to her Bre'n and waited.

F'lTiri stared at each Yaocoon in turn. They became uncomfortable. Some of them lowered their weapons. A few even retreated behind invisibility, leaving only the guns visible.

I'sNara stalked up to a weapon that seemed to hang in midair. "I see you, Tske," she said deliberately.

The Yaocoons gave a collective gasp. I'sNara had done the unspeakable.

"Can you see *me*?" she asked in a sweet voice. And vanished.

The Yaocoon behind the weapon materialized as he poured his energy into searching for i'sNara. When he could not find her, another Yaocoon joined with him, then another and another until five Yaocoons combined in a mental sharing that was both more and less than J/taal mercenaries could achieve. It was a mind dance of sorts, but limited to projecting or penetrating illusions.

The five cried out and pounced. I'sNara wavered into visibility, fighting their projected illusion of her as she really was. In the end she lost. She was forced to appear before them with no illusions. She had made her point, however. If she had wanted to kill them while they searched for her, she could have.

She had made her point too well. They tied her with a rope that had no illusion of softness. F'lTiri, too, was tied. Two Yaocoons had slipped up behind him while i'sNara taunted the others with her invisibility.

The same five who had unmasked i'sNara turned to concentrate on Rheba and Kirtn. The last shreds of their tomato, worm and vine illusion evaporated instantly, for they had no means of fighting the anti-illusion projection. The Yaocoons, however, did not stop. They continued to focus their projections on Bre'n, Senyas and Fssireeme, not realizing that the three were appearing as themselves.

When five Yaocoons could not penetrate the "illusions" in front of them, more Yaocoons joined in. Soon there were ten, then twelve, then twenty Yaocoons trying to nullify the alien appearances of Rheba, Kirtn and Fssa. It was futile. Illusionists could change the appearance of reality, but could not change reality itself.

"Redis," murmured one Yaocoon.

The word moved from one mouth to another, picking up speed like a stone rolling down a steep hill. "Redis, Redis Redis RedisRedis*Redis!*"

Weapons came up.

Fire leaped in Rheba's akhenet lines.

"No!" screamed i'sNara. "They aren't Redis! They aren't even Yhelles!"

Weapons paused. Yaocoons turned to look at i'sNara.

"They're from outside the Equality," she said quickly. "They were slaves with us on Loo."

The Yaocoons whispered among themselves, but not quietly enough to defeat the Fssireeme's hyperacute hearing.

"—believe her?"

"Unillusioned, she *looks* like Ara's memory of i'sNara."

"Yes, but the Stones—"

"He *is* f'lTiri. She *is* i'sNara. We were Libs together. I can't be mistaken!"

"A lot of Redis were once Libs."

"If we can't believe in our own unillusions, we might as well surrender to k'Masei right now."

The last was a snarl of frustration. The group broke apart, becoming more themselves, if startling colorations could be overlooked. One of the Yaocoons shivered and reformed, woman not man, chestnut-haired. She was tiny, perfectly formed without being unreal, and vivid.

"Ara," murmured f'lTiri. Then, "Where's my son?"

The woman Ara looked at the two Yhelles with little welcome. "A lot has changed since you were sold to Loo. *If* you are indeed the ones who were sold to Loo. K'Masei takes the illusions of former clanmates and uses them to haunt us."

Rheba walked forward a few steps, smoldering like a sunrise just below the horizon. "As you said, if you can't believe in your own unillusions, what's left?"

"I find it difficult to believe you're real at all," said Ara bluntly.

"Reality Street affected me the same way," admitted Rheba.

Ara's pale eyes glanced toward Kirtn. "*That's* not real. He's a sensualist's illusion." There was utter conviction in the woman's voice. She could accept Rheba, but not the tall man with her.

Rheba looked at her Bre'n, trying to see him with Ara's eyes. His copper skin-fur rippled over muscles that ensured grace as well as crude strength. Metallic copper hair curled against his powerful neck. His yellow eyes had a fire that rivaled hers in full dance. He stood like a clept watching an enemy, predatory purpose barely held in check, dangerous and fully alive. "Actually," Rheba murmured, rubbing her cheek against his arm, "he's a poet."

Kirtn smiled at her and whistled a seductive phrase out of a Bre'n courtship song. Her breath caught at the song's beauty, and his, but she managed to whistle the next phrase, a rising trill of longing that haunted the silence that followed.

Ara stared, riveted by possibilities that transcended cultural prejudices.

"Now you know how they destroyed the Loo-chim," said f'lTiri, his voice divided among too many emotions to name.

"And her fire. Don't underestimate that," sighed i'sNara.

"If he came from the Ecstasy Stones," Ara said finally, "I know now why we've lost so many to k'Masei's illusions."

"I didn't come from Stones, Ecstasy or otherwise." Kirtn's voice was rich with barely contained laughter. "You're as . . . unusual . . . to us as we are to you."

"That's more fantastic than any illusion I've known," Ara said. She looked at Rheba again. "Do you really burn?"

"Try me." Rheba's smile was challenging. She disliked Kirtn's effect on women. Irrationally, she blamed the women rather than the Bre'n.

Kirtn listened, slanted eyes unusually intense as he looked at his dancer. She was too young to be sexually possessive, yet she edged closer to it every day. She was too young to have akhenet lines arching over her hips, yet he had seen such lines, traceries of fire to come. She was too young to Choose, yet she gave off energies that kept him in a constant state of sexual awareness. Too young for Bre'n/Senyas passion. Yet . . .

He forced himself to look away.

"I don't think I will," said Ara, measuring Rheba's incandescent lines. The Yaocoon turned back to i'sNara. "Why are you here?"

"We told you. Our children."

"Your children aren't here," said Ara, regret and longing in her voice.

"So you say."

"You don't believe me?"

"I haven't seen their absence."

"What could convince you?"

"Join with me and f'lTiri to make a twelve. If we still can't find them, we'll leave."

Ara smiled but her voice was sad. "I'll join with you and you still won't find them. And you won't leave."

I'sNara hesitated, then accepted some words and ignored the rest. "Where are they?"

"With the Stones."

"Alive?"

"I don't know," said Ara in a strained voice.

"When did they leave?"

"Not long. Six days. We told them not to. We *begged*. They were strong in their illusions. We needed them for what was to come."

"Rebellion," said f'lTiri flatly.

"Yes."

The Yaocoons surrounding them made an uneasy, animal noise. Ara turned on them. "If the Tyrant can hear us in the center of our own illusions, then—"

"—we might as well give up," interrupted a thick voice. "You keep saying that. Are you sweating to be around your lover again? He'll be waiting for you in the Redis hall. The Tyrant never lets anyone go. No hurry, Ara, no hurry at all. Koro will still be there when the Final Illusion fades."

"Koro! What do you know about my son?" shouted f'lTiri.

"Ask Ara," said the man. "She's decided that her first illusion is the only one worth having. Even though he's an unillusioned traitor!"

Ara projected the appearance and stench of rotting meat on the speaker. He coughed and disappeared.

Before she could say anything, the thick-voiced man reappeared further away. "What about the other two?" he demanded. "They aren't tied."

Rheba stepped closer to Kirtn. He put his hands on her shoulders again, ready to partner her dance if it came to that.

"So tie them," suggested i'sNara when the other woman hesitated. "They won't object. I promise."

Kirtn eyed i'sNara doubtfully. "We won't?"

"No," said i'sNara in a firm voice. "We came for information. If we have to have our hands tied to get it then we'll have our hands tied."

"It doesn't matter," said Rheba to Kirtn in Senyas. "Plant fiber or plastic, I'll burn through it. Or," she added maliciously, "you'll break it in a display of Bre'n muscles that will make women moan."

"Shut up, dancer," said Kirtn amiably, holding out his hands to Ara. He smiled at the tiny woman and murmured, "I'm yours."

An illusion of incredible beauty suffused the Yaocoon woman.

Lightning smoldered in Rheba's hair. Kirtn glanced over at her and smiled like a Bre'n. He whistled softly, "There is no beauty to equal a Senyas dancer."

Her hair crackled ominously. It settled searingly around his neck, half attack, half caress. When she realized what she had done she made a startled sound. Her hair curled very gently across his cheek and lips, sending sweet currents of energy through him. "The zoolipt must be upsetting my enzyme balances. Apologies, mentor."

His eyes watched her with the hot patience of a Bre'n. "Accepted, dancer." Then, smiling, "Perhaps I told the Loo-chim the truth. We need to share enzymes from time to time in order to stay healthy."

Gold raced over her akhenet lines. She leaned against him, savoring textures and strengths that were uniquely Bre'n. She almost accepted the challenge and temptation implicit in his words. But his presence was so fierce that caution held her. He radiated like a Bre'n sliding toward *rez*. She stepped back, afraid of disturbing forces she could not calculate or control.

She turned and held out her wrists to Ara. "Tie me, then, if that's what it takes to make you feel good."

Ara stared from the uncanny Bre'n to the young woman smoldering in front of her.

"I won't burn you," said Rheba impatiently, damping the fires in her akhenet lines.

"You burn everything else in sight," muttered Ara. She accepted a strip of plastic held out to her by the thick-voiced Yaocoon.

Rheba waited with outward tranquillity while she was tied. The plastic bonds were cool, thick and loose. Ara was saying as plainly as words that she doubted the efficacy of bonds where Rheba was concerned. Ara turned to tie up Kirtn. She lingered so long over the job that Rheba's hair lifted in hot warning.

"What a marvelous texture," said Ara, stroking Kirtn's arm with appreciative fingers. "Is it real?"

"Yes," said Rheba, stepping close enough that Ara felt the heat from akhenet lines. "Like my fire."

Quickly, Ara backed away from both Senyas and Bre'n. She turned toward the illusionists, whose potential she understood. "Come with me."

"What?" said f'lTiri sarcastically. "You aren't going to tie us together in a Loo chain, slave to slave to slave in lockstep?"

Ara's appearance dimmed, making visible her inner embarrassment. "You're either enemies or you aren't," she said. "If you are, a Loo chain won't make any difference."

"Since when have Yaocoons tied friends?" F'lTiri held out his hands, accusing her with more than his voice.

"Since k'Masei the Tyrant," snapped Ara, angry with more than his words.

Unexpectedly, f'lTiri smiled. "I don't blame you, child. Koro loved you once."

Ara's face became the utter blank of an illusion waiting to form. She turned and began walking up what looked like a brook lined with Ghost ferns. The four bound people followed.

"Where are you going?" called the thick-voiced man.

Ara looked back. Her face was still an eerie blank. "To the clan hall. The full assembly will decide what to do with our . . . guests."

"What about them?" called the hoarse-voiced man, gesturing toward the gate. As though to underline his question, angry cries came from beyond the wall. The attackers beat on the gate with renewed force.

"If your paltry illusions fail," snapped Ara, "try real bullets."

In the silence that followed Ara's insult, the sounds of flesh thudding uselessly against steel sounded very close.

"Who *are* they?" asked Rheba, her voice rising above the noise of the men outside the gate. "Why don't they give up?"

Every Yaocoon turned to stare at her. Then, slowly, their illusions faded. They became more like themselves, appearing as they would before clanmates. Rheba stared in return, sensing that something had happened to disarm the Yaocoons. She turned questioningly to Ara.

"I believe," said Ara distinctly, "that you're just what you seem to be and you've just come from slavery on Loo."

"Good. But why?"

"Only an alien wouldn't know the Soldiers of Ecstasy."

Ara turned and continued up the stream that was a path.

"Fine words," muttered Rheba in Senyas, "but we're still wearing ropes."

XI

―――――――――

"Where are i'sNara and f'lTiri?" snarled Kirtn, towering over Ara.

The small woman's image blurred. When it reformed, she was out of his reach, watching him with dark eyes that held few illusions.

Kirtn flexed his bound hands. Strength rippled visibly through his massive arms. Rheba came to his side in a single smooth motion.

"Slowly, mentor," she whistled. "Even if you break the bonds, we don't know enough to escape yet."

His lips thinned into a bitter line. He was Bre'n, and frustrated everywhere he turned. He sensed the seductive violence of *rez* in the center of his bones. He looked at his dancer's eyes, cinnamon and gold, fear turning darkly at the center. The darkness hurt, for it was fear of him. Of *rez*.

He stroked her face with the back of his fingers, silently apologizing. "All right, dancer. Your way. But . . ."

"I know." Her lips burned across his before she turned around to face Ara. "Where are our friends?"

"Trying to fertilize a jungle."

"What?"

"The Yaocoon jungle is growing toward rebellion," said Ara dryly.

"Now? Tonight?"

Ara sighed. "That would be too much to hope for." She looked from Rheba to Kirtn's broad back. Even standing still, the Bre'n radiated savage possibilities. "I'sNara wants me to guide you back to your ship."

Kirtn spun around to face Ara. "No."

His speed and grace were so startling that Ara's image vanished completely for an instant. When she reappeared, she was out of reach.

"They said you killed the Loo-chim," whispered Ara. "Did you?"

"Yes," said Kirtn.

"Can you kill our Tyrant, too?"

"We're not executioners," he snarled.

Ara's mouth opened and shut soundlessly. When she spoke again, it was on another subject. "What do you know about Libs and Redis?"

"The Redis stole Ecstasy Stones so that everyone could share the good feelings," said Rheba when Kirtn refused to speak. "But the Redis didn't share, so the master snatchers who weren't Redis formed the Lib clan. Libs planned to steal back the Stones. They haven't had much luck."

"It's beyond Lib against Redis now," said Ara. "It's all of Serriolia. If someone doesn't help us we'll die. All of us."

"I doubt it," said Rheba coolly. "People have had a lot of practice surviving tyrannies."

"You don't understand." Ara's voice was soft. "This is a tyranny of love. There is nothing to hate, no leverage for rebellion. Everyone—*everyone*—who comes close to the Ecstasy Stones is caught by k'Masei. No," she said, when Rheba would have interrupted. "Listen to me. If your friends go to the Redis you'll never see them again."

Darkness pooled in Ara's eyes, a darkness haunted by dreams. Rheba had seen eyes like that before, Hiri's eyes staring out of a tarnished mirror. She felt pity for the tiny, beautiful illusionist who had found reality too painful to live with.

"I was just a little girl when k'Masei left the Lib hall to steal the Redis Stones, but I remember. He took our best Stones with him, Lib Stones. He thought they would protect him. Who could resist him when the Stones radiated love?

"When he left he was hazed in ecstasy, trailing love like a radiant cloud." Ara trembled at the memory. "The Stones. The Stones haunt my dreams wearing my husband's face, calling love to me . . . ecstasy."

Kirtn sighed. "K'Masei stayed in the Redis hall, didn't he?"

"He became their master snatcher. He stole Ecstasy Stones that had been clan secrets for thousands of years. He stole until the Redis had them all. If your illusions or reality didn't satisfy you, if you wanted to feel loved, you had to go to the Redis. To k'Masei."

Rheba saw Ara look at her own hands, small fists clenched so hard that muscles quivered in her arms. Her hands relaxed. Rheba was sure it was an illusion.

"At first it wasn't so bad," continued Ara. "People of all

clans would go to k'Masei, bathe in the Stones, and go back to their clans. But with each new Stone k'Masei stole, the experience changed. It deepened. It became . . . *necessary.*"

"And," said Kirtn sardonically, "people abandoned their clans to become Redis."

"Whole families," whispered Ara. "Children no taller than my waist. Gone."

"You make it sound as if they died," said Rheba.

Ara looked at her wildly. "How do you know they didn't?"

"Why would k'Masei kill them? Without them, who would he tyrannize? It sounds like a perfect match—people who want to be ruled and a man who wants to rule them." She would have said more, but her eyes chose that moment to itch with renewed ferocity.

Ara's appearance darkened and grew until it filled the small room where they were being held. "Nobody wants to be ruled!"

Fssa made a flatulent sound and stuck his head out of Rheba's hair. "Most people want to be ruled. They just don't want to admit it."

The illusionist's image deflated. She stared at the snake in astonishment. "It's real? It really speaks?"

"It really does," said Kirtn, glaring at Fssa. "Usually out of turn."

"What does a snake know about *people*?"

"That particular snake is a Fssireeme. His memories go back thousands of years."

"That doesn't mean he's right!" retorted Ara hotly.

The Bre'n said nothing, but skepticism was eloquent in his stance.

"If people want to be ruled, why does k'Masei need the Soldiers of Ecstasy?" demanded Ara.

"He probably doesn't, but they need him," said Kirtn impatiently. "I'll bet they're lousy illusionists. Strong arms and thick heads, right?"

"I—how did you know?"

"Fourth People are alike under the skin. Before k'Masei, I'll bet there wasn't a comforting illusion in the whole lot of them."

Ara's face settled into stubborn lines. "Koro did not want to be ruled."

"Koro? F'lTiri's son?" asked Rheba, abandoning her attempts to reach the itch at the back of her eyes. "Do you know where he is? Do you know where his sisters are?"

"With k'Masei, of course," said Ara bitterly. "They went to steal the Stones two days ago. I went with them. At least, I thought I was going with them. Tske tricked me. I followed his illusions rather than Koro's reality. By the time I found out, it was too late. Koro and his sisters were gone. They didn't come back. No one comes back from k'Masei." Ara looked from Rheba to Kirtn. "Now, are you sure you don't want to go back to your ship?"

"Yes."

"Then follow me."

Ara led them to the hall where the Yaocoon clan had gathered to discuss the attack of the Soldiers of Ecstasy, the appearance of two master snatchers and the aliens who had to be apparitions but were not. Rebellion was also on the agenda, but it was discussed in shaded illusions, if at all.

The Yaocoon hall seemed to be a jungle with no clearing. Plants of all kinds—and plants of unknown kinds—crowded one against the other. Fronds waved, flowers unfolded, fruit ripened in a riot of competing scents. The ceiling seemed to be an overcast sky. The heat and humidity were real, as inseparable from Serriolia as illusions.

Ara left Rheba, Kirtn and Fssa in the only corner that did not writhe with vegetable life. I'sNara and f'lTiri were nearby, defiantly wearing the illusions of the outlawed Liberation clan. She was shadow-drifted moonlight. He was darkness with only a hint of movement. Beneath those illusions lurked master snatchers, ready to slip between the cracks of human attention and steal the fabled Ecstasy Stones.

Rheba summed up her feelings with a whistle that descended from shrillness to silence in five beats. Kirtn took her bound hands in his. Lines glowed beneath his touch, sending restless messages through him. He rubbed his cheek against her gold-veined fingers. "Gently, dancer," he whistled. "Don't waste yourself on anger."

It was advice he needed as well. He rubbed his lips against her hot fingers and said nothing. After a few moments she sighed and gave in to his gentle persuasions against anger. She knew her Senyas logic was supposed to balance his Bre'n impulsiveness. She was young, though. She had already failed him once, when he had flashed into *rez* in a Loo dungeon. She could not let that happen again. But she did not know how to prevent it, either.

Some of her thoughts leaked to him. As always, danger heightened their ability to mind dance. He sensed her unease as a distant scream, echo and aftermath of *rez* still unabsorbed in her mind.

He kissed her fingertips before releasing her hands, afraid of what his thoughts might reveal to her in turn. She did not know that she had driven him into *rez*. Not her fault. She had no Senyas mother, no Bre'n mother, no paired akhenets to live among until gradually it came to her that Bre'n and Senyas akhenets were also lovers. He could tell her—and ensure their destruction. She would not refuse him, he knew that, and he also knew that was not the same as Choosing him. Dancer's Choice. Without that Choice freely made, akhenets lived under a sentence of death by *rez*.

He wondered what the Bre'n Face he had given her to wear was telling her, and if it could replace the tacit knowledge that had burned to ash on Deva. Even if the Face could teach her, when would she have the time or the tranquillity to meditate upon its messages? After she had come out of the long withdrawal that had followed the firestorm, she had vowed to find other survivors and build a new akhenet culture on a new planet. Since then, life for them had been one endless tumult beginning with a game called Chaos and culminating in a room full of illusions.

As though just discovering the strangers, the jungle quivered and swept toward Rheba and Kirtn like a hungry grove of Second People. Acid tendrils whipped down, coiling around fire dancer and Bre'n. A tangible sense of danger permeated the illusion. Rheba's akhenet lines ignited in molten warning.

"Enough." Ara's voice was a harsh wind ripping apart the jungle.

Gradually, the jungle straightened, becoming individual trees and flowers once more.

Ara stood on a raised part of the hall that was more balcony than stage. Her appearance had changed. She was taller, darker, more commanding. The last whispers and jungle rustles died away. Sure that she had the Yaocoon clan's attention, she changed again. She was herself now, small and vivid and somehow even more compelling.

"The two strangers you see are either real or twelves," said Ara. "They came with the master snatchers from the Liberation clan."

Noise rose, a sound like distant wind. The word "Liberation" was anathema, proclaimed so by the Tyrant. To speak it was dangerous. To shield Libs was to beg for disillusionment. Words flew like wind-driven leaves, proclaiming fear. The jungle rustled ominously. Poisonous-looking flowers unfurled long petals. Fruit ripened, then fell at the feet of i'sNara and f'lTiri and burst into putrescence.

"What a brave clan I joined," sneered Ara. "When courage is required, you hide and stink."

Anger whipped through the jungle.

"You plot and whine endlessly because it's so much safer than *doing* anything."

A roar of protest drowned Ara's voice. Fssa made himself into a megaphone that projected Ara's sadness and scorn throughout the room.

"You let a whole clan of master snatchers die one by one. Who will replace them? Who will steal the Ecstasy Stones now and free us all? Is it you, clan Yaocoon? Any of you?"

Protest died. Not even a leaf moved.

"Volunteers?" said Ara in rising tones of sarcasm. "Speak up. This illusion of silence is deafening."

The jungle glowered . . . silently.

"Hide and stink." The words reeked scorn. She looked out over the massed greenery. "I see you, Tske. Are you going to volunteer?"

A whirlwind of leaves spun up to the balcony, surrounding Ara. Leaves resolved into a man standing very close to her. He was nearly as wide as he was thick. None of it was fat.

"And I see you, Ara. Are *you* volunteering to be k'Masei's slave?" He leaned over her, whispering. "I have a better offer. Me."

Rheba recognized the hoarse-voiced man who had been so hostile to them at the wall. The last words he spoke were so soft that only Ara and the Fssireeme murmuring into Rheba's ear heard.

Ara ignored Tske. She stared out at the quivering jungle illusion. "Do I have to see each one of you before you see the truth? Is hide and stink the best you can do?"

The jungle whipped and shuddered. No one stepped forward.

"I see all of you," she said scornfully, "but I see nothing at all."

Rheba held her breath against the stench rising out of the jungle.

"Won't anyone go with me to steal the Ecstasy Stones?" cried Ara.

"We will!" said i'sNara and f'lTiri, leaping to their feet.

The jungle argued. Unnoticed, Rheba and Kirtn eased along

the edge of the room until they were next to i'sNara and f'lTiri. Fssa summarized the arguments he had heard:

"Those belonging to Tske want to send us in alone. The rest want to go with us on a raid. All of them are scared. The only thing they can agree on is that they're not ready to agree on anything."

"While they argue, our children could be dying." F'lTiri's tone was as neutral as his appearance, but no one was fooled.

"We'll go without the Yaocoons," said i'sNara. "Who needs an army of vegetables?"

"You'll need whatever you can get," Ara said succinctly, appearing beside f'lTiri. "No one comes back from the Redis hall."

"We did."

The jungle changed around them. It was no longer one solid mass of greenery. Openings appeared, ragged boundaries dividing Yaocoon from Yaocoon while arguments raged among the treetops.

The snake translated fragments he snatched out of the air:

"Do you want to die without even the illusion of a fight?"

"—her voice calling in my dreams. Ecstasy knows my name. I'm lost."

"—like all the others. Here one night, gone the next. It must be a truly Grand Illusion."

"The Tyrant's bleeding us clanmate by clanmate—"

"—dreamed again—"

"Stones on a mirrored table."

"—ecstasy reflected in a thousand faces."

"No one can go against k'Masei the Tyrant."

Fssa abandoned translating the cacophony, hissed, and said in cold Senyas, "They have as many mouths as a Fssireeme but they speak only the language of fools."

The Fssireeme's voice was like an iron bell. Silence spread out from him as Yaocoons turned to stare. Within moments, even the smallest plants took up the hush. A gnarled vine writhed across the jungle canopy. It curled lovingly around Ara, then coiled like a snake in front of Kirtn.

"I didn't give permission for you to leave your garden," said the vine in Tske's hoarse voice.

"I didn't ask." Kirtn's lips parted. Slightly serrated teeth gleamed.

The vine swelled. It quivered, ready to strike. Rheba's hair fanned out into a rippling field of fire. Kirtn was wrapped in flames. He laughed. Fire streamed from his mouth.

The vine wavered, then withdrew slowly.

The fire remained.

Uneasiness went through the jungle like a cold wind. The vine became a whip cracking, demanding attention. "We're not here to play illusion games," husked Tske. "The continuity of the clan Yaocoon is at stake. As reigning illusionist—"

"Only because Koro is gone," snapped Ara.

"—I've decided to use reason rather than illusion to settle the argument. You've all heard Ara." A mouth appeared on each vine leaf, sarcastic smiles endlessly repeated. "We've heard nothing but Ara wailing since her little Koro left."

Laughter and grumbles evenly mixed.

"You've all heard me when I argued with Koro. I thought it was a fool's project and he was a fool. I still think Koro's a fool," he added, "but a raid on the Ecstasy Stones by the Yaocoons is better than dreaming and screaming every night."

"That's what Koro used to say," muttered Ara to Rheba. "I don't trust this sudden change."

Ara was not the only one surprised by Tske's turnabout. Trees, shrubs and parasitic flowers rattled in consternation. Tske had been against a raid on the Redis since the idea had first been broached, long before Koro had been driven into Yaocoon's uncertain refuge.

Tske ignored the questions quivering in every rigid leaf of the jungle. "Those who want to go on the raid move toward the flowerfall." The vine pointed to the left side of the room. Suddenly, colorful flowers spurted out of the air and drifted to the floor, where they settled into fragrant piles. "Those who don't want to raid, leave the room. That's it. No more talk. Decide."

The jungle whispered among itself, then began tearing itself root from branch, flower from stem, vine from trunk. Illusions blurred and reformed until Rheba was dizzy from trying to sort out what came from which and belonged to whom. Many illusions vanished entirely from the hall, but many more stayed, voting for rebellion.

Rheba would have felt better if Tske were not among them.

XII

Whatever Tske's personal defects were, he was an efficient organizer. When he gave orders, illusions jumped. The scent of bruised flowers filled the air as Yaocoon after Yaocoon trampled petals underfoot, crowding forward to listen to the many-mouthed vine.

Rheba and Kirtn turned their heads slowly, counting illusions. "Fifty-two?" Her voice was hesitant.

"Sixty-four?" His voice was equally unsure. Neither one of them had much skill at numbering impossibilities.

F'lTiri overheard them. He leaned toward her and whispered, "Seventy-seven."

She sighed. "Right." Her voice echoed Scavenger Scuvee of the planet Daemen, brusque and resigned at the same time.

Kirtn smiled. Scuvee had been unpolished but likeable all the same. At least she had not tried to kill them, which was more than could be said of most Daemenites.

"Some are good illusionists," continued f'lTiri. "Young, for the most part, but strong. They don't like Tske leading the raid they've been planning, but they'll take orders. He's the best illusion they have right now."

With a grimace, Ara looked away. "I don't trust Tske."

"If I were you, neither would I," said i'sNara with a curt laugh. "But with this many Yaocoons as witness, he'll behave."

Fssa poured a running commentary into Rheba's ear. Most of it had to do with personalities and processes alien to her. Her lines rippled and winked restlessly, telling of energy held within her. She curbed her impatience, not wanting to provoke a similar—and more dangerous—impatience in her Bre'n.

"Eleven groups of seven," whistled Fssa. "Tske will lead our group. I don't know the name of the other Yaocoon who will be the seventh in our group. We'll be the last out the gate, holding the illusion of shadows and street over us.

Easier than invisibility and nearly as good. The other groups will project various illusions. Each will have a flower, leaf or fruit somewhere in it. That's more for us than for them. Clanmates can peel each other's illusions the way I peel new languages.''

Rheba made a grudging sound of appreciation. It was thoughtful of Tske to provide for nonillusionists. It might also be a bit risky for the Yaocoons to openly wear a badge of their affiliation. Perhaps outsiders could not strip away illusions with the facility of clanmates. She hoped so. She would hate to be responsible for putting Yaocoons in uniform so that the enemy could find them more easily.

"Tske wants the first three groups to go out and reconnoiter. He wanted just one group, actually, but they talked him out of it. Seven people aren't enough if they run into the Soldiers of Ecstasy."

"Ecstasy? Stupidity is more like it," muttered Rheba.

A second Fssireeme mouth formed, hissing agreement, while the first one continued translating without missing a syllable. Rheba listened, unconsciously tracing the outlines of the worry stones concealed within her pocket.

"If it's clear to the veil, they'll send back a messenger," continued Fssa. "Groups will leave at fifteen-second intervals. That should be far enough apart to keep the images from overlapping but not so far that we can't cover for each other."

"Overlapping images?" said Rheba doubtfully.

"Right," said the Fssireeme, in exact reproduction of Scuvee's voice. Then, "They didn't explain, so I don't know any more than you."

She shrugged like a Bre'n. The strategy and tactics of illusory raids were something she was forced to leave to the apparition in charge. "And after the veil?"

"They're still arguing about that one. Three groups want the honor of being first into the Redis hall."

"Fools."

"Probably." Silence from the snake, but not from the Yaocoons crowding around the vine that was Tske.

"What are they saying?"

"Insults. Redundant and unimaginative."

"Let me know if you hear a good one."

Fssa made a flatulent sound. Except for i'sNara, who had been a slave to the Loo-chim, illusionists confined their originality to their appearance. "Tske settled it. The groups are numbered now, one through eleven. We're eleven. Last in. They'll create the diversion and we'll do the sneaking and stealing."

"How?"

"That hasn't come up yet."

Rheba closed her eyes. When she opened them, Kirtn was watching her. "I'll bet it ends up a burn job," she said to him.

He smiled crookedly. "Most things do, when you're around." He worked his long fingers into the hair seething about her face. "That's why I Chose you, dancer. Even in your cradle you burned."

She leaned into his touch, stretching and rubbing against his hand. The resonances he set off within the energy she held were as enjoyable as the physical contact itself. It also kept her from thinking about the impossible theft they had volunteered to attempt. Ecstasy Stones. She had no use for them. She had her Bre'n.

A tendril of her hair curled out and settled around his muscular forearm. It was a touch that would have burned anyone except Kirtn. To him, it was a sharing of fire that went through him in an expanding wave of pleasure, marshaling and releasing the random energies that would otherwise eat away at his rationality until he dissolved into *rez*. Dancers danced because they could; Bre'ns shared that dance because they must, or die.

"The first group is gone," whistled the snake.

"What? Just like that?" said Kirtn. "No more planning than a few arguments and Tske's yapping vine?"

"The Yaocoons have been planning and arguing since their Ecstasy Stones were stolen years ago. They've run out of plans."

"But not arguments?" suggested the Bre'n.

"How did you guess?" said the snake acidly.

"They're Fourth People. The last thing we run out of is argument."

Kirtn's voice was haunted, remembering the verbal battles that had raged on Deva over whether it was better to flee the planet or stay and ride out the sun's unstable period. Ten years, twenty. No more than fifty at most. Then the sun would be benevolent again. But it had not happened the way Senyasi and Bre'ns had planned.

He was too young to remember much more than the last fifteen years on Deva. His Senyas and Bre'n parents had remembered, though. Now some of their memories were his. He laid his cheek on a burning strand of dancer hair, grateful that Rheba was too young to have his memories. Her own were bad enough.

Deva? It was both question and statement, spoken in his mind, wrapped in a complex of her emotions.

He curled a tendril of hot gold around his finger, letting Deva recede into the past again. "We're on Yhelle now. That's enough trouble without looking for more to burn."

Her eyes watched him, sad and wise and too gold for a dancer her age.

"At least they're going to untie you," said Fssa.

As one, Bre'n and Senyas looked at their wrists. Though they saw only a flicker of shadow and light, they felt the cool touch of a knife as it slid through their bonds.

"Thanks, whoever you are," said Rheba.

A fern no taller than her waist appeared. The fronds shivered and thinned, revealing a boy beneath. Rheba was so shocked to see a child rather than an adult that she forgot to return the boy's smile.

"Did you see that?" she asked in Senyas.

"Yes." Kirtn's voice was matter-of-fact.

"He's too young to risk his life on a raid against a tyrant that a whole clan couldn't touch!"

"The first time I sent you out against Deva's sun, you were younger than that boy." His voice was still neutral, but his eyes were like hammered metal.

"That's different. I was a dancer. I was bred for fire."

"And he's an illusionist, born and bred. I suspect the difference between your situation on Deva and his on Yhelle is more apparent than real."

"But the life of our people was at stake!" objected Rheba hotly. "We sent children against the sun because we had no choice!"

"It's the same with him." When she would have argued more, he cut her off roughly. "Think of what we've heard, dancer. No one who goes into the Redis clan hall comes back. *And one by one, everyone in Serriolia is being drawn into that hall.*"

She thought about it. She did not like any of her thoughts. She rubbed her wrists absently. The bonds had peeled off some skin despite the zoolipt's efforts to keep its host whole.

Or perhaps it was just that even zoolipt-healed skin itched with newness.

"I've got a nasty feeling that my zoolipt is going to earn its keep," she said finally.

"Don't count on the zoolipt too much," cautioned Kirtn. "I'm sure it has limits."

"Wonder what they are?"

"I don't want either of us to find out the hard way. Don't be careless, dancer."

"Me? You're the one that's a target as big as a spaceship. Nobody will even see me hiding behind you."

"Then you must have figured out a way to burn invisibly," smiled Kirtn, tugging gently on the electric tendril of hair he had wrapped around his finger.

Laughter ran brightly along her akhenet lines.

"The messenger just came back," said Fssa softly. "It's clear to the veil. Not a Soldier of Ecstasy in sight."

Groups of illusionists moved toward the door. As they moved, they changed. One group of trees, ferns and hanging flowers merged into the illusion of a single child batting a bright leaf from hand to hand.

Though Rheba knew there were eleven people in the group, she could not see them . . . unless they were that indefinable blurring of floor and wall, the not-quite-shadows gliding soundlessly out the door.

A cat condensed out of another group. Long-tailed, tawny, it turned to look at her. Its eyes were purple flowers carved out of gems. It stretched and moved with insolent ease after the boy.

"Beautiful," murmured Kirtn. "But I thought var-cats were legends."

"There's a lot of the Equality we haven't seen," said Rheba.

"Var-cats are real," whistled Fssa. "They were bred as a kind of mobile money in the Third Cycle. There aren't many left. Unstable."

Another group left the room wearing the illusion of an animal that even Fssa could not name. The beast was small and wore a pink flower tied to its tail. More child illusions left, quarreling over a ball that looked like a ripe melon. A woman walked away, tiny and black, wrapped in sensuality.

"Satin," breathed Kirtn.

Rheba's mouth thinned. Satin was the owner of the Black

Whole, the worst gambling dive in Nontondondo, which was the most licentious city on an utterly immoral planet. Satin was a psi master. She had sold them their Equality navtrix. She had also wanted Kirtn as a lover. And Kirtn had not said no as firmly as Rheba could have wished, for above all, Satin was alluring.

The woman turned. Between her breasts was a black orchid.

"Not quite Satin," sighed the Bre'n. "Satin is more . . . *alive*. But a woman of her race, definitely. I wonder where that planet is."

Rheba glanced sideways at him, a hot comment ready on her lips. Then she saw his yellow eyes watching her with unusual intensity. She bit her lip and said only, "And I wonder what we'll look like when we leave the room."

F'lTiri left the vine to writhe and yammer with its many mouths. He and i'sNara came over to Rheba.

"How much of that muddle did your snake pick up?" asked f'lTiri.

"Eleven groups of seven. We're number eleven. They'll provide a distraction while we snatch the Stones," summarized Rheba. "If anything was decided about our disguise or how in the name of the Inmost Fire we're going to pull off the theft, I didn't hear about it."

"Neither did I," said i'sNara grimly. She flapped her narrow white hand in a gesture of dismissal. "Just stay with me and f'lTiri. We'll peel the Redis hall illusions and get to the Stones faster than any clumsy Yaocoon. As for your disguises, you won't need any. Tske says that after your appearance on Reality Street, dancer and Bre'n pairs will be popping up all over Serriolia."

"He's probably right," said f'lTiri. "In any case, a good illusion for you two would take too much of our energy. Of course, you could stay here," he added with a hopeful lift of his voice.

"We never would have let you off the ship if we had known what would happen," put in i'sNara.

"We never would have let you off the ship either," retorted Kirtn. "But we did and you did. So let the dance begin." As he spoke, he pressed the harness stud that was also a transceiver. The stud remained inactive, telling him that no message was waiting to be deciphered by him.

Rheba saw him touch the stud, whistled a question and received a quick reassurance. No message. That meant that all was well on board the *Devalon,* because messages were reserved for emergencies. She was surprised to realize that she had been away from the ship for less than a half day. It seemed like a Loo week. Yhelle's illusions nibbled at the foundations of time as well as other perceptions.

The illusionists blurred. They reformed as a vague thickness between Rheba and the door.

"How can I follow that?" asked Rheba sharply. "If the Redis go in for textured glowstrips, I wouldn't be able to see you if you were standing on my feet."

"Watch," whispered f'lTiri.

Shadow shifted. Brightness turned and sparked at its center. Motes twisted and formed into a familiar shape, a Fssireeme with mouth open. It was a deft performance, done with only a few lines of illusion. Even Fssa was impressed.

"If you get lost, whistle and watch for the snake," murmured f'lTiri. Then, even more softly, "Be ready to burn, fire dancer."

Rheba's hair seethed and crackled, throwing off hot glints in the nearly empty hall. She let her lines gorge with energy, fierce gold racing over her body until it looked as though she wore a lacework of fire beneath her brief clothes. "I'm always ready to burn," she said quietly.

"If we get separated," i'sNara said, "go to the nearest veil. You can sense the direction of the veils, can't you? Their energies?"

Rheba remembered the discordant veil energies combing through her. She closed her eyes and tried to visualize the energy patterns of the hall, the compound, and finally the surrounding streets and residences. Then, like a distant disturbance, the curdling veil. "Yes . . . it's there. I don't like it."

I'sNara made a relieved sound. "See? I told you she could do it," she said to f'lTiri. "They'll be all right if something happens to us."

"But how do we use the veil once we find it?" asked Kirtn.

"Hurry up," snapped the vine that was Tske.

"All possible destinations appear one after the other," said f'lTiri quickly. "Just wait for Reality Street to cycle in. It's slower than our method of using the veil, but you don't have time to learn the other way."

The vine made a rude sound and turned into a shadow. "Follow me. Now!"

Rheba looked at her Bre'n. He shrugged, but his eyes had a feral gleam. Her akhenet lines echoed her heartbeat, a rhythmic pulse that grew brighter with each unit of deadly energy stored.

Side by side, dancer and Bre'n followed shadows out into the thickening night.

XIII

The gate swung shut heavily on its hinges, turning the wall into a seamless whole once again. In the deepening gloom outside the Yaocoon clan compound, Rheba flamed like a torch. She damped her burning somewhat but could not fade from sight unless she released a lot more energy, too much, in fact. She did not want to be caught cold if an ambush came.

Night seemed to conceal rather than cool the humid heat of day. She was too hot to sweat. Akhenet lines rather than perspiration carried away her body heat now. Kirtn's coppery skin/fur, however, was almost black with sweat. Where his weapon harness and Rainbow rubbed against his fur, traces of lather showed in pale streaks. Rainbow reflected dancer fire in every crystal facet, a molten necklace rippling against his broad chest.

"We're about as inconspicuous as a nova at midnight," said Kirtn grimly.

Ahead of them, various illusions merged invisibly with the night. A child's laughter, a cat's purple eyes, a flash of the black woman's fingernails, those were all Kirtn had to mark the unknown trail. Their own group was invisible to him.

"I'm glad the veil isn't far," he said very softly as the land dipped beneath his feet.

His empty weapon harness annoyed him. In Serriolia, guns were an admission of failed illusions. Except for a few pragmatic Yaocoon rebels, only Soldiers of Ecstasy carried guns. There had been no weapon for him. It was a situation he planned to remedy with the first soldier he got his hands on.

They scrambled down the decline to the stream, using Rheba's akhenet lines to see by. She would have made a ball of cold energy and sent it ahead to light their way, but feared being even more conspicuous than nature had made her.

When they got to the edge of the stream, they stopped. Kirtn watched the night with wide yellow eyes that were better adapted to darkness than gold-veined dancer eyes. He neither saw nor heard anything, not even the footsteps of the rest of their group. Calling out to them was tempting but foolish. So was blundering blindly up the opposite bank of the stream.

"Do you sense anything, snake?" whispered Kirtn.

"Water. Shallow, only a few strides across. Incline. Something at the top that could be trees."

"Could be?" asked Rheba, her voice barely audible.

"Dancer," Fssa murmured patiently, "on Yhelle, they could be anything."

"Including Soldiers of Ecstasy?" she snapped.

"Including—" Fssa convulsed, reshaping himself into an array of scanning devices.

Balanced on the breakpoint of dance, Rheba sensed the Fssireeme's changes and even, very slightly, the energies radiating from and returning to him. She grabbed Kirtn's arm. He looked at her and saw the odd shapes of Fssa beneath her glowing hair. He froze, trying to make no sound that would obstruct the snake's search.

Fssa's whistle was a mere thread of sound. "I don't like it. Not the trees—they're real enough—but beyond. Sounds."

"What kind of sounds?" asked Kirtn, his voice so soft that only a Fssireeme could have caught the words.

"Fourth People sounds. But no rhythms."

"That doesn't make sense, snake."

"Fourth People walk in patterns and talk in patterns, and patterns have rhythms. These sounds don't."

"Maybe the trees break up the patterns of sound," whispered Rheba.

A hiss was the snake's only answer. Then, sharply, "I know about echos the way you know about energies. These are *wrong*."

"Maybe it's an illusion," suggested the Bre'n.

Fssa made a sizzling sound, Fssireeme anger.

Kirtn looked at Rheba. His eyes were hot with reflected dancer fire. Hers were growing more gold with each heartbeat.

"Ambush?" he whispered.

"Surely Fssa would have heard something."

A scream, stifled in the first second, yet unmistakable.

They crossed the stream in a single leap and ran up the opposite bank. As they gained the top, she sent a white sheet of energy ahead to light the way, knowing that it was possible to hide in blinding brightness as well as in darkness. Not only would the wall of light illuminate what was ahead, it might catch attackers with their illusions down.

Frozen in the unexpected light, illusionists and Soldiers of Ecstasy slipped in and out of illusion in dizzying blurs, adjusting their appearances to the demands of light instead of darkness. Motionless huddles of clothes lay strewn across the clearing between trees both real and illusory. Some of the shapes on the ground wore gray uniforms, but only a few. Most wore the rags of people whose appearance depended on illusions woven over a threadbare reality.

Black against dancer light, shadows formed and reformed around Redis and Soldiers, trying to bring them down. But there were so many more Redis than shadows, and the Soldiers' white eyes saw through illusions with frightening ease. Shadows slid to the ground and puddled into ragged, motionless bundles.

With the ambush discovered, there was no further need for stealth. Guns appeared in Redis hands. Muzzles flashed and vented death. More shadows screamed and became illusionists slack upon the ground.

Flames seethed out from Rheba, licking among the gray uniforms of the Soldiers of Ecstasy. Hands holding weapons were burned to the bone. Five Soldiers, then, twelve, screamed and cradled their hands. The clearing shivered and changed as more uniforms poured out from between the trees.

Rheba answered with another wash of flame. To her horror, she saw that some of the uniforms were facades forced upon Yaocoons by superior Redis illusionists.

She had burned three of her own people.

Kirtn whistled shrilly, demanding that i'sNara and f'lTiri show themselves. There was no answering flash among the roiling shadows, no snake shape calling wordlessly to them.

Rheba lifted her hands and sent lightning to dance among the fighters. Uniforms retreated, harried by shadows. The ground sizzled and stank and finally grew sullen flames. Smoke rose, concealing the shadows that remained. It was all she dared to do until she had some way of telling Yaocoon illusionists from Redis.

Kirtn leaped into the smoke, looking for friends. He quickly discovered that conscious or not, the Soldiers of Ecstasy wore real uniforms, as befitted their lack of illusion talents. He suspected that some of the badly dressed illusionists fallen throughout the clearing were also Redis, but had no way of being sure. He searched through the casualties with ruthless speed. He did not find anyone he recognized.

Fire sizzled past him. Something yelped and retreated, dropping a gun. He scooped it up, learning its mechanism by feel and firelight. Muzzle, barrel, stock, trigger. Guns varied little from culture to culutre. Their design was implicit in their function.

He put his back to a real tree. Rheba set barriers of flame burning in an arc behind him. Fssa whistled a shrill imperative that ended with two names. If i'sNara and f'lTiri were conscious, they would come to the Bre'n.

For a moment, the only sound in the clearing was the hot crackle of fire. They had broken the back of the ambush, but were still far from safe. Warily, Rheba moved to join her Bre'n. They formed a triangle with the tree as their apex. Fssa scanned ceaselessly.

Shadows began to gather around them, black moths drawn to an alien flame. Rheba could not be sure that the winged shadows were friends; neither could she burn them down as enemies. Seething with barely controlled energy, she searched approaching illusions for Yaocoon clan signs.

A leaf flickered at the edge of one shadow. A lush curve of flower bloomed briefly in another. A fern quivered and vanished in a third pool of darkness. A fourth shadow approached. It displayed neither flower nor fruit, stem nor branch, nothing but tone on tone of darkness shifting.

Dancer fire rained over the shadow. It vanished, leaving behind nothing, not even a cry of surprise.

"Fssa?" she asked.

"A projection. The illusionist was somewhere else," answered the snake.

"At least the illusion couldn't carry a gun."

Kirtn stared at the shadows between trees and said nothing. There were plenty of Soldiers of Ecstasy still around. He doubted that they would carry nothing more deadly than an illusion in their hands.

Shadows continued to flow toward them, revealing tiny flashes of plant life as they came. No snake shape appeared, though many shadows gathered.

"Why aren't they shooting at us?" asked Rheba in a voice that was a harsh whisper. "Are they blind?"

"In the past, killing aliens caused more trouble than it cured," hissed a nearby shadow. "You never knew how powerful their planet might be. Besides, we're shielding you as much as we can. He's a tree and you're moonlight.''

A bullet whined by, burning itself in a tree no more than an arm's length away.

"It would help if you threw less light," the shadow muttered.

Fssa hissed a stream of Senyas directions in Rheba's ear. Blue-white fire leaped from her fingers, scorched across the clearing and danced among trees on the far side. Men screamed and threw down guns too hot to hold.

"On the other hand," said the shadow, "throwing light isn't always a bad idea."

Kirtn's smile was a predatory flash of teeth. He, too, was comforted by dancer fire.

"That's it," the shadow whispered. "Everyone who could get here has. Let's break for the veil."

"What about i'sNara and f'lTiri?" asked Rheba.

"I don't see them. But then, they're nearly twelve and I'm only a nine."

"Is Ara here?"

"No."

"What about Tske?"

"I'm Tske," hissed the shadow. "They're holding the veil for us, but they can't hold it forever. Hurry. If we waste any more time here they'll go on without us."

"What about them?" whispered Rheba, gesturing toward the people lumped up in the dark clearing.

"The ones who are unconscious will wake up with a headache. That always happens when you're forcefully unillusioned. The ones who were hit are dead. The Tyrant's bullets are a thin metal shell wrapped around the Equality's most potent poison."

Rheba grimaced. The more she heard of k'Masei, the Redis and the Soldiers of Ecstasy, the less she wanted to be near any of them. As self-appointed keepers of a planet's love, they were as unlovely a group as she had seen anywhere but Loo. "Lead the way," she snapped to the shadow that was Tske.

Her akhenet lines flared as she walked, telling of energy held in reserve. She called in more with each step, weaving it out of moonlight's pale solar reflections. The Soldiers of Ecstasy might have abandoned this battle, but somewhere ahead the war still went on.

At least she hoped it did. Otherwise i'sNara, f'lTiri and their children were lost.

"How did we get separated from i'sNara and f'lTiri?" she whistled in Bre'n, no more than a tiny thread of sound. "I thought we were together when we went out the gate."

"We stopped at the stream."

"But not for long."

"Long enough, apparently," whistled Kirtn.

Uneasiness shivered in each Bre'n note, telling more clearly than words how he felt about being escorted toward an unknown enemy by a contingent of nameless shadows. In Serriolia, deluding a nonillusionist was so easy that even children were embarrassed to stoop to it. He hoped that the same held true for the Tyrant, but doubted it. Tyrants stooped to anything within reach.

Fssa whistled mournful agreement. His sensors were better equipped than eyes for seeing through illusions, but not much better.

Rheba trotted after the barely visible shadow illusion that was Tske. He flickered in and out of the trees ahead of her. The way was rough, more a trail than the broad street she remembered following to the Yaocoon clan wall. Her memories were not to be wholly trusted, however; things changed without warning or apology in the streets of Serriolia. Even so, she had a persistent sense of wrongness, of things out of place.

Her eyes itched fiercely, adding to her malaise. Everytime her eyes had itched recently, it meant trouble on the way. Her hand closed around Kirtn's wrist. Her uneasiness went through him in a soundless mental cry. Her sense of imminent peril joined them in shallow mind dance, more emotion than words.

Wrongness.

?

Veil too far. Her emotions were a silent cry of warning, of danger unseen, of sounds unheard, of blind worlds where only the sighted survived. But she was blind and so was he.

Find the veil. A mentor's command, cold and binding.

Rheba stopped. Gold licked up and down her arms, dancer power flowing as she sought the uniquely discordant energies known as the veil. She felt her mentor's presence behind her, his hands on her shoulders refining her dance.

There.

Veil energies danced dissonantly on his nerves. It seemed neither near or far, but he was not a dancer to weigh forces, only a Bre'n.

Wrong. Too far. With her silent words came emotions, a feeling of futility in a world full of shadows.

He let go of her. "Fssa." Kirtn's whistle was almost a keening. "Do you sense anyone ahead besides Tske?"

The snake changed, glittering violet quills, a silver ruff, black cups that shone oddly, metallic ripples coursing through his length. "Nothing."

"The veil?"

"Oh, it's there. It's always there. It winds in and out of everything in Serriolia. But we're going away from the part we were headed toward before."

"Is there anyone or anything behind us?" For all its softness, Kirtn's whistle was urgent.

"Just the illusions we gathered in the clearing. At least, I think they're the same ones. It's very hard to be sure."

Rheba's hand closed hotly around his wrist. Words and emotion seared him, but when she spoke, her voice was controlled. "Tske," she whispered, calling ahead to the shadow leading them.

"Hurry," was their only reply.

"We're going the wrong way!"

The shadow blurred, then raced back toward them. "Don't be ridiculous," hissed the shadow. "I know my way around Yaocoon territory better than any illusionless alien. Now *hurry*!" He turned back the way he had come.

"That's the wrong way," insisted Rheba, raising her voice, knowing that Fssa would automatically increase the volume of his translation. "The veil we want is over that way"—a bright-gold finger pointed to Tske's left—"and that's the way I'm going!"

The shadow snarled. Suddenly the night seemed to darken. Soldiers of Ecstasy leaped out from behind trees, wave after wave of gray uniforms and glittering white eyes. The ground shook and roared, giving birth to yet more soldiers. As Kirtn and Rheba turned to flee, shadows twisted, condensed, white eyes gleaming. No Yaocoon clan symbols gleamed this time, only metal gun barrels.

The shadows following them had been Redis illusionists, not Yaocoon raiders. She and Kirtn had been neatly trapped.

XIV

Before any shadow could move, Rheba exploded into flames. With part of her mind, she called down fire on everything within reach. The rest of her mind reached for the nearest energy source that could sustain the demands of her dance. While fire raged within the trees and not-trees, she tried to drag power out of the veil.

The energies were unlike anything she had ever tapped before. Discordant, dissonant, grating terribly on every natural rhythm in her dancer body, the veil's power came to her more as an attacker than as an ally. She struggled against the clashing energies, forcing them to bend to her needs in an act of will that left her blazing.

New akhenet lines ripped through her flesh, but she felt nothing except the hot demands of her dance. Her Bre'n flowed through her, steadying her erratic fire. Even with his presence, the veil energies arced dangerously at the edge of her dance.

Grimly, Rheba fought to control the forces she must use to fight free of the ambush.

Shadows flowed closer, stitched through with the gray threads of uniforms. Bullets whipped by the dancer's burning body, warning of soldiers growing bolder. Kirtn poured more of himself into her dance, giving her both strength and balance to use in her fight to reshape the veil's bizarre energies.

He smelled the stink of his own fur and flesh scorched by unbridled energy. The pain was like a vicious light searing his brain. He ignored it as Bre'ns throughout time had always ignored pain.

He risked a quick glance over his shoulder. Where Tske should have been, there was a skirmish line of soldiers. Behind them were more soldiers, and more, line upon line of gray pouring out of the night. Illusion? Reality? Something in between?

Dancer.

With the single word spoken in Rheba's mind came a picture of themselves, the burning center of a growing circle of gray.

Kirtn sensed her reply flowing up through his palms where they rested on her shoulders. A backwash of discordant power tore through him, but he did not lift his hands. He bent himself to the needs of her dance, controlling her body so that her mind was free to grapple with fire.

A feeling of relief raced through Rheba as Kirtn took more of the burden of the dance on himself. It was dangerous for a Bre'n to carry too much of the dance, but Kirtn was unusually strong. And she needed every bit of his power now.

She matched her rhythms to those of the veil, sucking energy to her in a single dangerous rush. She could not fully control the veil, but she could hammer its energies into a deadly weapon. She had to work with reckless speed. She could not hold onto the veil long without burning herself to the bone. Nor could Kirtn bear so much of the dance for more than a short time.

Her hands lifted. Incandescent light leaped out, light that swept through trees and flesh and night with equal ease. She pivoted in a circle with Kirtn at its center, sweeping her surroundings with deadly energy, trying to burn through illusions to whatever reality might lie beneath.

She watched the resulting blaze with eyes that were almost wholly gold. And she saw shadows between the burning trees, shadows sliding over burning ground, shadows lifting guns.

But the bullets were not shadows at all.

As one, she and Kirtn threw themselves aside. At the same instant she released a brilliant burst of light, hoping to blind the soldiers who were even then sighting down gun barrels. Bullets stitched harmlessly through the night. The Soldiers of Ecstasy were dazed by dancer fire, but that would pass very soon. Then she and Kirtn would be targets once more.

She reached for the veil again, determined to draw enough energy to make the area a fiery hell where only Bre'n and Senyas could survive. She sensed Kirtn's soundless protest at the danger she was calling into herself. But he did not try to stop her. Whatever the veil's danger, it was not as great as the Soldiers of Ecstasy.

Raw energy poured into her. Her akhenet lines burned

hotter and hotter, trying to channel the dissonant power of the veil. She screamed but no sound came, only a gout of searing fire. Desperately she threw away the terrible energies, raining death around her. Grass and small bushes exploded into flame. Trees, rocks and the very air itself smoked. Still her dance raged, demanding more fire and then more, a Senyas hell created for Yhelle illusionists.

Kirtn's lips writhed back from his teeth in an agonized grimace, but he did not stop her dance. Nor did he release his grip on her, though his fingers blistered and fur smoked. She was dancing at the farthest edge of their control, yet she *was* controlled and that was all that mattered. If he flinched in the face of her fire they would both be consumed.

Hell leaped around them in every shade of fire. Trees exploded into flame, dirt smoked, rocks shattered. Illusions screamed, but their sounds were lost in the consuming roar of unleashed fire. Triumph flickered through Kirtn's pain. They were winning. If they could sustain the dance for a few more moments the Soldiers of Ecstasy would scatter like ashes in a hot whirlwind.

Then he felt his dancer change beneath his hands, akhenet lines guttering light and dark, hot and cold, warm and cold. Cold. She was falling. He staggered and barely managed to keep both of them upright. Wrenched out of dance, he was dazed, disoriented, stunned by the slack weight of dancer in his arms.

Rheba?

There was no answering flicker, no stir of recognition, no warmth of companionship in his mind.

He put his lips against her throat, seeeking a pulse. He found it easily, a strong, steady beat of life. Relief came in a rush of weakness. He knelt and held her, turning her face away from the flames that still twisted up into Serriolia's uncertain night.

Eyes narrowed into yellow lines, he searched the spaces between the fire for Soldiers of Ecstasy. He saw only uneven light, ashes, darkness. Yet he knew there had been neither time nor fire enough to burn all their enemies. Or had the massed uniforms been merely illusions? Had she danced herself to unconsciousness for no more than a Redis trick?

A glittering, white-hot head poked out of her tangled hair. Fssa's low whistle called to him in Bre'n notes rich with concern. "Is she all right?"

He answered without looking away from the night and fire that surrounded them. "Yes."

"What happened? One moment wonderful, hot energies and the next—nothing."

"I don't know." Kirtn's whistle was very soft, his eyes restless, probing shadows for illusions living between real flames. "We danced more viciously on Loo. She danced more violently on Daemen, alone, and did not faint." As he whistled his fingers moved over her, searching for burned-out akhenet lines. Fear lived in his whistle, but his hands were steady. "Her lines are whole. She's burned and so am I, but the zoolipt is taking care of that."

Dizziness spiraled through him, followed by a thought of how wonderful it would be to stretch out on the resilient forest floor and sleep. Impatiently he threw off both the dizziness and the desire for rest. The dance had drained him and its sudden end had been like being dropped out of a building, but he was far from the end of his strength.

He felt a sense of persistence, of turquoise seduction weakening his resolve. He had not sensed/tasted that color so clearly since he had floated in a pool on Daemen, buoyed by a fluid that was not quite water, tone on tone of blue, but most beautiful of all was the vivid living turquoise that was a Zaarain construct gone wild.

He blinked and had trouble opening his eyes again. It would really be so much better if he slept. . . .

"The zoolipt!" whistled Kirtn, consternation and anger and the beginning of fear in each clear note. "It stopped her and now it's trying to put me to sleep!"

He looked at his palms, knowing they had been deeply burned during the dance. They were healing, just as his dancer's hands and arms were healing. They owed that to the zoolipt inside them. It liked their "taste." After hundreds of thousands of years of Daemenites for breakfast, lunch, dinner, and midnight snacks, Senyas and Bre'n were exotic fare for the zoolipt. It would keep them alive far longer than their normal spans, healing them until its skill failed or it finally became tired of their taste. Then they would die and the zoolipt would look for a new treat.

Until then, the zoolipt would do everything within its unknown powers to keep its palate happy, including cut them off from a dance it saw as too dangerous. The zoolipt, rather than dancer or Bre'n, would make the choice as to what was or was not worth risking death to achieve. It was the Daemen's own Luck that they had been fighting more illusions than soldiers. Otherwise dancer and Bre'n would be dead now, killed by a meddling zoolipt's kindness.

He did not realize that he was thinking aloud until he heard the snake's soft commiseration. Fssa's Bre'n whistle not only harmonized and sympathized, it pointed out that nothing was free. He and Rheba had live-in doctors. A great convenience . . . until they disagreed on what was best for the "patient."

Fssa's whistle changed into a shrill warning. "Something is approaching behind the flames!"

With a speed that few but Bre'ns could achieve, Kirtn put Rheba behind him and drew his weapon. His burned hand sent searing pain messages to him as the gun's hot metal butt slapped against his palm. Dizziness swept over him like black water, a zoolipt protest. He swore in savage Bre'n and ignored the unwanted advice. The dizziness came again, narrowing reality to a tunnel leading into night. He felt consciousness sliding away as he spun toward the tunnel's mouth. He would sleep as she slept, defenseless, brought down by a blob of protoplasm that was too stupid to accept injury now in order to avoid death later.

The thought of being forced to abandon his sleeping dancer to whatever waited beyond the flames hurled Kirtn to the breakpoint of *rez*. Black energy sleeted through him, energy drawn from his own body without heed to the cost. Black flames leaped. Unchecked, they would consume him cell by cell. *Rez* was the antithesis of survival; it was the pure, self-devouring rage of a mind trapped in a maze with no exit.

Abruptly, the zoolipt retreated. It was ignorant of Bre'n psychology, but it was not stupid. If it persisted, it would drive its host straight into the injury or death it was trying to avoid.

Control returned to Kirtn, but it was too late. Through the barrier of dying dancer fire he saw a circle of uniforms. "Real?" he whistled curtly to the Fssireeme.

Fssa sent out sonic probes, sifted returning signals with an array of cones and quills, and sighed. "Yes and no. Not all of the guns are real and most of the people are illusions, but they keep shifting."

"Thanks," said Kirtn sourly. He did not know how much

ammunition remained in his stolen weapon. He did know it was not infinite. He could not afford to waste ammunition on illusions. There was also the uncomfortable fact that while he was shooting at an illusion, real bullets would be coming his way.

"I'm sorry," whistled the snake, each note vibrating with shame.

"Not your fault," Kirtn whistled, stroking the still-hot Fssireeme and watching the growing gaps between the flames. The attack would come soon.

"Alien!" The call came from beyond the flames. The voice was harsh, husky, speaking in Universal.

Instantly, Kirtn's weapon covered the spot where the voice came from. There was nothing but smoke and shrunken fires.

"Alien!"

The voice came from behind him. He spun and saw nothing at all.

"Alien!"

The voice was at his elbow, but when he turned he was alone.

"You can't—find me—alien!"

The voice came from three directions in rapid succession, but when Kirtn whirled to locate the speaker, there was nothing in sight but the unmoving soldiers.

"I could have killed you, alien."

The words were soft, so close that Kirtn felt the speaker's breath. "Tske," said Kirtn, recognizing the voice.

The man laughed and appeared just beyond Kirtn's reach. Kirtn shot three times and the man laughed again, unhurt.

"I'm behind you."

Kirtn did not turn.

"You're learning."

Tske condensed out of the night, three of him, then five, then eight surrounding Kirtn, flickering in and out of life like fire. Kirtn waited. He knew that projecting illusions cost energy. If Tske kept bragging in multiple images he would eventually wear himself out. Then he would find that Bre'n strength was more real than apparent.

"Throw the gun down."

Kirtn hesitated, then hurled the weapon at the nearest soldier. It was a long throw for anyone but a Bre'n. The gun smacked into flesh. The soldier cried out and Kirtn smiled. That one, at least, was not an illusion.

A knife gleamed out of darkness. Rheba jerked suddenly.

A red line slid down her arm, blood flowing. Kirtn leaped forward, swinging his arms wide to catch something he could not see. It was too late. Whoever had wielded the knife was gone. He looked at the gash on her arm and wanted to kill. Blood slowed, then stopped as the zoolipt went to work on the wound. Kirtn's lips lifted in a snarl. He still wanted to kill.

"It would be a lot more pleasant if the soldiers didn't have to kill you," said Tske reasonably. "You have a formidable ship, and I'm sure your friends on board would be unhappy to lose you. But the Soldiers of Ecstasy are also formidable, and rather stupid. Don't push them any more, alien. They don't like your illusion or your furry reality."

"What do you want?" snarled Kirtn.

"A day or two. Then, if i'sNara and f'lTiri succeed, I'll give you to them and welcome!"

"And if they don't?"

"I'll take you to your ship."

Kirtn did not believe anything except that Tske was afraid of the alien ship looming in the port. The illusionist was hoping that i'sNara and f'lTiri would fail. The Yaocoon would not like to have witnesses to his treachery against his own clan. If the two ex-Liberationists did come back, Kirtn doubted that he or Rheba would be alive to meet them.

Yet it was also true that Tske did not particularly want them dead or he would have killed them during the confusion of the first ambush instead of merely leading them away from the rest of the group.

With a feeling of frustration and unease, Kirtn heard people closing in. The soldiers muttered among themselves, illusion and reality alike. He could not understand their words, for Fssa was not translating. The snake was listening, though. Cups and quills gleamed on Rheba's head like an eerie crown.

"I'm telling the truth," said Tske persuasively. "You think I'm afraid of what you'll tell your friends if they survive." The illusionist laughed. "But you can't prove I'm Tske. I could be k'Masei the Tyrant. What better face for the enemy to wear than that of the opposing general?"

Kirtn stared at the circle of Tske illusions, trying to see the truth. Tske—or whoever owned that sly, teasing voice—was right. There was no way for a nonillusionist to see the truth. Alive, he and Rheba were inconvenient but not especially threatening. Dead, they could open the door to a host of alien problems.

It was a comforting thought. He wished he could believe it. He was still wishing when a blow from behind hurled him face down into the ashes of dancer fire.

XV

Rheba awoke to the stench of rotting mush. It was not the smell that had brought her out of unconsciousness, however; it was the relentless itch behind her eyes. She reached up to rub her face, only to find herself spreading a liberal portion of muck across her cheeks. The foul textures of garbage brought her upright. Her last memories were of clean flames, not sludge.

"Kirtn?" she asked, her voice hoarse. She coughed and tried again. "Kirtn?"

She looked around, ignoring the fierce itch behind her eyes. She saw darkness relieved only by the faintest phosphorescence from the rotting garbage. She combed her fingers through her hair. "Fssa?"

There was no answer. She shook out her hair. "Where are you, snake?"

From the darkness came a soft slithering sound. Fssa's sensor's glowed as his head poked out of a garbage pile.

"What are you doing over there?" demanded Rheba. "Where's Kirtn?"

"Your zoolipt shut down your energies so completely I couldn't stay in your hair," said Fssa, answering her first question. "The warmest place for me to be was in this compost pile." The snake's tone shifted downward. "I don't know where Kirtn is. They hit him from behind after you fainted. Then they carried both of you away. When they dumped you here I fell out of your hair. I didn't see what they did with Kirtn."

"They?"

"The Soliders of Ecstasy. And Tske. At least," sighed the snake, "I *think* it was Tske. These illusionists make my sensors reel."

Rheba sent lines of light radiating out from her body until she could see the dimensions of her prison. She leaned forward, coughing as her movements released foul gases from the decomposing garbage beneath her. Her eyes burned and itched. She ignored them.

The room—if it was what it appeared to be—was a hexagon about as large as the *Devalon*'s control room. Dancer light illuminated every corner and stinking garbage mound. No matter how hard she stared, she could not see Kirtn's familiar form.

"What happened before they hit Kirtn, snake?"

The question was in flat Senyas. Fssa answered in the same tone and language. "You stopped dancing. Do you remember that?"

She hesitated. "Yes. But I don't remember why." She ran her hands over her body. Akhenet lines shimmered like golden opals just beneath her skin. "I'm not burned out. No cold or empty lines. I've danced harder than that before and not fainted."

"Kirtn thinks your zoolipt stopped you. You were burning yourself up."

"But not dangerously! Not yet! If I'd lost control or Kirtn had flinched it would have been different, but we were winning!"

"The zoolipt only knew you were burning."

She made a searing comment about the zoolipt's intelligence. Fssa wisely said nothing.

"Is Kirtn hidden here beneath garbage or illusions?" asked Rheba finally.

"I probed. If Kirtn's here, I can't find him."

"Can you tell what's beyond the wall?" she asked, trying to keep her voice steady. She had lost everyone she loved but Kirtn when Deva burned. To lose him, too, was unthinkable. She fought the panic streaking along her akhenet lines in sullen orange pulses as she listened to the Fssireeme.

"The wall is real. It interferes with my sensors. I can get some sonics through, but the returning energy isn't clear enough to tell the difference between what's out there and what the illusionists want us to think is out there."

"Is the wall made of wood, plastic, stone or metal?"

"Wood."

She made a sound of satisfaction. She took back the light she had created. The compost room became very dark. Then a flush of yellow akhenet light suffused her body. She took heat from rotting garbage and braided it into a thin line of fire. Heat streamed from her fingertip as she pointed toward the farthest wall. Smoke curled invisibly, stinking worse than anything that had come before.

Just when she thought she could not bear the stench any longer, a section of wood as big as her hand leaped into flame. The wall burned through quickly, leaving behind a dazzling shower of white-hot sparks.

Fssa did not need to be told what she wanted. He poked his head out of the still-burning hole and probed what was beyond. In the twin illumination given off by embers and dancer lines, he changed shapes like a fluid fantasy wrought in every metallic color known to man. Finally he returned to his snake shape.

"More garbage," he said succinctly.

Rheba's answer was another line of fire eating whitely at another wall. The snake slid over to the fire and used his head to punch through the weakening wood. The heat was nothing to the Fssireeme. He could swim in magma with the ease of a fish gliding through a pond.

"Machinery. A recycler, from the shape. Disconnected, though. I don't think there's any energy loose for you to use."

She did not squeeze past the lump in her throat to ask if Fssa had seen Kirtn, knowing that if he had, it would be the first thing the Fssireeme said. The fire that leaped from her hand was bright and vicious. It attacked a third wall, burning through it before Fssa could help.

Even as the snake reached the third hole she turned to a fourth stretch of wall. She would have incinerated the whole hexagon, including the garbage, but she did not know where Kirtn was. An unconscious Bre'n had no more protection against dancer fire than any other race of Fourth People. Until she knew where Kirtn was being kept, she would have to be careful.

She refused utterly to consider the possibility that her Bre'n was dead.

"Guards," whistled Fssa.

Instantly Rheba let go of the fire she was creating and darkened her akhenet lines. Fssa flared out, using himself to patch the hole so that no one beyond could see the dancer burning within. He resumed probing, hampered but not incapacitated by his role as living plug. He formed a whistling orifice in the lower third of his body and resumed describing what his sensors revealed to him. "Soldiers of Ecstasy."

"How can you tell if you can't see the uniforms?" asked

Rheba, sending another line of light at the fourth section of wall. It did not burn well. It was either wetter, thicker, or of a more resistant wood than the other three.

"Their eyes are different. Odd energy patterns. Unique."

Rheba remembered the few times she had been close enough to the soldiers to tell the color of their eyes. White. All of them. She had assumed that it was merely an illusion, a badge of their allegiance that separated them from other Yhelles. Now she wondered. Was there some mechanism that bound them to their tyrant k'Masei, a bond reflected in their white eyes?

Her own eyes itched wildly, then she felt a wonderful cool sensation. She shivered in relief. Maybe the zoolipt had finally figured out how to take care of whatever was causing the intolerable itching.

Even as she had the thought, her eyes itched again. The itch was mild, but definite. She swore and turned her attention back to the still-smoldering wall. It was nearly opposite the third hole she had burned, the one that Fssa was covering with part of his body. If she went to work on the fourth wall again, and Fssa moved, the guards outside would be sure to see the light and investigate.

She did not want that, at least not until she knew if Kirtn was nearby, perhaps even within reach. She would much rather be with her Bre'n when she faced the guards than have either of them face the white-eyed Soldiers of Ecstasy alone.

She crawled across the slippery garbage toward Fssa. "Finished?" she asked.

"Yes. If he's out there, he's not in any of my frequencies."

"Take the heat out of the embers."

With a Fssireeme's total efficiency, Fssa sucked all the unwanted warmth from the wood around the hole in the wall.

"I'll cover the hole," said Rheba. "You go to work on the fourth wall."

With her back over the charred part of the wall, she sent a streak of fire across the stinking garbage. The fourth wall smoldered and flamed. Fssa measured the heat, centered on the greatest area of weakness in the wooden boards and rammed his dense-fleshed body through the wall. Minute embers fell over him like incandescent snow.

"He's here!"

Fssa's excited whistle brought her halfway to her feet before she remembered the guards outside. As Fssa surged through the small opening in the fourth wall, she turned and plastered garbage over the hole she had been covering with her body. Some of the garbage fell out, but more of it stuck. Very quickly, the hole vanished beneath oozing refuse.

"He's alone," whistled the snake hesitantly. Then, in a single ascending trill of exultation, "He's alive!"

Relief went through Rheba in a wave that left her dizzy. She swallowed hard and tried to control her shaking body. After a moment, she succeeded.

"Protect him, snake," she demanded in Senyas. "I'm burning through."

She sent a double-handed stream of fire across the compost pile. Fire fountained, bringing wood to its flashpoint so quickly that there was little smoke. She held the fire, drawing heat out of the rotting garbage to feed her dance. When she was through, the deeply piled refuse was cold and the wall was only a memory outlined in cherry embers.

Fssa, who had spread himself like a fireproof tarpaulin over the Bre'n, sucked up the last of the fire as he shrank back to his normal, heat-conserving shape.

She slid and staggered across the compost pile until she was next to Kirtn. She wiped slime from her hands and then ran them over his body, searching for any wounds. She found no burns or injuries, nothing but copper fur coming away in patches and sticking to her hands. Yhelle's humid heat was making Kirtn shed like a cherf. Other than that, he did not seem harmed. But he was too still, and his breathing was too shallow.

Carefully, she made a ball of light and used it to examine him. With gentle fingertips she probed beneath the hand-length copper hair on his head. Behind his ear she found a horrible softness where hard Bre'n skull should be. Blood was oozing beneath his hair, blood thick between her fingers.

She made an odd sound and withdrew her hand. Very gently she eased his head onto her lap and prayed to childhood gods that the zoolipt inside him would be able to heal his wound. She tried not to tremble, afraid of disturbing him even though she knew that it would take more than her shaking flesh to drag him up from the darkness a soldier's club had sent him into.

From beyond the burned wall came voices, people talking, a ragged murmur that had no meaning to her. At the edge of her awareness she sensed Fssa shifting, changing, dragging sounds out of the air and transforming them with Fssireeme skill into other words, words she could understand if she wanted to.

She did not listen. Nothing mattered to her but Kirtn's slack body—not the guards, not the cold slime creeping over her legs, not even her own imprisonment. Considering her precarious situation, her attitude was irrational; but where Kirtn was concerned, she was no more rational than a Bre'n teetering on the edge of *rez*.

After a time the snake ceased his soft translations. He kept on listening, however, dividing his attention between her small, stifled sounds and the voices beyond the wall.

Kirtn groaned. Immediately the ball of light near his face brightened. Rheba bent over him. With an inward flinching, she eased her fingers into his hair. No viscous blood met her touch, no crushed skull, and only a trace of swelling that vanished even as she discovered it. His zoolipt was nearly finished.

She held her breath and waited, still afraid of wounds she could neither see nor feel.

His eyes opened clear and yellow. They focused on her instantly. She felt his consciousness like a special fire spreading through her. His face blurred and ran as the tears she had been fighting finally won. She reached up to wipe her eyes. His hands closed around her wrists.

"Don't. You'll get whatever you have on your hands in your eyes." He hesitated. "Just what *do* you have on your hands?"

"A little garbage. Some of your blood." Her voice broke. "And a lot of your fur, you great shedding cherf!" She tried to shake tears free of her eyes but could not.

"Here," he said. "Let me."

"Your hands are no cleaner than mine."

He sat up and pulled her close. She laughed raggedly and cried and held him with arms that were more gold than brown. His lips moved over her eyelids, drinking her tears with a delicacy that made her shiver.

"Are you really all right?" she whispered. "It's not a dream?"

"No . . . but I've dreamed like this more than once."

She shifted so that she could look up at his face, trying to sort out the emotions rippling through his voice. He smiled as his mouth slid down her cheek.

"And you, dancer," he breathed against her lips, "are you all right? Have you ever dreamed like this?"

A golden network of lines ignited over her body as she tasted the salt of her own tears on his tongue. She fitted herself against him and savored his mouth like a rare spring wine.

Fssa's apologetic but urgent whistle separated them. "I know you two have to share enzymes once in a while," he said delicately, "but you'll have to find a better time. Some Redis are on their way here."

Kirtn spoke without looking up from the half-closed, half-gold dancer eyes so close to him. "Carrying garbage, no doubt," he said, acknowledging the truth that his sensitive nose had been shouting at him ever since he woke up.

"Nothing that healthful," said Fssa in curt Senyas.

The snake's tone got their attention. Bre'n and Senyas focused on Fssa in the same swift movement. Fssa's sensors noted the change. When he spoke again, his tone was less cutting but no less urgent.

"I tried to tell Rheba earlier," said Fssa, "but she wasn't listening. The Redis are only keeping you here until there are more of them to work on you. As soon as the last of the false Yaocoon raiders come back, there will be enough."

"Enough for what?" said Kirtn. "They could have killed us before now if that's what they wanted."

"They don't want to kill you. The Redis—or k'Masei's Soldiers—are really frightened of your ship. They haven't been able to trick Ilfn into opening the door, and the ship itself is interfering with their attempts to project illusions inside the control room."

Kirtn's hand went to the slime-covered stud on his weapon harness. There was no tingle of response, no signal that any messages had been sent. In fact, there was nothing at all, not even the slight warmth that indicated the stud was alive.

"Are you sure?" Rheba asked Kirtn, though he had said nothing aloud. She brushed aside Kirtn's hand and probed the stud with subtle dancer energies. "Nothing," she said to him in Senyas. "It's dead. Probably the fire warped it." Then, to Fssa, "How do you know that the ship is under attack?"

"The soldiers outside are talking about it," he said patiently. "They're scared invisible of you, but they're hanging on until the Stones are through with the rebels."

Then what happens?"

"The Stones will be able to concentrate on you. They won't kill you, but you won't be dangerous anymore. You'll open the *Devalon* for them and everything will be safe again.

A whole shipload of Redis converts will be there for the making.''

"That's absurd," snapped Rheba. "It will take more than looking at a few crystals to make us into Redis."

"The soldiers are sure you'll convert. You won't be as satisfactory to the Stones as converted illusionists. Apparently aliens are . . . resistant . . . to love. Even so, it's better than killing you and then having to deal with a ship that can baffle illusions."

Kirtn stared at Fssa's opalescent sensors. "You keep talking about the Stones. What about k'Masei the Tyrant? Doesn't he have a say in all this?"

Colors rippled over Fssa in the Fssireeme equivalent of a shrug. "The soldiers only talk about the Ecstasy Stones."

"Do they say what conversion is like?" asked Kirtn uneasily.

"Oh yes, they're quite specific." But the snake said nothing more.

"Go on," said the Bre'n, his voice as grim as his eyes. The Daemenites had believed in scuffing up their living-god offerings before throwing them in the turquoise soup—fresh blood helped to pique the zoolipt's interest. He wondered if something similar was part of Yhelle's conversion rituals. "Just what does conversion involve?"

For a moment it seemed that Fssa was not going to answer. He darkened perceptibly. When he spoke, his voice was thin and sad. "Conversion is just like being disillusioned."

"But we're not illusionists," protested Rheba. "Nothing will happen to us."

"The energies Yhelles use to control illusions are quite similar to the energies you use to control fire," whispered Fssa, so dark now he was almost invisible. "When the Stones are through, you'll still be alive. *But you'll never dance again.*"

XVI

Rheba did not need to ask what Kirtn thought of Fssa's words. The Bre'n's bleak fear and rage swept through her akhenet lines like a new kind of energy. If she could not dance, he and she would soon die—or wish they had. Was that what disillusionment meant to the Yhelles, too?

For the first time she had a visceral appreciation of what i'sNara and f'lTiri had risked in order to trace their children. No wonder f'lTiri had not wanted Rheba and Kirtn to join the rebels.

"I could probably handle whatever machine does the probing," Rheba said in a hesitant voice.

"You have to see it first," Kirtn said in a cold mentor's voice. "And what if it isn't a machine? What if it's a psi master like Satin?"

"She couldn't control me, or you either."

"She could have killed me." Kirtn's tone was uncompromising. He used Senyas to emphasize the blunt realities of the situation they faced. "We can't count on burning our way free, either. Your zoolipt . . ."

Though he said no more, they both heard his words in the silence of their minds: *If you burn too hard, your zoolipt will stop you and never know that it killed you.*

"The rebels might win," she whispered.

He did not bother to answer. Neither of them thought much of the rebels' chances, particularly since it seemed that the rebel leader was a traitor called Tske.

"I'm not going to sit here like a lump of muck," snapped Rheba, pushing away from her Bre'n.

He laughed humorlessly. "Neither am I, dancer."

"Right," said Fssa, his voice an exact duplicate of Master Scavenger Scuvee.

"Wish I had some of the zoolipt's gold dust," Kirtn said, remembering the yellow drifts of aphrodisiac that one of Daemen's zoolipts had created to reward its worshipers for especially tasty sacrifices. "That would separate illusions and people in a hurry."

"You might as well wish that the communication stud worked and we could call the ship to our rescue," pointed out Rheba.

"Or that the J/taals could help us, or even the rebels," sighed Fssa.

"Yes, yes," said Rheba impatiently, closing her itching eyes and rubbing them with a relatively clean knuckle, "but I've noticed that off-planet things don't work very reliably on Yhelle. Illusions confuse us hopelessly. We need something *of* Yhelle to defeat the Tyrant and his white-eyed Redis."

A soothing feel of coolness washed behind her eyes, followed by an exultant sense of affirmation deep within her mind. Startled, she looked at Kirtn. He was looking at her with equal surprise.

"You didn't think/say/feel that?" they asked each other simultaneously. Then Kirtn said slowly, "It was in *your* mind, dancer."

An eerie feeling crept along the back of her neck. Her hair rippled and whispered hotly. Someone or something was in her mind, trying to—what was it trying to do?

The itch behind her eyes was suddenly increased tenfold. She cried out and would have clawed at her eyes if Kirtn had not grabbed her hands.

"Maybe it's just an accident," he said, but his voice held a mentor's skepticism of coincidence.

She writhed, trying to break free of his grip long enough to scratch her maddening eyes.

"It can't control you, dancer," he said harshly. "Even Satin couldn't do that. Maybe it's just trying to talk to you."

Instantly cool relief washed behind her eyes, followed by another sense of affirmation. She shuddered and sighed. "Maybe. But it picked hell's own way of doing it."

"I don't sense anything new," said the snake, sensors blazing as he washed both of his friends in soundless radiation, seeking anything unusual. He found only muck and flesh surrounded by a dancer's unique energies . . . and an odd twisting echo that he dismissed. He had first sensed the echo on Reality Street as Rheba bent over a fascinating Ghost fern. When the echo persisted whenever they went, he had decided that the echo was the cumulative signature of Serriolia's illusionists. "Could it be the zoolipt?" asked Fssa, reshaping himself into his usual form.

"It's not the zoolipt," said Rheba bitterly, remembering the dance that had ended too soon. "The zoolipt doesn't ask, it *acts*."

Relief was still cool behind her eyes. She basked in it. Then she opened her eyes, startled by a thought that was definitely her own. "That's it! Itch is trying to communicate!"

A delicious feeling came into her mind, relief and laughter and pleasure combined into shimmering exultation.

"Itch?" whistled Fssa. "Is that a What or a Who?"

Kirtn just stared. "Itch?" he asked, his tone that of a mentor, demanding.

"I don't know what else to call it," said Rheba, "but if that itching keeps up, I'll have a few suggestions that would make a cherf cringe."

The itching stopped instantly.

Rheba smiled like a predator. "Message received. Now get your little histamine fingers out of my brain so I can think!"

Kirtn watched Rheba with eyes that reflected the uneasy surges of her akhenet lines. Plainly, he suspected that she was in the grip of a subtle illusion. His only concern was whether or not the illusion was destructive. Considering what had happened to them since they had left the ship, he was not particularly hopeful. With few exceptions, Serriolia's illusions were not benevolent to outsiders. He was afraid that Itch was just one more manifestation of the Tyrant's pervasive powers.

His dancer smiled and put her gold-bright hand on his cheek. "I don't think it is malevolent. Just itchy."

"The zoolipt isn't malevolent, either," he pointed out, "but its goals aren't necessarily ours."

"If I could make Itch go away, I would. I can't. So we'll just have to figure out how to live with it until it gets whatever it wants or gives up and goes back to wherever it came from."

"And what might an itch want?" said Kirtn in a tone that attempted to be reasonable.

Rheba shrugged irritably. "I don't know, and right now I don't care. It will have to wait its turn." She held her breath, expecting an onslaught of itching. Nothing happened. She let her breath out in a relieved rush. Apparently Itch was capable of cooperation.

"Maybe," suggested Fssa tentatively, "maybe what Itch wants is to help us against the Tyrant k'Masei and his soldiers."

"How?" Kirtn demanded.

Simultaneously, a feeling of pleasant coolness bathed Rheba's eyes. "Itch likes the idea of helping us," she said.

Kirtn threw up his hands. Arguing with a dancer, a Fssireeme and an Itch was beyond even a mentor's çapabilities. "No wonder Bre'ns go crazy," he muttered. He turned to Fssa. "If we burn our way out of here, are there too many guards to fight before Rheba's zoolipt gets nervous and shuts down the dance?"

Before the snake could answer, Rheba winced and fought not to rub her eyes. "Itch says no."

"No what?" demanded Kirtn coldly. "No there are too many guards, or no Itch doesn't want us to leave?"

She considered carefully. "No there are too many guards."

Kirtn swore with a poet's vicious skill. Then, "I suppose we're just supposed to sit here and scratch and stink.'

She winced and itched. "No, that's not it."

"Then what in the name of Fire does that damned Itch want us to do?"

There was no response, though she waited for several moments. Then she realized what the problem was. "The question's too complex for Itch. We're stuck with a binary method of communication. Yes or no, pleasure or itch."

"Sweet burning gods," whistled the Bre'n sourly. "With everything else, we had to pick up an idiot hitchhiker!" He rubbed his hands through his copper hair and sighed. "Yes or no. Not even a maybe. We could be a long time establishing even the most rudimentary understanding. I hope the Soldiers of Ecstasy aren't in a hurry to begin disillusioning us."

"I could ask Rainbow if it knows anything about life forms like Itch," offered Fssa hesitantly, knowing that every time he communicated with the ancient crystals it caused Rheba inordinate pain. "If Rheba thinks it would be worth it, that is," he amended.

She looked with open distaste at the double strand of large crystals hanging to the middle of Kirtn's wide chest. Neither sweat nor muck nor shedding Bre'n hair stuck to Rainbow's polished faces. Endless colors winked back at her in a silent beauty that belied the savage headaches that came to her each time the snake spoke to the Zaarain library.

"No," said Kirtn, his voice rough and final. "If the soldiers came while you were communicating, Rheba would be in too much pain to dance. We'd be as good as dead."

Rheba hesitated. "Itch agrees," she said finally. She frowned, trying to remember what she had said before she realized that the itching behind her eyes was more than a random allergic phenomenon. Something about using Yhelle to defeat Yhelle's illusions.

The backs of her eyes radiated soothing coolness. So far, Itch was with her. The only question was, where were they going?

Nothing, neither itch nor pleasure.

Rheba sighed. "The only thing we have of Yhelle that might be useful is an illusionist or two," she said aloud, thinking of f'lTiri and i'sNara.

She groaned and knuckled her eyes. Itch did not agree with that thought.

Fssa rippled with dark metallic lights. "More voices," he whistled softly. "More Redis coming. Soldiers, too. They're arguing."

"What about?" asked Kirtn.

"The soldiers won't let anyone in until the Stones are through with the rebels. The Redis illusionists want to move now."

"How much time do we have?"

"None if the Redis win. Not much if the soldiers have their way. Only three rebel illusionists are still at large."

"I'sNara and f'lTiri?" asked the Bre'n hopefully.

Fssa made a thin human sigh. "It doesn't matter. They're still caught within the Redis clan hall. No one leaves Tyrant k'Masei's presence without his permission." The snake's sensors blazed as he turned toward Rheba. "Why in the name of the First Speaker didn't Itch choose *me* to talk to? Surely one of my languages would work!" He brooded in somber metal shades, then whistled coaxingly. "What are you trying to say to Itch, dancer?"

"I'm trying to tell her that we don't have anything of Yhelle to use against Yhelle illusionists," grated Rheba, fighting not to rub her abused eyes. "Not our weapons or our clothes or our brains—nothing we have with us is Yhelle."

Kirtn's eyes widened, then narrowed to slanted yellow lines. His hand shot out, twisted in her clothes, then reappeared. On his palm caged crystals shone black between traceries of dancer light.

"The worry stones!" said Rheba. "But what good are they against Soldiers of Ecstasy?"

"Don't ask me," snapped Kirtn. "They're Yhelle, though. Does Itch approve of using them?"

"Yes," said Rheba, blinking rapidly and smiling. "It's

ecstatic.'' Rheba frowned at the sullen stones. ''I don't know
why, though. Depressing lumps of crystal.''

On an impulse, she allowed the golden cage surrounding
one of the larger stones to dim. Despair flowed out from
between the thinned lines of light like a dark miasma, a night
that admitted no possibility of dawn.

Kirtn made an eerie sound of Bre'n sadness. Rheba glanced
at him, startled. She could sense despair emanating from the
stone, but it was despair at a distance, merely a possibility.
But to the Bre'n, despair was a probability on the verge of
becoming all too real.

Fssa mourned with a sound like wind blowing back from
the end of time.

Hastily, Rheba fed energy into the dim cage around the
worry stone. The stone fought the only way it could, silently,
viciously, pouring out dispair. But the cage brightened, turning the stone's energies back on itself. Inside the cage, light
energies pooled, building like water behind a dam, pressing
silently for release.

Rheba was surprised to see that her hands and lower arms
were as gold as the cage she had built around the stones. Her
body was hot, each line radiant. She suspected that somehow
her akhenet lines gave her a measure of immunity to whatever
emanated from the worry stones. She also suspected that the
longer the stones were restrained, the stronger they would
radiate on their release. The thought was not a comforting
one.

A whistle of relief came from Kirtn as dispair was caged by
light. He shook his head as though coming out of water.
''Next time, warn me.'' He looked thoughtful. ''If it affects
the Yhelles the way it affected me, it might help us after all.''

''Yesss,'' hissed Fessa. ''That's it! Something about the
worry stones' emanations must upset the Yhelles. It affected
me, too,'' he added as an afterthought.

''Worry stones are an uncertain weapon,'' said Kirtn. ''We
don't know the range, power or duration of their effect. But
they're all we have.''

''I'm not sure I like them,'' murmured Rheba, watching
the stones' dark glitter, ''but they fascinate me. Their energies are tangential, bittersweet.''

She stared at the stones and waited for Itch to comment.
Nothing happened. She sighed. ''I guess the worry stones
aren't what Itch wanted after all.''

No more had she thought it than the back of her eyes felt

like sand. "Correction," she said through her teeth. "Itch wants the worry stones."

"Itch can have them," muttered Kirtn.

He did not like the dark, greasy shine of stone through dancer fire. He did not like the bleak winter memories they had called up out of the depths of his ancestral Bre'n mind.

"All right, Itch. What do I do with these black beauties?" asked Rheba.

Nothing happened. It was not a yes or no question.

"Dancer," said the snake softly. "May I borrow your energy? I want to scan something. Maybe . . ." Fssa stopped talking and began changing shapes as he scanned the various walls.

Rheba looked at the snake, not understanding what he wanted. Then she realized that he had been out of her hair for some time. The heat of rotting compost was not much for a Fssireeme's requirements, especially when he was changing shapes.

She scooped him into her hair. "You don't have to ask, snake."

He whistled thanks with one part of himself while the remainder flashed through a familiar yet still dazzling variety of metallic blue quills, scarlet metal vanes and silver mesh constructs. Using the energy that she naturally radiated, he could probe the surroundings more deeply than when he was dependent on his own energy alone.

Voices came through the thick wood walls, angry voices. She did not need Fssa to translate. The argument over when to disillusion the prisoners was reaching the point where it would either be settled or become a brawl. For once, she sided with the Soldiers of Ecstasy; more time might not save Bre'n, Senyas and Fssireeme, but less time would surely work against them.

Fssa's head snaked out of her hair. His sensors looked like opals set in platinum filigree. "The fifth wall doesn't have any guards," he whistled, "and the ones on the fourth and sixth walls are drifting off to listen to the argument. I can't be sure, but I think there's nothing between us and a segment of the veil except a few buildings."

Rheba's eyes began to itch lightly.

"I could throw my voices—and a few insults—into the group by the first wall," continued Fssa. "When the fight begins, we can burn through the fifth wall and run for the veil."

She squinted and fought not to rub her eyes. "Itch doesn't like the idea," she said quietly.

Fssa said something in a language Rheba had never heard.

Kirtn did not know the language either, but he had an idea of what the Fssireeme was saying. "I agree," he said grimly. "First the fight, then the wall. And if Itch doesn't like it, Itch can suck ice."

Fssa brightened into iridescence. He formed several mouths, paused to gather his best insults and then slid them through the wall in a nearly invisible, multivoiced assault.

The fight broke out within seconds.

"Burn it," said Kirtn, pointing toward the fifth wall.

"Itch doesn't want—"

"Burn it!" demanded the Bre'n roughly, all mentor now, unyielding.

Rheba swore and burned the wall to ash in a single out-pouring of flame. Kirtn kicked through the glowing skeleton of boards, oblivious to the embers that seared fur and flesh. She followed in a rush, akhenet lines blazing, trailing a snake's hissing laughter.

They ducked between two buildings and listened. No one had followed. Soldiers and Redis were too busy pounding on each other to notice that the focus of their argument had escaped.

Rheba closed her eyes, ignoring the itch. She sensed the direction of the veil as a brittle brush of discordance. The itch increased in intensity, telling her that her unwanted hitchhiker did not want to go toward the veil. Too bad. A lot of things had happened to Rheba that she had not wanted either.

"This way," she whispered, tugging at Kirtn's hand.

Together, they eased around a corner of the building—and straight into a mass of white-eyed soldiers.

XVII

For a wild moment Rheba hoped that the soldiers were only illusions. The hope passed in a flurry of shouts and raised clubs. Desperately she grabbed for stray energy. There was very little for her to use. It was night and only a tiny moon was in the sky. She could braid fire from the warmth the ground was giving up to the sky, but it would take many minutes to transform such meager forces into a weapon. She had bare seconds. With an explosion of searing light, she loosed all her energy in a single wild instant. Fire streamed out from her, flames washing over the soldiers in hot tongues. Heat left black scorch marks on gray uniforms.

Soldiers screamed and clawed at clothing that had become too hot to wear. Weapons smoked in their hands, burning them. Incandescent light blinded them. Men in the front ranks fell to the ground, kicking and crying out to their gods.

Kirtn yanked Rheba aside and began running. He knew what she had done, knew that draining herself was the only thing she could do under the circumstances—and knew that it would not be enough. Only the closest soldiers had fallen. Some of the others were dazed, partially blinded. The rest were already in pursuit, weapons raised, white eyes seeking enemies. At least her akhenet lines were dull now, offering a less obvious target.

Fssa's head lifted above Rheba's flying hair. He swiveled methodically, sensing both where they had been and where they must go. What he found made black run in waves down his supple body.

"There are more soldiers ahead," he whistled in tones that cut through the sounds of pursuit.

"Where?" demanded Kirtn. "Right? Left? Center?" His yellow eyes pierced shadows that could be enemies.

"Yes," said Fssa simply.

Kirtn heard the shouts and pounding feet behind. There

was no escape in that direction, either. Rheba twisted out of
his grip and spun to face the closer soldiers.

"No!" he shouted. "Your zoolipt won't let—"

His words died as he saw what she was doing. She held
both hands in front of her, palms up, fingertips sorting over
the worry stones. Pale dancer light crawled over her fingers.
Inside the light, pools of darkness waited.

Rheba looked up, measuring the distance to the approaching soldiers. She poured all but one stone into her left hand.
Her right arm came back, then snapped forward. The stone
she threw was no bigger than the tip of her smallest finger. A
golden lacework enclosed the stone's darkness, but as the
crystal tumbled among the soldiers, she sucked the cage
energies back into her akhenet lines.

There was no fire this time, only freezing darkness, yet the
Soldiers of Ecstasy fell as though burned to the bone. Their
mouths gushed terrible rending cries, wordless agonies that
marked their passage into darkness. The silence that followed
was almost worse, an icy black blanket that seemed to mock
even the possibility of light.

Above her head, Fssa mourned in the eerie sliding notes of
Fssireeme threnody. Though he floated in dancer hair, his
body was as black as the space between galaxies.

Rheba heard his keening as though at a distance, a wind
twisting through hidden caves. She was not as affected as the
Fssireeme was. The uncaged worry stone gave her a feeling
of melancholy rather than tragedy. She responded only in a
mild way, like someone hearing the travails of a stranger.

Beside her, Kirtn whistled a Bre'n dirge she had never
before heard, minor-key notes singing of death, rhythms of
entropy and extinction. The pure, grieving notes affected her
as no worry stone could. But she ignored his song, ignored
the tears it drew down her face, ignored everything except her
own hand holding the quintessence of despair caged behind
dancer light.

Around her, soldiers fell like rain.

More? she asked silently, her fingers hovering over the
smallest remaining worry stone as Bre'n grief turned like a
razor in her heart.

A coolness soothed her hot eyes.

Which direction? she asked, taking the small stone and
turning slowly, seeking a target.

Pleasure came, tiny and distinct.

She saw nothing in the direction indicated by whatever

lurked in her mind, but she did not hesitate. Her arm came back once more. Once more she hurled caged darkness through the night. Once more she took back dancer light and loosed despair.

Illusionists screamed and shattered out of invisibility. Their screams thinned and died as quickly as they had come. It took longer for their feet to stop beating futilely against the ground.

Silence came again, silence more profound than death, for dead men do not grieve.

More? she asked, shuddering and hoping that she had done enough. She would rather burn flesh than minds. Flesh healed, eventually.

The itch came back. It almost felt good, for it told her that she did not have to loose more worry stones. Tentatively, she walked toward the first group of fallen soldiers. She wanted to retrieve—and cage—the stone she had hurled at them. Even so, she held her breath, expecting Itch to object behind her eyes. Nothing came, neither pain nor pleasure.

She moved among the soldiers like swamp fire, burning fitfully, more sensed than seen. The worry stone nagged at her awareness, a black hole sucking away at her mind. She dragged a soldier aside. His body was wholly slack, yet he was alive—if meat that breathed could be called living.

The stone lay beneath him. A chip, a bare fragment of a once larger stone, yet it had brought down more Soldiers of Ecstasy than she could count in the darkness. She wondered if it was always that way, if grief always far outweighed ecstasy. After Deva, she could believe that was true.

Quickly she caged the stone, and her dark thoughts with it.

The soldiers did not move. If bridling the worry stone made any difference to them, they did not show it. She stared at the huddled bodies near her and wondered if it would not have been better to burn them to ash and gone. Certainly it would have been cleaner.

Her eyes itched lightly, telling her that she was wrong.

Or was Itch simply trying to make her feel better?

The question was unanswerable, even in a binary system. She sighed and turned toward the place where the illusionists lay. Fssa's soft keening fell from her hair like twilight over a mauve desert. Though he understood the artificial nature of his grief, he could not wholly control his response to the stones.

Kirtn was less affected. He no longer sang the poetry of
despair, though it lived behind his yellow eyes. He walked
next to her without speaking, knowing that she was being
drawn to the only remaining source of the bleak emanations.
When she stopped, he stopped, waiting.

With an apologetic glance at her sad Bre'n, she bent over
and retrieved the second stone from beneath an illusionist's
ragged robe. The stone was four times the size of the first she
had thrown. She began to draw dancer fire over its black
faces. Gold sputtered and died. It was then she realized that
the stone's power increased geometrically with their size.

And this stone did not want to be caged again.

Silently, she gathered the slow warm exhalations of the
earth and braided them into fire. The energy was thin,
dissipated, nebulous. It was almost more trouble to gather
than it was worth. It certainly was not enough for her
purposes.

The stone drank the budding cage almost casually, black
consuming threads of gold.

Her right hand stretched high over her head as she tried to
slide between clouds to touch the pale moon. After a long
time, moonlight twisted, thickened, ran over her fingers like
ghostly water. Yet she was far from full, far from having
what she needed for the demands of the cage. Her fingers
began to shake. She was using almost as much energy to feed
her small dance as she was retaining to build a cage for the
stubborn worry stone.

Her body ached, protesting. Akhenet lines surged raggedly.
Yet she had no intention of leaving the stone unmuzzled. She
did not need the itch behind her eyes to know that she must
cage the stone's energies once more.

Bre'n hands touched her shoulders, Bre'n breath stirred
warmly in her hair, Bre'n strength ignited her akhenet lines.
She drank Kirtn's presence until it filled her and wan moonlight
burned sunbright in her hands.

She gave her body over to his control while she danced
across the many faces of darkness. Sadness called to her. She
ignored it, drawing laughter in thin lines of fire. Whorls and
arcs and graceful curves danced over black planes, fire pulsed
in traceries as strong as they were fine. The cage uncurled,
gold on gold, incandescent against the stone's night, burning
until each face of darkness was confined.

With a sigh, Rheba blinked and looked at the caged stone
in her palm.

"Thank the Inmost Fire you didn't use one of the big stones," said Kirtn, pulling her against his body, trying to forget the unholy grief he had known before she danced.

"Thank Itch," said Rheba. "I was going to unwrap the big ones, but she made my eyes burn so badly I couldn't see to choose."

Fssa's head dangled low, caressing her cheekbone where lines of power still smoldered. "Is it safe? Are the soldiers dead?" he whistled, sensors gleaming as he searched the nearby ground.

"We're safe from these men, though Itch says they aren't dead," answered Rheba. "But then, Itch's idea of life might not be ours."

An uneasy silence followed her words.

"We're going back to the ship," said Kirtn, his voice flat. "We can't help i'sNara and f'lTiri until we have weapons we can trust. Which way is the veil?"

"That way," said Fssa and Rheba together, finger and slim head pointing to the right. "But," she added, "Itch is telling me not to go that way. Or maybe she doesn't want us to go back to the ship."

Kirtn did not bother to answer. He started walking to the right. "Pick out a small stone or two," he said, peering into darkness as clouds closed over the pale moon. "Just in case we find more trouble than you can burn."

Reluctantly, Rheba sorted through the stones sealed in her pocket. Her fingertips found the third-smallest stone; it was bigger than her thumb. She hesitated, then pulled the stone out of her pocket. She did not want to unleash such a large stone, but suspected that the stones she had just used would not be back to their full strength yet.

"What about i'sNara and f'lTiri?" she asked, not objecting, merely wanting to know his plans.

"We could call in the Yhelle Equality Rangers," offered Fssa.

Kirtn made an untranslatable sound. So far as he was concerned, the only thing the Rangers were good for was making state-of-the-art navtrices. "We'll use the J/taals. The clepts could probably track i'sNara and F'lTiri through any illusion this side of reality."

Rheba's eyes itched fiercely but she said nothing. The anger in Kirtn's voice told her that this was not the time to argue with him, much less try to thwart him.

Fssa was not so used to Bre'ns. "Didn't i'sNara say that if we used J/taals, every hand on Yhelle would be against us?"

"Do you think we'll notice the difference?" whistled Kirtn sarcastically.

Fssa flushed shades of darkness and withdrew into Rheba's comforting hair.

When Kirtn was not looking, she rubbed her eyes. Whatever Itch wanted, they were not doing it at the moment. She swore silently and hurried toward the veil, stopping only when Kirtn eased around buildings to check for stray Soldiers of Ecstasy. The way they went was not difficult; as far as she could tell, the illusion of a paved walkway matched the reality beneath her feet. Apparently the Yaocoons did not wrap illusions around their outer holdings as fervently as they did around themselves and their clan hall.

The veil gleamed and sparked fitfully in the distance, looking rather like stripped atoms twisting over a planet's magnetic poles.

Rheba's skin prickled as her akhenet lines moved, reflecting the dissonant energies ahead. She was not looking forward to tangling with the veil construct again. She wished that it were dawn, that Yhelle's sun would rise and pour its silent cataracts of energy over her. But dawn was far away. She would have to face the veil armored only in cloud-thinned moonlight.

There was nothing near the veil, no place to hide. It looked like a trap baited with the hope of escape. With shrinking skin, she approached the end of the walkway.

"Now what?" whistled Fssa, his question as soft as a breath sliding between strands of her hair.

"It's supposed to be like a showcube," murmured Rheba, "only instead of pictures from home, the veil shows various clan symbols. When Reality Street comes up, we go through."

As soon as their presence registered on the veil's tenuous energies, it shimmered and made a portal. Inside the oval was the image of Ecstasy Stones glittering on a mirrored table. The sight was chillingly beautiful, light in all of its colors flashing and turning, calling to them in the voices of everything they had ever loved or hoped to love.

Rheba's eyes stopped itching. Coolness flowed like a benediction.

"Redis hall," said Kirtn hoarsely.

"Itch," she whispered. "Itch wants us to go there."

Kirtn's hand closed bruisingly over her wrist, as though he feared she would leap into the veil. "No."

She did not move or protest. She, too, was afraid of the alien who communicated with her only in terms of pleasure or pain, an alien who seemed to want her to enter the stronghold of the Tyrant who wielded disillusionment and death against his enemies.

Silently, Bre'n and Senyas waited for the veil's portal image to shift as it had when they stood on Reality Street, two aliens impatient for their first glimpse of untrammeled illusions. It seemed like a lifetime ago, but it was barely more than a day.

The portal image did not change. Ecstasy Stones called to them, seducing them in tone on tone of rainbow pleasures.

Senyas and Bre'n waited. The image remained the same, stones glittering with promise, chiming with all the possibilities of ecstasy.

"Maybe this is the wrong place to go through," suggested Rheba, biting her lip when renewed itching attacked the back of her eyes.

Kirtn said nothing.

The veil shimmered and remained unchanged.

Kirtn turned to walk back the way they had come. She turned with him, but could not control the sound that escaped her lips as an agony of fire scraped behind her eyes.

Nor was that the worst of it. Where he and she had walked between buildings there was only darkness now, darkness and the hollow gliding of unfettered wind. She did not want to walk into that emptiness, for she knew in her soul that it had no end.

"No," she whispered when Kirtn walked forward.

He neither turned nor acknowledged her voice. Fssa's sensors reeled as the snake probed the nothingness ahead. At that moment, Kirtn staggered. He leaned forward, feeling ahead with his hands as though a wall had sprung up between him and whatever lay beyond his fingertips.

"Either this is a class twelve illusion," mourned the snake in a minor key, "or what we came through before was a twelve." He sighed thinly. "Not that it matters. On Yhelle, reality is a matter of opinion."

Kirtn strained, muscles knotting and moving under his copper fur, pouring all of his Bre'n strength into the wall. Nothing moved, at first. Then slowly, gradually, Kirtn gave way. The invisible wall pushed him backward, toward his dancer, toward the Ecstasy Stones shimmering in the veil's unchanging portal.

Abruptly, he straightened and leaped sideways along the wall. It took no more than a touch to tell him that the wall was in reality a crescent. He and Rheba were caught between its horns. The wall curved toward him, narrowing the space that separated him from his dancer and the veil gleaming behind her.

Gently, inexorably, the crescent contracted, pressing Senyas and Bre'n closer to the portal where Ecstasy Stones waited in deadly multicolored silence.

There was no escape. The veil energies closed over Kirtn and Reba, sucking them into the tyrant K'Masei's stronghold.

XVIII

There was nothing on the other side of the veil but an uninhabited slidewalk curving toward a distant glow. The Redis clan territory displayed no blatant illusions, no sweeping conceits, no wry deceptions replacing reality.

Not even buildings. The area beyond the veil was so empty that it made Rheba's skin move and tighten. She had seen places like this before, on Deva, scorched ruins where dancers had not been able to hold at bay the leaping sun. But there were not even ruins in the Redis territory, nothing except the sinuous invitations of the slidewalk.

"I don't like it," she said flatly. Her akhenet lines surged in ragged pulses, unsettled by her recent passage through the veil. The slidewalk rippled like a river of pearls waiting to be strung.

Kirtn smiled down at her. "It's not as bad as it looks, dancer. The Stones . . . I think the Stones aren't what we were told. They don't want to hurt us."

She looked up him with eyes that were cinnamon and skeptical. "How can you tell?"

"Can't you feel it?" he murmured. "They're as gentle as a summer dawn. They're love, not hate."

She closed her eyes. When they opened again they were gold and more than skeptical. Fear glinted, fear and a dancer's power gathering. Her hand closed around Kirtn's wrist. Fear, proximity and love for her Bre'n forged a fragile mindlink between them. For an instant she shared with him echoes of joy and laughter gliding. . . .

But only for an instant. Her touch dimmed the Stones' allure. The echoes of ecstasy faded. Kirtn shook himself and looked at her with eyes that were caught between regret and fear.

"Psi masters," Rheba said hoarsely, her fingers hard and trembling around his wrist. "They were in your mind, as Satin was in your mind on Onan. Don't trust them!"

"At least they weren't trying to rearrange my brains," said Kirtn in a tight voice, "or disillusion me."

Fssa hissed with pleasure. He was all the way out of Rheba's hair, supported only by a coil around Kirtn's strong neck. "The Stones are lovely, dancer. Like my Guardians' dreams of swimming Ssimmi's molten sky/seas."

"You too, snake?" she said, both frightened and oddly angry.

"Yesss. But your energies interfere." He sighed like a child asked to choose between sweets. "If only Kirtn were hotter. Then I could have fire and the Stones, too."

Rheba frowned. Her akhenet lines quivered and ignited. With an effort, she stilled her fears, murmuring litanies in her mind until her lines faded to whorls of transparent gold.

"Mentor," she said slowly, carefully, "Don't trust the Tyrant's Ecstasy Stones. No one who goes to the Redis hall comes back out. Remember that."

"I'm trying to," Kirtn said. Suddenly he buried his hands in her seething hair. "Hold me, dancer," he whispered. "The Stones are so very beautiful. . . ."

For an instant she stood without moving, lost, for he had always been her strength. Then her arms went around him in a gesture both gentle and fierce. With an instinct far older than her years, she built a network of energy around her Bre'n, pouring herself through him in a sweet rush of fire that even the Ecstasy Stones could not equal.

He shuddered and lifted her off her feet, holding her as though he were afraid it was the last time. Then his mind was free, not even a wisp of alien ecstasy remained; but ecstasy was there, unity of dancer and Bre'n.

Slowly he let her slide down his body to stand again on her own feet. "I'm all right now, dancer. The Stones . . ." Darkness turned uneasily in the depths of his yellow eyes. "They won't fool me so easily again."

But unspoken between them was the question: *Was it simple deception the Stones offered, or was it something more?*

"Or something less," said Kirtn wryly, lips half curved, half smiling at his dancer. Patches of copper hair clung to her skin and clothes, held there by her sweat. He brushed futilely at the fine, tiny hairs. "Sorry, dancer. I've gone and shed all over you."

Rheba smiled, but she wanted to cry. "What's a dancer for if not to help her Bre'n shed?"

Kirtn's fingers moved as though he would hold her again, sweet fire and energy pouring. Then he closed his eyes and stepped back. She watched, waiting. After a moment he opened his eyes and tried to smile.

"They're back, dancer. But I know them, now." He turned to step up on the slidewalk, then looked over his shoulder at her. "You're more than they could ever be to me."

"Wait!"

Her voice pulled him back from the slidewalk's smooth gleam.

"I—we—have to know more about the Stones before we get any closer to them."

"We know that the closer we get, the more powerful they are," said Kirtn in Senyas, blunt and sardonic at once.

She took Fssa and put him on the ground. "Put Rainbow around him." Her voice was strained. Only Kirtn's vulnerability to the Stones could have driven her to the extreme of requiring communication between Fssireeme and Zaarain construct.

Reluctantly, Kirtn pulled Rainbow off his neck. He knew the cost of the alien conversations for Rheba when she was within their range.

She took the caged Stones out of her pocket and put them close to Rainbow, but not touching. Although she was not sure her energy cages could prevent Rainbow from pirating the stones for its own uses, she hoped to discourage such theft.

"Snake, ask Rainbow if it knows what these stones are, if they can be controlled, if they're real or illusion, alive or machine, anything that can help us. And," grimly, "be quick about it."

She retreated rapidly as Fssa assumed the fungoid shape that he used to communicate with the fragmentary Zaarain construct. There was not time for her to get beyond the reach of the Fssireeme's savage energies. Nor did she think she should. Fssa, too, was vulnerable to the Ecstasy Stones' allure.

Kirtn followed her, putting his body between his dancer and the odd pair on the ground. Even dense Bre'n flesh could not deflect the bizarre communication between Fssireeme and Zaarain crystals, but a dance could. His hands slid into place on her shoulders. Flames licked up from her akhenet lines, concealing dancer and Bre'n, disrupting the flow of alien energies.

Still, Fssireeme-Zaarain communication was not painless for her. It never was.

When the dance ended, blood trickled down her lower lip. Kirtn, too, was affected, but not nearly so much as his dancer. What was agony to her was merely discomfort to him.

"Well?" she said, walking back to Fssa. Her voice was thin, her face pale against blazing whorls of akhenet lines.

The snake whistled lyric Bre'n apologies for hurting her.

She brushed them aside as she did the drops of blood on her lips. "Did Rainbow know anything useful for once?" she demanded.

"Rainbow is only fragments," Fssa reminded her softly.

She groaned. "Useless pile of crystal turds. Doesn't it know anything at all?"

"Some of the worry stones are Zaarain," said Fssa in hasty Senyas. "Some aren't."

"What are they?"

"Rainbow doesn't know. Remember, it was knocked to pieces and sold as jewelry across half the galaxy after the Zaarain Cycle ended."

"So we can assume that the non-Zaarain stones came from a later Cycle," said Kirtn, picking up Rainbow and replacing it around his neck. The double strand of crystals dimmed as it got farther from the worry stones.

"Yes. Rainbow wants some of them," added the snake.

Kirtn grunted, remembering Rainbow's blinding scintillations when it was thrown among Zaarain crystals on Daemen. "I could tell by the glow that it was interested."

"Which does it want?" said Rheba thoughtfully, looking at the worry stones on the ground.

"The big ones."

"I should have guessed," she said with a grimace. "The better to take my head off, I suppose."

"It's sorry it hurts you," the snake whistled miserably.

She sighed, wondering if it was the Zaarain or the Fssireeme that apologized. "Anything else?"

"The non-Zaarain crystals are alive," whistled the snake.

"Alive? You mean energized?" asked Kirtn, looking at the worry stones with new interest.

"I mean nonmachine life," said Fssa, switching to unambiguous Senyas.

"Biological life?" said Rheba incredulously, scooping stones and snake off the ground at the same time.

Fssa made a frustrated sound and switched back to Bre'n. Sometimes ambiguities were the essence of truthful communication. "Alive as Rainbow is alive, only more organic. They're haunted with Fourth People. They're . . . *alive*."

The Bre'n harmonies the snake created said more, telling of growth that was not quite organic nor yet lithic, intelligence that encompassed one more dimension than Fourth People acknowledged, a form of life flickering between the interfaces akhenets called time and death.

Rheba sighed, wondering if she knew more or less about the worry stones than she had before a Fssireeme described the impossible in the voices of Bre'n poetry. "Can they be controlled?" she asked, thinking as much of the Ecstasy Stones as the sullen crystals in her hand.

"Only for a time. As you guessed, their energies build geometrically inside the cage every few minutes. You won't hold those much longer. They can be neutralized, though."

"How?"

"Rainbow didn't know. It only knew that balance must be possible or whatever lives in—or through—the stones would have shattered long ago."

After a long moment, Rheba jammed the stones deep in her pocket. She looked at the slidewalk, then back at the veil. Though they were still within its field, no portal showed on the veil's face. It was as though there were no other possible destinations on Serriolia except the Redis clan hall, so no other portal was needed.

Deliberately, she walked toward the blank veil. The air in front of her thickened into a wall. Simultaneously, her eyes itched so badly that she cried out and flung herself backward.

"What's wrong?" said Kirtn, grabbing her when she would have fallen.

"Itch," she said succinctly, then shivered when the itch was replaced by coolness and a wisp of something that might have been an apology. "And the veil. Neither one wants me to go away from here. I guess that only leaves the Tyrant and his white-eyed minions."

And the Ecstasy Stones.

But neither of them said that aloud. It was simply there between them, words shared in the silent depths of their minds.

With an inward shrinking that did not show, Rheba mounted the slidewalk. Kirtn leaped up lightly beside her. Rainbow bounced against his chest with a flash of crystal faces. She tried not to shudder when she looked at the Zaarain construct. It might have more in common with the Ecstasy Stones than was good for any of them.

"Can we trust it?" she asked tightly, clicking her fingernail against a vivid sapphire stone that rolled in the hollow of Kirtn's neck.

He took her hand and soothed it with his lips. "Rainbow doesn't want to hurt us," he said. "Neither do the Ecstasy Stones."

"Neither does the zoolipt," she shot back, "but it nearly got us both killed."

He sighed because there was no answer to her fears. She could not feel the rising purity of the Stones, ecstasy reflected, born and reborn on a thousand flawless faces . . .

"Mentor!"

Her voice called him out of his waking dream. He smiled sadly, for himself and for the dancer he loved who could not see ecstasy when it was spread out glittering before her.

Kirtn!

Ecstasy winked and sighed and vanished beneath a cataract of dancer fire. He blinked, saw the slidewalk, a nacreous ribbon stretching between emptiness. Ahead, nothing more than a silver-blue glow beckoning.

With an enormous effort he shook off the languid seduction of the Stones. "I'm all right, dancer. They're very subtle, but I'm on my guard now."

She said nothing, only looked at his eyes. They were clear and yellow again, no longer glazed with inwardness. Her fingers uncurled from his wrist. Itching assaulted her eyes. Hastily she grabbed his wrist and was rewarded by coolness.

He looked at her, puzzled and amused. "I wasn't going to run off."

"I know. Itch just wants us to keep in touch. Literally."

He whistled to himself, more thoughtful than surprised. "Does that mean you can't trust me?" he asked in Senyas.

She hesitated, but no messages formed behind her eyes. "I don't know. Itch isn't saying anything either way."

"What about Fssa?"

She felt her hair quickly with her free hand. "Still there. I think as long as he stays in my hair he'll be immune."

But her eyes itched even as the words formed on her tongue.

"Then what should I do?" she hissed beneath her breath to the Itch behind her eyes. "Tie the snake in a knot?"

The itching faded. She had the clear feeling that it was not an answer, merely a temporary erasure so that she would be able to feel new messages written on the back of her eyes.

Kirtn tugged gently at her hand. His eyes were fixed on the silver-blue glow ahead. Clearly he was impatient with the slidewalk's leisurely pace. She, on the other hand, would have been glad never to get where the slidewalk was taking her.

She looked over her shoulder and felt her lines flare. She would have to go forward, because two steps behind her was nothing at all, not even the slidewalk's pearl shimmer. It was as though the world ended. The veil itself had vanished as completely as though it had never existed. She could not even sense its penetrating, dissonant energies.

With a feeling close to despair, she turned from the emptiness behind her to the unwelcome radiance ahead. Shapes were condensing out of the glow, curves of flashing light, crystal geometries rising plane after plane, all bathed in a subliminal humming of emotions neither demonic nor divine, yet somehow more compelling than either or both together.

From her hair a Fssireeme sang of beauty in a chorus of Bre'n voices. She looked at Kirtn, afraid that he would be swept out of her reach into the Stones' crystal embrace.

"I'm here," he murmured, smiling down at her. "But hold on to me. If the Stones don't get me that silver-tongued snake will."

The slidewalk increased its pace until her hair was whipped by wind. Abruptly, she regretted not jumping off while she could. She looked at her Bre'n. Lines of strain were etched on his face. As though at a great distance, she sensed something calling to him, something inhuman and superb, devastating perfection.

"Kirtn?" she asked softly.

"Nothing." His voice was curt. Then he shrugged. "The Stones. They're unspeakably beautiful, but I like to choose my lovers—*or my gods*."

"Fight them."

"I am." Silence. Then, almost wistfully, "Don't you feel them, dancer?"

She said nothing, for she had finally seen the slidewalk's destination. Her fingers clamped around his wrist harshly enough to draw a grimace even from a Bre'n. Just ahead, the shining ribbon they rode ended in a burst of pearl light. A figure stood waiting for them, dark within the radiance that was endemic to the Redis territory.

The slidewalk stopped so suddenly that Bre'n and Senyas were thrown off their feet. They scrambled upright—and found themselves looking into f'lTiri's triumphant smile.

A million hot needles dug into the back of Rheba's eyes.

XIX

"F'lTiri?" asked Rheba, happiness and uncertainty mingling in her voice.

"Of course," said f'lTiri, laughing as he reached for his friends.

His hands were warm and firm as they clasped first Kirtn's arm and then Rheba's hand. The voice was the same, the lips, the laugh . . . but she would have felt better if she had never heard of class twelve illusions. Even so, she smiled and returned f'lTiri's greeting, for she very much wanted it to be him.

Her eyes itched savagely. Something inhuman began singing deep in her mind. Hastily she let go of f'lTiri. The singing, if not the itching, stopped.

"Where's i'sNara?" she asked, clutching Kirtn's wrist as though he would run away despite his previous assurances.

"With the children," answered f'lTiri. His smile was happiness condensed into a single curving line. "We were so wrong about the Ecstasy Stones. They're . . ." F'lTiri groped for explanations that did not exist in the Yhelle language.

Rheba's lines ran hot, then icy, for f'lTiri was speaking Yhelle instead of Universal. Fssa was translating automatically, inconspicuously, so that she could understand f'lTiri.

But before this moment, f'lTiri had never spoken anything except Universal to them.

"The Stones are so wonderful," sighed f'lTiri. "Come. I'll take you to them."

Rheba did not need the torment behind her eyes to know that something was more or less than it seemed. Was f'lTiri the unwilling—or even willing—captive of Ecstasy, or was he a class twelve illusion from sweet smile to dusty sandals? She stared into his eyes, looking for answers. She saw nothing except her own fiery reflection. It startled her, for she had not realized that she was burning.

"Dancer?" murmured Kirtn in Senyas. Then he added a

Bre'n trill that asked why she burned when there was no danger near.

She looked at f'lTiri and said only, "We're not ready to see the Stones yet. We were trying to get back to our ship when the veil brought us here."

Not quite the whole truth, but enough for her purposes.

F'lTiri smiled again, redefining joy in a single gesture. Rheba stared, fascinated. Even the boy she had known as The Luck had not smiled quite so perfectly, and he had been the culmination of Cycles of genetic selection for charm and good fortune. But The Luck's sweet surface had been only half of his unique truth. She suspected that it was the same with f'lTiri.

She looked away from his compelling smile. Her lines burned hotly, fed by fear and the energy that pervaded everything with a blue-white glow.

"Oh, the veil," said f'lTiri, dismissing it with a twinkle of his illusionist eyes. "It gets independent every now and again. We're illusionists, not engineers, and the veil construct is many Cycles old. It always works again, though, if you give it enough time. Unless there's something urgent at the ship for you to attend to . . .?"

She looked at Kirtn. He said nothing. His face was hard, his eyes narrow within their golden mask. She could sense the conflicting energies within him, her own and f'lTiri's racing along sensitive Bre'n nerves, competing for his attention.

Casually, as though it were an oversight, she let flames leap from the hand nearer f'lTiri. After a momentary hesitation, f'lTiri jerked his fingers away from Kirtn's arm. She sensed the conflict within her Bre'n diminish. With a smile of her own, she faced the Yhelle illusionist.

"Now that you, i'sNara and your children are safe, Kirtn and I have to get back to the ship." Rheba's words sounded unconvincing, even to her. "There are other Loo slaves on board the *Devalon*," she added quickly, "other promises to keep. They're as eager to see their homes again as you were to see yours. Or," she added, thinning her smile to a bare line of teeth, "*more* eager. You were reluctant to come home again. Remember?"

F'lTiri's smile shifted, then resettled into indulgent lines. "I'sNara and I were very foolish."

"The veil," reminded Rheba gently. "Fix it for us."

"I can't."

"Is that the way the Tyrant keeps his subjects in place?" asked Rheba.

F'lTiri's smile widened. "K'Masei isn't a tyrant. He's just impervious to love."

She smiled sardonically. "That's as good a definition of a tyrant as I've heard."

"No tyranny, just ecstasy," murmured f'lTiri dreamily. "You must see the Stones, Rheba. They are . . ." His voice dissolved into another incredible smile.

She turned away from him. As she looked over her shoulder she realized that the slidewalk was gone. Where its pearl ribbon had once been there was nothing at all, not even a small glow. She closed her eyes and tried to sense the direction of the nearest coil of veil. All she found was energy pouring out of the radiant center of the Redis hall—if those crystal curves could indeed be called something so mundane as a clan hall.

Deliberately, she tried to touch the core of whatever powered the hall. It was like trying to hold an oiled ball on her fingertip; whenever she approached a balance point, the ball would slide away. She could only drink the source of energy indirectly, like taking light reflected off another surface instead of going directly to the luminous core. Perhaps if she were closer to the source she could tap it more directly.

At least her eyes had stopped itching while she tried.

"Ready?" asked Kirtn, when he saw her attention return to the moment.

"Ready for what?"

"The tour."

"What tour?"

"The one f'lTiri is going to give us," said the Bre'n patiently.

She looked at f'lTiri. Her eyes itched terribly. She looked at her Bre'n. The itching abated but did not go away. She frowned and sent dancer energy coursing through Kirtn, trying to chase the confusion she sensed beneath his benevolent smile.

F'lTiri made a small sound and stepped back from Kirtn. Only then did Rheba realize that the illusionist had been touching Kirtn's arm. The unexpected surge of akhenet energy must have scorched the illusionist's fingers.

Kirtn moved as though walking out of deep water. He focused on the dancer eyes staring up at him. He whistled a slow apology. "They're strong, Rheba. Each time I close one

door they find a new one to open. But they can't get around
your energy. Burn for me, dancer. Burn for both of us.''

''And the tour f'lTiri is going to give us?'' she whistled,
letting the minor key and her touch tell him that she would
burn for him beyond the ice at the end of time. ''Do we go
with him like slaves broken to the training lead?''

His mouth turned down at her reminder of the Loo-chim's
razor leash. Were it not for the zoolipt's mindless healing, he
would have worn a collar of scars for the rest of his life. ''No
razor restraints here. Just . . .'' His voice died. He could not
describe the temptations of Ecstasy.

Her mouth echoed the bitter curve of his lips. She heard his
thoughts as clearly as she had heard his whistle. ''Be grateful
I can't hear their call. If I could, we'd be up to our cracks in
ice and ashes.''

''Are you ready?'' asked f'lTiri serenely.

''No, I'm not ready to see the Ecstasy Stones.'' Rheba's
voice was as clear and hot as the flames licking over her
akhenet lines.

And then her voice broke, for the ground had changed
beneath her feet. The distant building composed of radiance
and crystal arcs loomed in front of her now. A scarlet slit
opened in the lowest curve of wall.

''No,'' she said, pulling back.

F'lTiri stood patiently. ''I'm not taking you to the Stones,''
he murmured. ''Just a tour of k'Masei's hall. Then, if you
still don't want to know Ecstasy, I'll take you back to the
veil. The Stones don't force,'' he added softly. ''That's not
their way.''

Rheba glanced sideways at her Bre'n's strained face and
had to bite her lip to keep from answering. A coolness behind
her eyes rewarded both her restraint and her conclusion about
the Ecstasy Stones' gentleness. Having Itch's agreement was
a two-sided weapon, though; she was not sure just whose
interests Itch had at heart—assuming Itch had something that
passed for a heart.

''Well, Itch'' she whispered beneath her breath, ''should I
go or stay?''

There was a mixed flash of itch-cool.

''No tour?'' breathed Rheba. She grabbed her eyes. ''All
right,'' she hissed. ''I'm going!''

Coolness and a distant breath of apology.

Grimly, Rheba tightened her grip on Kirtn's arm. He smiled

despite the pain of her hand grinding flesh against bone. He shifted so that their fingers interlaced in an unbreakable clasp.

She looked at the man who might once have been f'lTiri. "Make it a short tour. I've already seen enough of Yhelle to last me until I die."

F'lTiri smiled and turned. As he did, the crystal hall shifted and reformed around them. The Redis, unlike the Yaocoons, apparently believed in advanced machinery. She sensed speed and movement and wild rush of energy nearby. Her hair rippled, questing outward in blind, precise seeking, tendrils reaching for the power that leaped endlessly around her.

Kirtn whistled and clenched her fingers until they ached. "Dancer," he whistled, off-key in his urgency, "the Stones are much closer now. They may not be coercive, but in the name of Fire they're addictive! *Burn!*"

She loosed a torrent of energy through him, scourging his nerves and purging his mind. He staggered, caught himself and held her fiercely against his sweating body. Rainbow's hard facets cut across her cheek, but she did not complain, simply held on and burned.

F'lTiri watched, smiling with blind affection. For the first time Rheba saw that his eyes were white.

Fssa shifted beneath her seething mass of hair. Though she could not see him, she knew the snake was changing shapes as rapidly as a thought, tasting the various wavelengths that pervaded the hall. She hoped he could understand them better than she could. The sleeting variety of energies was enough to make her dizzy. Only one was familiar, the dissonant cry of the core that powered the veil.

"Find anything, snake?" she whistled.

"Ssimmi is in here . . . somewhere . . . where?"

The Fssireeme's longing whistle squeezed her heart. He had mourned his lost home far longer than she had been alive. Nor did she have any way to take him home. Ssimmi was not known to any of the navtrices she had queried. The snake's planet was lost somewhere among the galaxy's billion stars.

If Fssa could find Ssimmi's equivalent on Yhelle, who was she to tell him it was merely an illusion?

"Is there anything else here?" she asked softly. "Is the hall an illusion?"

The snake sighed and retreated into her hair. "Yes, but what's beneath it is no different."

"I don't understand."

"Neither do I," whistled the snake plaintively. "There are

crystal walls and floors and halls and all, but not where we see them.''

"Could you find our way back out of here?''

"I . . .'' The snake changed again, tugging gently at her flying hair. "No,'' sadly. Then, "But it's so very beautiful here, dancer. Why do you want to go back?''

"Are there other ways out of here?'' she asked, ignoring his question.

The snake's most human sigh slid past her ear. "Stripped of illusion, this place is a maze of light and competing energies.''

She glanced aside at Kirtn, wondering how he was holding up in his struggle against the seductive Ecstasy Stones. His face was hard and closed as a fist. If she had not been touching him, she would have thought he had no feelings at all. But she was touching him. His conflicting desires raced over her with a discordance that was like passing through the veil again and again.

Rainbow shone like a double string of molten crystal. It seemed impossible that the Zaarain construct could glow so hotly and not burst into white flames.

"Are you ready to see the Ecstasy Stones?'' asked f'lTiri, his voice as white as his eyes, as white as the hall and the floor, the blinding maze closing around Bre'n and Senyas and Fssireeme alike.

"No,'' said Rheba, striving to make her voice calm.

"There's nothing to fear,'' smiled the illusionist, voice and words a single curve of light. "Ecstasy doesn't hurt you.''

He leaned forward. As his fingers brushed Kirtn's arm, conflicting currents of energy raced through the Bre'n, numbing him and shocking his dancer. For an instant their interlaced fingers loosened.

The air around Rheba crackled harmlessly, but it was not so easy for Kirtn. Ecstasy pounded him like a mountain storm, all but shattering him. He staggered against her, renewing their contact once again. He clung to her with hands that were too weak to belong to a Bre'n.

F'lTiri laughed gently, ignoring Rheba, looking only at Kirtn. "Be like the sea grass, my strong friend. Bend to the waves. Only rocks break.''

Fire leaped from Rheba, an immaterial whip meant to scorch rather than injure, for she was still not certain whether f'lTiri or an illusion talked to her.

"We've seen enough," she said harshly. "Take us out of here."

White eyes turned and regarded her with blind intensity. Her lines went cold, then leaped. If this had once been f'lTiri, it was not her friend now.

Dancer fire swept out, caging f'lTiri as she had caged the worry stones. He cried out, writhing. Nondancer energies sparked and spat around him, trying to sustain patterns her fire had disrupted. F'lTiri's appearance melted and ran like mercury, eyes white in a shapeless puddle of gray.

"Take us out of here!" demanded Rheba, speaking more to whoever controlled the Ecstasy Stones than to the apparition that could have been f'lTiri.

Walls became mirrors and glided inward, shrinking as floor and ceiling shrank, closing in on her, trying to burn her with her own reflected fire. It was a mistake, like throwing fuel on a raging fire. She took the reflected energy and wove it back into her dance, strengthening the immaterial cage around the illusionist.

He screamed and changed before her eyes, f'lTiri again, then i'sNara, then a boy with i'sNara's eyes and a half-grown girl with f'lTiri's smile. She did not need to know their names to recognize the illusionists' children. Then he became more people in dizzying succession, Yhelle after Yhelle with no distinction as to sex or age, an agonized throng caught in one quicksilver illusion, flickering in and out of being like a flame in a wind.

And each illusion wept to be free.

"*Let us go!*" screamed Rheba, backing away from the plastic entreaties.

Hot shards of ecstasy probed her, looking for weaknesses in her akhenet lines. She screamed again. Flames exploded around her and the multifaced illusion. She burned bright and pure, pouring power into the cage of energy she was weaving around what had once worn the appearance of f'lTiri. As the network of fire thickened, the cries faded to whimpers.

Silence came as the cage imploded.

When Rheba was no longer blinded by the flames in her eyes, she saw an unknown illusionist dead at her feet. Whoever had died, at least she had not killed f'lTiri. She shuddered, glad that she did not know the man.

In a last spasm of death, his slack hand opened. A caged crystal rolled free. It burned so savagely that the dancer energies restraining it looked dark by comparison. Rheba stared, puzzled by the too-dark dancer fire before she realized that she had inadvertently caged an Ecstasy Stone.

"Kirtn," she said, reaching out to take his arm, "Look at—" Her voice stopped when her fingers closed around nothing at all. She looked around frantically. "Kirtn? *Kirtn!*"

Nothing answered her scream.

"Snake!" she cried, combing her fingers frantically through her hair. "Find him with one of your shapes!"

Her fingers came up as empty as her heart. Fssa and Kirtn were gone. She was alone.

XX

For an instant Rheba was paralyzed. Around her was nothing but fire reflected and reinforced by a thousand mirrors. At her feet was the dark face of death. It was Deva all over again, a hell she had revisited too many times in her nightmares. She was a child once more, helpless, her arms and face blistered by the same fires that had consumed her parents before her eyes.

Kirtn had ended that nightmare by running in and sweeping her out of the burning ruins of her childhood. But he was gone now. There was no one to take her out of the smoking ashes of despair. This was a new nightmare, a worse one. A hall of mirrors where only death and a fire dancer were real.

There was nothing to do but dance, alone.

Flames of pure gold swept over her body as she began her dance. Her hair was a seething corona, her hands incandescent with akhenet lines. She took the wild energy of the Redis hall and sychronized it into coherent light. Then she took the light and used it to shatter the illusions reflected endlessly around her.

Mirrored walls and floor shifted, shrank, tilted, trying to turn her weapon against her by changing the angle of the returning energy. Light scattered wildly. Part of her own dance rebounded, burning her. She wished futilely for Kirtn's sustaining partnership or Fssa's protective ability to absorb heat, but she had only her fear and her dance.

So she danced while the walls slid closer, the better to turn her own fire against her.

Grimly, she transformed random energy into disciplined fire. She concentrated on a single wall, not caring whether it was real or illusory, certain only that somewhere beyond the mirrors lay a way out. She danced savagely, yet well within her own control. She had not forgotten the zoolipt. She did not want its interference, however well meant. She knew if she stopped dancing the walls would close in and crush her. She doubted that the zoolipt knew it, though.

For that reason she did not try to tap the dissonant core that was the major source of the hall's power. She had to satisfy the demands of her dance with the energies sleeting freely through the Redis clan building. She was not sure she could control the core if she did tap it. If she could not, she would incinerate the hall and herself with it—unless the zoolipt stopped her dance. And it certainly would stop her if she approached the core as she should, slowly, learning its nature by burning herself when she guessed wrong.

There was only one way she could evade her unwelcome monitor. She could simply grab the core. There would be a single searing instant of holocaust unleashed before the zoolipt could intervene, a dancer burning out of control, burning to ash and gone. Only as a final resort would she crack the core and die, destroying everything within reach of her fire, including Kirtn lost somewhere beyond the mirrors.

Until that moment came she would dance, and hope.

As though at a distance she saw herself a living flame in the center of deadly energies, and the room shrinking around her. In front of her a mirrored surface shattered and smoked blackly. The wall on which the reflective illusion had been based burned with the acrid smell of plastics and the cleaner scent of wood.

Instantly the other mirrors blackened. Whoever controlled the illusions must have realized that the mirrors were aiding her dance. She assumed k'Masei shaped the illusions. It was like a tyrant to use illusions to enslave and kill.

There was a pause, a sense of ingathering like the silence before a storm shifted and attacked from a new quarter. Instinctively she built a defensive cage of energy around herself, for she had no Bre'n to protect her back.

Suddenly a cataract of invisible demand beat on her. Her defensive cage bristled and flamed until she stood like a torch in the center of a starless night. There was no light around her that she had not created, no companionship except her own dance. Part of her mind screamed for her lost Bre'n; but the akhenet part of her coldly ransacked her surroundings for a power source great enough to vaporize illusions.

Her immaterial questing brushed a familiar energy source, a simple electromagnetic generator that powered the Redis

food machines. The machines were off, cold, but the generator itself vibrated with life.

She drained it between one breath and the next.

She burned.

A new figure formed in front of the metal-reinforced wall
she was trying to destroy. A man, tall and powerful, more
familiar than her own hands. Kirtn. She leaped toward him,
incoherent with joy. He laughed and hugged her—

—and she screamed, for there was nothing inside his mind,
nothing more to him than the textures of flesh and fur, yellow
eyes, and his warm lips speaking Yhelle words she could not
understand. Not Kirtn. Illusion.

Yet she could not bring herself to burn it down. She shaped
her dance so that deadly fire divided around the false Kirtn.
Behind the Bre'n illusion the wall smoldered and smoked,
slowly catching fire. Streamers of fire from her reinforced the
reluctant flames.

Kirtn's image expanded suddenly, blocking off the wall.
Her dance faltered when his image smoked and burned and
screamed Yhelle pleas she could not understand. She closed
her eyes and ears and let fire rain down. If the Tyrant k'Masei
wanted to protect that wall with Kirtn's likeness, then she
wanted to reduce the wall to a smoking memory.

The screams stopped. She opened her eyes and saw a sheet
of fire where the wall had been. The illusion of Kirtn was
gone. Automatically she fed the flames, streamers of energy
pouring out from her as the wall consumed itself.

She did not know how much longer she could dance before
the zoolipt stopped her. The stench of her own hands burning
was strong in the air. She knew she should feel pain, but did
not. The loss of Kirtn consumed everything else.

The wall trembled, then began to collapse. From behind its
rapidly cooling metal skeleton came a scream. A running man
crossed the room and dove beneath the surface of a bathing
pool. The scream, more than the water, saved his life. She
had seen too many Senyasi and Bre'ns burn to death beneath
Deva's unstable sun. Reflexively she called back her fire. In
the next instant she cursed herself for being conned by yet
another of the Tyrant's endless illusions.

She was alone in a room full of steam. She waited until the
cooler air of the hall took away the hot vapors. Behind her
was a passageway lined with scorched, broken shards. Around
her a luxurious room emerged from dissipating steam. To her

right a man bobbed to the surface of the bathing pool and watched her with more curiosity than fear.

"Where did the Stones find your template?" he asked in Yhelle. When she did not answer, he repeated the question in Universal.

"I'm real," she said in the same language, "as k'Masei will find out to his grief."

"You speak Universal! You're not an illusion!"

Rheba looked at him curiously.-"Why does speaking Universal make me real?"

"The Stones only speak Yhelle, so their illusions only speak Yhelle, too."

The man's voice was reasonable. It was only his words that did not make sense; Ecstasy Stones did not speak at all. She was about to point out that fact when she remembered how she had recognized that Kirtn was an illusion. He had spoken Yhelle. Her thoughts continued to their inevitable conclusion as she walked toward the man in the pool.

"You're real, too," she said.

"Of course," he said in a startled voice, as though it had never occurred to him that someone might mistake him for an illusion. "Are you finished?"

"Finished?"

"Burning things. I'd like to come out. They never get the water warm enough for me."

She felt laughter twist in her throat. With an effort she controlled herself, recognizing the difference between humor and hysteria. "You must be real," she said in a strangled voice. "You're crazier than any illusion I've seen yet." Then, realizing that he was still waiting, "Come out. I won't burn you."

Shivering, the man walked out of the pool. He was her height, thin, and as pale as every Yhelle she had ever seen shorn of illusionist facade.

He wiped off excess water with his hands, shivering violently. "I don't suppose you could dry me off without scorching me? Or start a small fire?" he asked in an apologetic tone. "It's cold with that draft where the wall used to be."

She reached for a rich robe that was draped over a nearby chair. Her hand went through both robe and chair. She made a startled sound and examined the rest of the room closely. Beneath a thin sheen of illusions, the room was a spartan cell. She looked back toward the shivering man and opened her mouth to ask a hundred questions.

He shivered miserably. In the silence she could hear his teeth chattering. He would not be able to answer her questions until he was warm enough to unlock his jaw. She would have to dry him off despite her tiredness. Dancing alone had drained her of everything except fear for her Bre'n. If she helped the half-mad illusionist, would he help her in return?

"Hold still," she said, concentrating. She had not had to dry off anyone for a long time. On board the *Devalon*, the ship's machinery took care of such things.

The air around the man shimmered and shifted. Flames appeared above his skin and hair, close enough to warm but not to burn. The flames startled him into moving incautiously. He yelped as the fire came too close. Instantly the flames vanished. He waited without moving, but the fire did not reappear.

"Dry enough?" asked Rheba, fighting weakness and the zoolipt's seductive tugs on her eyelids.

"Thanks," he said, making a small gesture of embarrassment. He smiled shyly. "This is the first time I've been warm since they threw me in here." He looked beyond her. "Where's your guide?"

"Dead."

His face brightened. "How did you do it?" Before she could answer, questions poured out of him. "Don't you feel any pressure? Don't you want to go back into the hall? Don't you see pictures of Ecstasy Stones in your mind? How can you just stand there? Aren't they calling to you? Don't you just *have to* go to them?"

"The Ecstasy Stones don't affect me," she said, pushing back a yawn with a half-burned hand that healed even as she noticed it. "Why are you—"

He laughed and clapped his hands, interrupting her. "Another immune! No no, let me talk," he said quickly, all but babbling with joy. "It's been so long. You can't know how lonely it's been with only my own thin illusions and the Stones' constant whispering. Do they know you're here? Oh, that's what you were fighting, wasn't it? Don't worry, pretty stranger." He began skipping in place, giggling. "They can't control an immune, no no no, they can't, no no—"

"That's enough!" snapped Rheba, corking the man's bubbling hysteria with a snarl and a warning surge of fire.

"Sorry," he sighed, chagrin and joy warring on his face.

Another gesture, apology and self-deprecation in a graceful turn of his pale hand. "You just don't know—"

"—and I don't care," interrupted Rheba brutally. All she cared about now was her Bre'n and a Fissireeme more fantastic than any Yhelle illusion. "Do you know a way out of here?"

He tipped his head one way and then another as though seeing her for the first time. "Would I be here if I knew a way out?" he asked gently.

"*Is* there a way out?" she countered swiftly, realizing her mistake in phrasing her question.

"Oh yes. The Stones always give you a choice."

"Good," she said grimly.

"Not really. You don't know what the choice is."

"But you're going to tell me."

The man tipped his head back, studying a ceiling that was no different from the floor. "You can worship the Stones. Then you won't want to leave anymore and the problem of choice is solved."

Rheba grimaced and made a gesture of rejection.

"Or," continued the man, looking at her with eyes that were green-flecked brown, not white at all, "you can be disillusioned."

"Worship or disillusionment? Some choice." She looked back at him with eyes that were more gold with every passing moment. If she were not so tired she would be burning. As it was, tiny flames flickered raggedly over her akhenet lines. "Which did you chose?"

"Neither. I'm immune." He smiled unhappily. "So they took away my clan instead. I don't worship and I'm not disillusioned—but I might as well be for all the good I can do against *them*."

The room began to turn slowly around her. It was not an illusion. The zoolipt was warning her that she would be better off sitting down. She began to fight, only to be attacked by itching behind her eyes. It seemed that Itch and the zoolipt could collaborate at times. The thought did not comfort her much as she collapsed on the floor's hard surface.

She pushed herself upright, ignoring the grainy feeling in back of her eyes. She had to get out of here and find Kirtn. The first part of the thought brought a redoubled attack from Itch. The second part, finding Kirtn, brought a bit of relief. Was Itch trying to tell her that getting out of here right away was not the same as getting closer to finding Kirtn?

Blessed coolness. Itch agreed. Rheba groaned with relief.

"Are you all right?" asked the man, bending over her, but cautiously. She was still radiating heat from her strenuous solo dance.

"All right," she sighed. "Tired."

"Oh, then you'd better rest. You won't be able to steal the Stones unless you're strong and alert."

"Steal the Stones?" she asked, feeling like a wan echo of the illusionist.

"Of course." Then, anxiously, "Isn't that why you're here? To steal the Ecstasy Stones for the Libs?"

"No, I—" A savage attack of itching doubled her over, clawing at her eyes. *"Stop!"* she cried.

Itch stopped.

The man waited, his expression that of mingled curiosity and fear. "You aren't here to steal the Ecstasy Stones?" he asked, disappointment clear in his voice.

She sensed Itch poised behind her eyes, waiting to strike. "I didn't think that was why I came here," said Rheba cautiously, speaking more to Itch than to illusionist, "but I'm willing to negotiate. I want my Bre'n—and my friends—alive and free."

Itch made no move to disagree.

The man, who knew nothing of what lay behind her eyes, asked, "Did your friends go to the Stones?"

"I think so. As soon as I let go of Kirtn, he ran away. He must have taken Fssa with him, or else the snake followed. As for i'sNara and f'lTiri . . . they came to steal the Stones."

"Were they immune?"

"I doubt it."

The man made a sad gesture. "Then they won't be back. None of them. What the Stones seduce, they keep. If you want your friends back, you'll have to break the Stones' power by stealing some. Individually, they're not nearly as strong as they are collectively."

Rheba remembered the single Ecstasy Stone she had inadvertently caged in the hall. She looked at the man in sudden speculation. His eyes had not changed, still brown flecked with green, not white. His own eyes, not Stones' reflections. Yet—"Who are you? How do you know so much about the Stones?"

"Oh," he made one of the self-deprecating gestures that

she was coming to associate with him, "I'm the master snatcher who brought the Stones together."

"You? But I thought k'Masei the Tyrant was the one who gathered all the Ecstasy Stones."

He smiled lopsidedly. "That's me. But my name is k'Masei the Fool."

XXI

Rheba's glowing lines dimmed and sputtered out from sheer surprise. She could not believe that the modest, gently crazy illusionist in front of her was the fearsome man known as k'Masei the Tyrant.

"You?" she said weakly, looking at his odd eyes and rumpled hair and trying not to laugh. "Tyrant?"

"Is that really what they call me now?" he asked in a sorrowful voice. "That's even worse than being called a fool. What else do they say about me?"

"I was told," she said carefully, "that you were the Liberation clan's master snatcher."

He smiled wistfully. "I was."

"I was also told that you were a traitor to your clan." Her voice was even, her eyes intent. "I was told that you took the Libs' best Ecstasy Stones and gave them to the Redis."

K'Masei sighed. "The Libs still don't understand, do they?"

"They never will," she said bluntly. "They're dead."

He winced. When his expression smoothed again, he looked older. "I—" He cleared his throat and began again. "There are some things you should know if you're going to try to steal Ecstasy Stones. You *are* going to try, aren't you?"

"I don't have much choice, do I?" muttered Rheba. Her lips thinned to a line as she thought of Itch's torments. It was better than thinking about Kirtn, caught and held by forces she did not understand. Anything was better than thinking about that, even Itch. "I'll do whatever I can to free my Bre'n," she said. Her voice was calm but her akhenet lines pulsed, telling of dancer agitation.

"What's a Bre'n?"

She opened her mouth but no easy words of explanation came. Finally she said simply, "A man."

"Slave?"

"*My* Bre'n, but not my slave. Just as I'm *his* dancer." She looked at the massed, intricate lines of power swirling up from her fingertips to her shoulders. "He's as much a part of me as my arms. More. If you cut off my arms I'd still live."

"Then I can't talk you out of going after the Stones?"

"I thought you wanted me to steal them."

"Oh, I do. It's just . . . you're quite beautiful, you know. Can't they send someone ugly?"

Rheba choked off an impulse to laugh and cry at the same time. "I'm alone. There's no 'they' sending me after the Stones."

"Then you're not Lib?"

"I told you. All the Libs are dead."

He looked away for a long moment. When he looked back, his eyes were more dark than green. "In that case," he said, "you'd better listen very carefully. The more you know about the Stones, the better your chance of surviving. Although," he sighed, "I must tell you that you've little chance at all. Certainly none that I'd wager my worst illusion on."

"I don't have any time to waste listening to tales," said Rheba, ignoring the sudden itch behind her eyes. "Kirtn—my Bre'n—" Her voice squeezed into silence.

"The Stones won't hurt your Bre'n," said k'Masei. "At least, not right away. I'm not even sure that the Stones mean to hurt anyone at all. They're just"—his pale hands described random curves—"ignorant. Or maybe they don't care."

"How much time does Kirtn have?"

"Once, I would have said months. Then it was weeks. Days. Now . . . surely an hour or two?" He looked sadly at her. "Is your Bre'n strong?"

"Yes. Stronger even than he looks, and he would make four of you."

"Then," sighing, "if he doesn't go crazy he'll be all right for a few hours."

"I won't wait that long."

"Listen to me," he said, turning suddenly and bending very close, so close that she saw her akhenet lines glowing in his eyes. "Getting yourself enchanted or killed won't help your Bre'n. They nearly got me, and I'm immune too."

"Immune. What does that mean?" she said impatiently.

"You don't feel the Stones calling to you? Not at all?"

She frowned. "Since Kirtn has gone . . . sometimes, far away, I hear beautiful singing. I'd like to go and find it. Is that what you mean?"

"Is it hard to resist going out and looking?"

"No. Just an urge that comes and goes."

He smiled. "You're lucky. It's worse for me, but I'm used to it. That's what immunity is. They can't control your mind. That's what made me a master snatcher. As you can see"—a wave toward the room's slender illusions—"I'm not Serriolia's best illusionist. But I'm not bemused by Ecstasy Stones, either. My friends would dress me up in their best illusions, I'd sneak into other clans, and I'd come back with Ecstasy Stones.

"I decided," he said, settling onto the floor next to her, "that in order to break into the Redis clan hall, I'd have to come under cover of the Stones that the Redis didn't own."

"What went wrong?"

"Oh, nothing." He smiled wryly. "It went all too well. I brought a double handful of Ecstasy into the Redis hall. When I got there and saw the Redis Stones, I realized that there were more than I could carry in a single trip. The only logical thing to do was to leave my Stones there."

"Logical?" said Rheba, her voice rising.

"I told you I was a fool." K'Masei sighed. "I didn't know then that the Stones could get into your mind. I thought it was my own idea to leave my Stones there. Then I thought that if only *every* Ecstasy Stone in Serriolia was brought to the hall, the love would overflow to the point that it wouldn't matter who possessed the Stones—Redis or Libs or Yaocoons. Everyone would hold them in common and we'd be just one big happy clan. And maybe, just maybe, I'd be able to feel the love that everyone else was raving about."

He closed his eyes. "Only a fool believes in his own illusions. By definition, I was a fool." His eyes opened. He stared at her. "Are you sure you're real?" he asked softly. "I don't want to believe in any more of my own illusions."

"I'm real," she said impatiently. "What happened after you finished stealing Ecstasy Stones? When did you realize you were being used?"

"When people stayed and starved rather than leave the Stones. Ecstasy seems to be . . . addictive." He shivered, though he was dry and the room was warm again. "I tried to separate the Stones, to make it the way it used to be. But it was too late. The Stones had learned about illusions, or maybe they had always known. Anyway," he said softly, "they're very good. When I went to separate the Stones, they were never where they seemed to be. They wrapped illusions around me until I nearly strangled.

"When I woke up, they told me that if I tried to separate

them again, they'd kill me. They liked being together, you see.''

"They told you that? They really speak?''

"Oh, not in so many words. I just had a very clear feeling that they would kill me if I came into their physical presence again. I could be wrong. I could be a coward as well as a fool. But if I'm not wrong and I go back to the Stone room, I'm dead. That might solve my problem but it won't free Serriolia.'' He looked at her, sad and smiling at the same time. "You see, unless someone does something about the Stones, all of Serriolia will be sucked into them. All of Yhelle's best illusionists. Then we'll be as helpless as fish in a desert.''

"Are Ecstasy Stones a race of First People?'' asked Rheba. Before k'Masei could answer, Itch went to work on her eyes. So far as Itch was concerned, the answer was no.

"I don't think so,'' said k'Masei. "But I'm no expert on the Five Peoples.''

"What do the Stones want with the people they attract?''

"If I knew that, I might know how to stop them. All I know is that the Stones use people, somehow. I've seen things . . . illusions are rampant in Serriolia, more and better illusions than we created before the Ecstasy Stones were united. But such illusions should be impossible, because nearly all the illusionists in Serriolia are here, held by Ecstasy Stones. If illusionists aren't creating what I've seen, the Stones must be.''

Rheba stared at his pale, earnest face. He seemed to expect some comment from her, but she did not know what to say.

"Don't you understand?'' he said, leaning very close to her again. "Except for the Yaocoons and a few resistant members of other clans, *there is no one left in Serriolia*. Only illusions roam free. When the Yaocoons are absorbed and the city is enslaved, what next? The rest of Yhelle's city-islands? The whole planet? Maybe the whole Equality?''

"How do you know that only illusions inhabit Serriolia?'' said Rheba, concentrating on the part of his words that she thought might help her free Kirtn. She did not understand the rest of what k'Masei was saying. Nor did she care to. She wanted her Bre'n; she would have him no matter what she had to burn. "How do you know who's free and who isn't? Aren't you a prisoner here?''

"The veil window still works,'' said k'Masei, indicating

the far wall with a nod of his head. "At least it used to.
Lately all I've gotten is the Stone room."

"That's all anybody gets out of the veil," she said bitterly.

"What do you mean?"

"The veil only goes to Redis territory unless you're strong
and smart enough to wrestle another portal out of it. We
weren't." She surged to her feet with startling speed. Her
lines of power flickered raggedly. "Show me the Stone room,"
she demanded.

"Wait. I haven't told you everything."

"Then talk while you show me," she snapped. "We're
wasting time."

Itch disagreed. Rheba snarled soundlessly. K'Masei, assuming he was the focus of her anger, hastened to activate the
veil window.

"Is it two-way?" she asked, standing next to him as colors
blurred and ran over the oval face of the window. "Can the
other side see through to us?"

"No. But—" His voice died abruptly.

Frowning, he concentrated on the veil window. His hands
moved over buttons that could have been controls. Colors
twisted, slid down diagonals of white, blurred, shuddered and
did everything except make a coherent picture.

K'Masei muttered something in Yhelle. Rheba suspected
that even if Fssa had been present, he would not have translated the words. She leaned closer, eyes straining to make
something out of the jigging, incoherent colors.

"They won't let me see anything except *them*," said k'Masei
hoarsely, but he tried another combination anyway. Then,
with a final hissed phrase, he abandoned his attempt to control the veil window.

Immediately, shapes condensed out of chaos. A room came
into focus, a room huge beyond reason and crowded beyond
bearing, a room where no one moved, no one spoke, a room
where all eyes were focused on a mound of glittering crystals
resting on a mirrored pillar.

No. Not quite a mound. The piled crystals hinted at symme-
tries foreign to Fourth People, manipulations of space that
existed just beyond Rheba's ability to see or perhaps even
imagine. There were arches . . . or were they arcs of light?
There were stairs that went up forever, yet terminated below
the level of the first step. There was a tunnel that expanded
into infinity and at the same time doubled back, chasing and
catching itself through dimensions that had no names.

The piled Stones had built, and were still building, a crystal universe in miniature. Or was it merely a miniature? Could it be something much greater that she simply lacked the eyes to see?

Rheba forced herself to look away from the endless crystal fascinations of the Ecstasy Stones. Only then did she notice the sea of faces adrift in the huge room, a sea whose only shore was the glittering island that she would not look upon again.

Nebulous eddies of light connected the Stones with the faces of their worshipers. Many of the faces close to the Stones were emaciated, mouths slack, eyes dead white. Farther away, pressing inward, the faces gradually became more human, colors of flesh and eyes that were alive.

Two of the faces at the edge of the crowded room were familiar: i'sNara and f'lTiri. She looked at them for only an instant, though. Towering above them was her Bre'n, a bemused Fssireeme dangling from his neck and a Zaarain construct scintillating brilliantly across his chest.

But Kirtn was motionless, a man bound hand and soul in unspeakable ecstasy, beyond even the reach of his dancer; she would touch him but she could not.

Kirtn, where are you?

Gradually Rheba became aware of k'Masei's voice speaking softly to her, trying to call her back from whatever terrible place she had gone.

"It wasn't always like that. People used to come and go, eat and sleep, do something other than . . ."

. . . *hang suspended on the Ecstasy Stones' shimmering promises.* Her thought was like bile, like the bitter fear congealing into ice along her akhenet lines, darkness where light should be.

"Then something happened. Too many people, maybe. Or just enough. The crystals . . . changed. The biggest ones went dark. Dead, I guess."

Rheba's eyes itched in denial, but she said nothing. She could not. Like her Bre'n, she was suspended in the endless moment of discovery. Unlike her Bre'n, it was not ecstasy she savored but the agony of losing him.

"After that," continued k'Masei, "the Stones were calmer, less powerful, I guess. Then one of the Soldiers of Ecstasy came into the Stone room. When he left, he was carrying the dark stones. I don't know where he . . ."

. . . *took them to the Liberation hall, despair rather than ecstasy for enemies of the Stones.* Her eyes itched, denying her conclusions. She hardly noticed. Kirtn was filling her mind, her enthralled Bre'n like ice flowing where fire should be.

". . . doesn't really matter. Without the dark stones, Ecstasy was rampant. People would come drifting into the room, dazed with love, and they would stay until they died. I think the Stones didn't understand Fourth Person physiology. After a while they learned, though. They let people come and go, eat and drink and sleep, but not often and not enough."

Cold crept over her body, sliding through veins and lines, the antithesis of fire claiming her as she stared at skeletal faces, dulled eyes, slack mouths drooling . . . and one of them would be her Bre'n unless she . . . but what could she do, a dancer alone? What could anyone do against alien ecstasy?

Her eyes burned, tears and cold and itching alike.

"The more people who came, the greater the Stones' power. And the greater their power, the more people came," said k'Masei, letting out his breath in a long sigh. "Cycle without end, but not aimless. The Stones have a purpose. I'm sure of it. I just don't know what it is."

She hardly heard through the fear beating in her veins. And the itching . . . the itching would drive her crazy before the Stones drove Kirtn out of his mind. *Or were Itch and Ecstasy Stones one and the same?*

"When the Stones talk to you," she said hoarsely, grabbing his arm, "what does it feel like?"

"What do you mean?"

"If they don't communicate with words, how do you know what they want?"

"You just . . . know."

He frowned at the grim picture revealed by the veil window and moved as though to shut it off. Her fingers tightened with a strength that drew a sound of protest from him. She did not hear, or if she heard, she did not care. He moved away from the cutoff switch and stared at the alien woman whose eyes had become wholly gold.

"How do you know what the Stones want?" she demanded. She did not want to ask outright about Itch, but she did not have time or temperament to be coy, either. "Do you feel hot or cold when the Stones speak? Does it sound like rainbows or silence? Do your teeth or knuckles hurt? Does your scalp itch? How about the back of your eyes?"

K'Masei, who had been looking more and more puzzled, brightened at her last words. "I don't know about the rest, but when Ghosts talk to you, I'm told that it makes the back of your eyes itch."

"Ghosts?" she said hoarsely. "Ghosts? Ice and ashes! The last thing I need now is some freezing fairy tale riding my mind!" She groaned and said beneath her breath, "Itch, is it true?"

Coolness spread behind her eyes, telling her that it was true. Itch was a member of that near-mythical division of life called Fifth People; or, irreverently, Ghosts.

Shuddering, Rheba put her face in her hands and wondered what else could go wrong.

XXII

"What else do you know about Ghosts?" asked Rheba, lifting her head to confront the man who called himself k'Masei the Fool.

"Why? The Stones aren't Ghosts," he added quickly, as though to reassure her.

"The back of my eyes itch," she said succinctly.

"Oh," he said, looking at her as though she were an interesting specimen and he a collector. "Do you have a Ghost?"

"Yes," snarling, "and the damn thing itches enough to drive me crazy!"

K'Masei blinked and backed away a bit, startled by her vehemence. "It's just trying to get you to listen. After a while it will give up and go away. Ghosts can't talk to us, but they keep trying. They're harmless, though," he said soothingly. "We've had them as long as we've had Ecstasy Stones and they haven't hurt us yet. The Ghosts, I mean."

Rheba winced, hardly reassured. The Ecstasy Stones had not hurt the illusionists for eight Cycles, either. But that had changed, drastically. "What else do you know about Ghosts?" she said, not sure that she wanted to hear.

K'Masei half closed his eyes as he concentrated. His lips moved while he sorted through his memories of history and legends in a low voice. "Twelfth Cycle? Tenth? No. Ninth. We've had Stones and Ghosts since the Ninth Cycle. In fact, legend has it that they came to Yhelle together, riding in the ship of our greatest explorer. I can't remember her name. She also brought those odd ferns. Did you see the elegant ferns on Reality Street?"

Rheba remembered her delight in the plants and cursed herself as a fool. Apparently she had inhaled a Ghost as well as the fern's fey fragrance.

K'Masei smiled vaguely and made a dismissing gesture. "But that was a long, long time ago. Nobody knows anything for sure about Ghosts except that they exist and the best time to see them is during a thunderstorm.'' His smile thinned. ''We don't know much more than that about the Stones. At least, we didn't up until now. We thought they loved us.''

''You were wrong,'' said Rheba dryly.

''Yes. We believed in our own illusions,'' said k'Masei, lips twisting in a bittersweet smile. ''Epithet for a race of fools.''

She stared at the veil window, listening to k'Masei with only half her mind. Kirtn was there, unmoving, trapped. And she was here, restless, a Ghost riding the back of her eyes. Friend or enemy, both or neither—what stake did Itch have in this game being played with deadly crystal markers? *What do you want from me, Itch?*

There was no answer, of course. It was not a yes or no question.

Why me?

But that was the wrong kind of question, too.

Rheba gathered her mind as she had been taught to gather energy. When she no longer felt like laughing or crying or screaming, she asked the only question that mattered to her: *Will you help me free my Bre'n?*

Coolness came, sweet delight and . . . anticipation? Apparently Itch would be pleased to ally herself with a Fourth Person.

Rheba wanted to ask how Itch could help against the compelling perfection of the Ecstasy Stones, but it was the wrong kind of question again. No simple answer. And, perhaps, no answer at all. Itch was as alien as the zoolipt, and even more ignorant of her needs. The best she could hope for was that Itch would stay out of her way when she began to dance. That was more than the zoolipt had managed to do.

Suddenly, blue flashed across the faces of the Ecstasy Stones, riveting her attention on the veil window. Around the edges of the room, faces blurred and moved like statues sunk beneath disturbed water. Something had happened, something that stretched the hold of the Ecstasy Stones over their worshipers.

In that fluid instant Kirtn quivered, a wild animal straining at a leash. His mind was an ache in her bones, his anger and fear and rage, Bre'n rage sliding toward suicidal *rez*. Then the blue blush faded from the Stones and her Bre'n was motionless once more. She was alone with echoes of agony quivering in her marrow.

But she had learned something. Though the Ecstasy Stones held her Bre'n, he was not pleased by their embrace.

She stared at the screen with unblinking eyes, eyes where fire grew with each breath, each heartbeat, energy streaming into her, answering her unconscious demands. Pale-gold flames coursed over her akhenet lines, telling of energy doubled and redoubled and redoubled again, answering silent dancer commands.

Her hands were gold now, no flesh showing, replete with fire. Yet still she stared at the veil window. If she burned the Redis hall to the last glass tile—

She jerked her head and cried out as Itch attacked her eyes. "Shut up!" screamed Rheba. "I can't think with you clawing at my eyes!"

Itch retreated, but no coolness came. The Ghost was waiting to see where Rheba's thoughts might lead. The implication was clear. If Rheba's thoughts went where the Ghost did not want to go, the itching punishment would return.

Half-wild, Rheba looked at the beautiful hell framed by the veil window. She sensed k'Masei staring at her, wanting to know what she was going to do, but she had no more time to talk to either tyrant or fool. She had to think, and think not as a dancer but as a Senyas engineer.

She knew her own power. She could transform the Redis building to slag, and the Ecstasy Stones with it; but this was not a Loo dungeon or a Zaarain machine that stood between her and her Bre'n. Think. What would happen to the worshipers when Ecstasy shattered and its shards burned to bitter ash inside their minds? Would the Fourth People die as the Stones died . . . or would something worse happen to the captives of Ecstasy?

A cool glow of agreement suffused her eyes, telling her what she did not want to know. Something worse would happen to the captives, to Kirtn. It would have been so much easier simply to burn the hall to ash and gone. If she was not allowed to do that, what could she do?

And what of the Ghost, friend or enemy or both or neither? What could such a being do, a Fifth Person who inhabited some bizarre interface between reality and illusion, part of both and belonging to neither?

She shook her head, turning her hair into pure flames. She must do somethimg. She must do—what? What could she do?"

(listen)

If she could just—

(listen)

With an anguished sound, she looked away from the veil window where Kirtn was being cruelly slashed by ecstasy, bleeding until he died. Her hands clenched. Even through fire, she felt sharp edges of crystal cutting between her akhenet lines. She opened her hands. Caged worry stones pooled darkly between lines of fire.

Why had she taken them out of her pocket?

(free them)

The idea came to her like a whisper among raging flames. Before she had time to consider, she began taking back the fragile cage around one of the worry stones. At that instant she realized the whisper had come from behind her eyes. Akhenet lines blazed. Instantly she was wrapped in a defensive cloak of energy that was similar to the glowing cage around the worry stones.

"What are you, Itch?" she said between her teeth. "Are you one of *them* after all?"

No answer came, neither itch nor cool nor that slight sense of waiting she had come to associate with the Ghost's silent anticipation of the right question.

"Can't get to me now, can you?" asked Rheba, triumph burning as brightly as fire in her voice.

Nothing answered her except k'Masei, his voice strained, fearful. "Where did you get those?" he asked, staring at the worry stones lying darkly within her fire.

She looked at him with eyes that burned, but he hardly noticed.

"Are they the same?" he muttered, bending over her hands and peering between pale fire and akhenet lines. "They're the right sizes. They look the same except for the weird gold lines around them." Excitement rose in his voice. "Are they?" he demanded of her, touching her and burning himself and not caring. "Are they the ones the Soldiers of Ecstasy took out of here?"

He was almost shouting at her, more animated than she had ever seen him. "I got them from the ruins of the Liberation clan hall," she said.

K'Masei made a long sound of satisfaction. "They're the same." He laughed softly. "The same!"

"What do you know about them?" she demanded, holding a radiant hand beneath his nose. She was almost afraid to hope that she had finally found something she could use to free Kirtn. "Are they a weapon?"

He looked at her with wide dark eyes. Excitement drained out of him. "I don't know," he admitted. "All I know is that the Stones didn't want them around or they wouldn't have sent them away." He sighed. "Seeing them here . . . can't you understand? It's the first time something has gone wrong for the Stones."

Rheba stared at the worry stones in her hands. For a moment she had hoped she had found the answer. Now she would have to defeat the Stones in another way, one at a time, the way she had done in the burning hall outside.

But there were so many Ecstasy Stones to cage one by one, each sucking away her power. She might do it if the zoolipt did not interfere. Might. It would stop her if she burned too hard, and she would have to burn very hard to cage even a few of those Stones. The zoolipt did not understand that it was better to dance and chance fiery extinction than to live in icy eternity without her Bre'n. . . .

When she looked up, K'Masei flinched away from her eyes. She hardly noticed. "In the hall," she said, her voice too cold for a fire dancer, "there's a dead illusion holding a crystal. Bring the crystal to me."

She did not see him go. She stood watching the veil window through the vague flickering that was her defensive shield against Ghosts. Kirtn had not moved since that one tiny instant when blue raced through the room. No one had moved. Nothing looked alive but the eerie glittering crystals heaped on the mirrored table, bizarre pseudolife building an interface between universes that had never been meant to touch.

Only Rainbow seemed to move. It had become a double strand of uncanny light suspended from Kirtn's neck. Rainbow scintillated pure colors, but none so primal as the yellow blaze of Bre'n eyes. She had seen that color before, when his mind was poised on the edge of *rez*, death refined and purified into the color of rage in his eyes.

She remembered Satin, the deadly psi master who had wanted Kirtn to warm her nights . . . Satin had said that she could kill Kirtn but not control him. What if the Stones were no different? What if Kirtn tore his mind apart fighting against what *he* could not control while she stood and watched and wondered what a mad triangle of Ghost and zoolipt and fire dancer could do?

"Here," said k'Masei, thrusting his hand toward her. "Take it."

Slowly her eyes focused on him. He was more pale than

before, sweating and trembling. There was a wildness in his eyes like a trapped animal. Like Kirtn. With shaking hands, she put all but one of the worry stones into her pocket before she held out an empty palm to k'Masei. He gave her the Stone hurriedly, snatching back his hand before he burned himself on her skin.

"They didn't want me to give that Stone to you," said k'Masei, sagging against a chair whose illusions of comfort were all but transparent. Fear and triumph fought to control his face. "But I brought it anyway."

"Thank you," she said absently, staring at the two crystals in her hands. One dark, one light, both caged in dancer fire. She thought of the battle in the hall, when she had poured enormous energy into building a cage around an illusion, only to discover that she had trapped an Ecstasy Stone.

Just one small Stone. So much energy to restrain it. Just one. Unwillingly she measured the heaped brilliance shown by the veil window against the fingernail-sized crystal in her hand. So small. So much effort. There must be a better way to defeat Ecstasy Stones than one by one by one. Perhaps if she knew more about the Stones. . . .

She stood for a long moment weighing each crystal in her hand, stone and Stone, dark and white, despair and killing Ecstasy. In the end she chose the dark, for despair was no stranger to someone who had survived Deva's death.

"What are you going to do?" asked k'Masei, fear and hope squeezing his voice until barely a whisper was left.

"The Stones use energy. I'm a dancer. I use energy too." She looked up, saw that he did not understand. "I'm going to learn what makes these crystals live. I'm going to try to untangle their patterns. Energy. That's all that life is. Energy."

She saw that he still did not understand. Fssa would have; Fssireemes knew energy as well as Senyasi dancers did. But Fssa was with Kirtn, suspended in killing Ecstasy. And she was here, alone but for a man who was neither tyrant nor quite fool, merely human and very afraid. For a moment she pitied him, knowing what was about to begin.

"Run," she said quietly, speaking through lips where akhenet lines glowed like fine burning wires. "I'll give you a minute, maybe two," and she closed her eyes against the sight of Kirtn torn between *rez* and Ecstasy, for if she looked much longer at her Bre'n she would burn out of control, "but no more; I can't give you more time than that." She looked at the failed illusionist with eyes that blazed. *"Run!"*

But he still did not understand. He sat, staring at her.

"They won't let me," he said finally.

She looked at the sullen stone in her hand and thought of the Soldiers of Ecstasy and Redis illusionists who had fallen to a stone smaller than this. "When I release this you'll die," she said simply. "I'd work on the Ecstasy Stone first, but I'm afraid the others will use it against me. I'm too close to them to take that chance. Distance matters to them. They couldn't control Kirtn until he came here." She turned the full force of her dancer eyes on the slight man who sat watching her. "Run away, k'Masei. There aren't any illusions left here for you."

"Don't you understand yet?" he said. "I can't. I'm a prisoner here. Like you."

"I'm sorry," she whispered, looking away from the eyes of the man she would probably kill. She would not mean to, but he would die just the same. "I have to know what these crystals are. I don't know any other way to defeat them. I do know I can't control the worry stone without burning out every wall in the room. . . ."

He tried to smile but could not. He understood now. She would burn as she had when his wall melted. Only this time there would be no wall to protect him from her fire.

She reached for the electromagnetic generator she had used fighting the illusion and his Stone. Energy answered her touch, humming in husky resonance to her need. Apparently she had not damaged the machine when she drained it of power. She hesitated, looking again at the pale illusionist who had the bad luck to be trapped between a dancer and a Bre'n.

"Get in the pool," she said pityingly. "When I start to dance—"

He was moving before she finished. He remembered how he had first seen her, the center of a firestorm that melted steel. He landed in the bathing pool with a splash that sent water curling across the floor, wrapping cool fingers around her bare toes. She hardly noticed, for energy was pouring into her.

She began to burn.

XXIII

The stone lay like a black tear in Rheba's palm. Slowly, carefully, she thinned the intricate energy barrier that reflected the worry stone's emanations back on itself. Though she felt nothing to show that the cage was being drawn back into her akhenet lines, k'Masei begin to groan.

Darkness oozed from the stone, absorbing light so completely it seemed as if there was a hole in her hand leading to absolute emptiness. There was nothing for her to see, no lines of energy for her to unravel and understand. Baffled, she closed her eyes, straining to see the crystal with other senses. All she found was numbing despair welling up, cold to the bottom of the universe.

The stone ached in her hand, freezing her wrist, sucking light out of her akhenet lines. She took more power from the engine, sending it into overload as it met her demands. She noticed only distantly. Her mind was fastened on the needs of her intricate dance and the heat sink in her palm.

She probed with immaterial fingers of energy, trying to discover the nature of the worry stone, why it was a hole in the bottom of the universe draining away light and life, a shortcut to entropy's final triumph.

Hints of a black network, power flowing, fleeting outlines of entropy. So close, but she could not see. She needed more power, a deeper dance, her Bre'n's strong presence.

Fire leaped wildly, upsetting the balance of her dance. She drove all thought of Kirtn from her mind as she had driven all meaning from k'Masei's cries coming from beyond the flames. She could dance deeply alone. She must, or she would dance alone until the zoolipt let her die.

Power flowed into her, power drawn from a laboring engine. She sensed the limits of her energy source but could do nothing except hope that she learned what she needed before the engine melted itself into a crude metallic puddle. She had to know what the worry stone's dark lines were. She had to trace that freezing network drawing warmth downward and the stone expanding blackly, consuming everything . . . hope frozen eternally in crystalline lattices of entropy and despair, burned-out pathways of light and desire, a cold that frozen time itself into motionless.

The patterns were there, black on black, terrible and clear. She had no words to describe them, but she did not need words. She had her dance.

Energy flowed between dancer and crystal, energy that began to melt the engine's heart with too-great demands. But the dance must go on. The white building lights dimmed, then went black. Rheba noticed the change only remotely. She was the hot core of fire, needing no illumination but her own.

The worry stone glimmered darkly on her incandescent palm. The stone was uncaged, yet no longer overpowering, exuding only melancholy rather than unbridled entropy. She could cage it again with a casual thought, gold veins braiding over blackness; but she did not. It had taught her what she needed to know, the crystal's indescribable melding of mind and energy and time. There was no need to cage the crystal again, damming and geometrically increasing energies she could neither name nor control.

She looked at her left hand, where the dead illusion's Ecstasy Stone waited to be examined in a holocaust of dancer fire. The Stone was . . . changed. The veil of dancer light that had caged it was gone. The Stone's polished crystal faces beamed benignly, winking and whispering of her beauty. She was reflected in all the Stone's faces, her smile outshining their crystal brilliance.

Nowhere could she see the annihilating perfection that was the essence of Ecstasy Stones.

She put stone and Stone side by side in her hand. They were no longer absolute black and terrible light. They were simply rare crystals whose changing bright and dark faces had a symmetry that was reassuring rather than frightening.

(balanced)

Her head jerked as the whisper caressed the back of her eyelids. Her Ghost shield was gone, consumed by the far greater energies that had poured through her.

(others)

The Ghost's sigh was reluctant, but not as reluctant as

Rheba's hands digging the other worry stones out of her pocket. They were utterly black beneath their fragile cages of dancer fire; and with each second the stones would get blacker, colder, deeper, the quintessence of entropy growing in her hands.

She stared in horrified fascination. She knew that if she released the stones now even she would not be immune to their power. Yet she had no other weapon to use against the massed Ecstasy Stones.

"Where are the Stones, Itch?" she murmured. But even as she asked, she sensed a subliminal pull, a mindless calling that came through the wall where the veil window displayed the agonized face of her Bre'n. "That close?"

Coolness in her mind.

For a moment longer she hesitated, considering whether or not to build another Ghost shield.

(please)

A sense of more than one voice, a chorus of pleas asking, promising, reassuring her that she did not need a shield.

Blue rippled across the veil window like a soundless cry. Close to the mirrored table two worshipers twisted and fell forward, their boneless attitudes telling of death more clearly than any words could.

(hurry)

She did not need the spectral whispers to know that the Ecstasy Stones were forcing the issue. Even as her hair began to lift, seeking other energies to draw on, the faceted universe the Stones were building blurred. When it was clear again, it was somehow larger. And three more people lay dead.

She reached for the electromagnetic engine, but nothing answered. It was as dead as the worshipers who had lived too long at the focal point of Ecstasy.

She sensed another source of power, one she had hoped to avoid. The veil. Its energies were incompatible with dancer rhythms but very powerful. She needed that power. Without it her dance would end before it began and Kirtn would be frozen forever, caught between conflicting universes.

For a moment she gathered her dance, shaping and strengthening it for the violence to come. She could not ease up to the veil, courting its partnership in choreographed moves of advance, touch and retreat. She would have to attack, tearing the veil's power out of accustomed pathways and sucking it into her own akhenet lines in one terrible instant.

It was the most dangerous way for a dancer to deal with

asynchronous energy, but it was the only way she could evade the zoolipt's jealous guardianship of her body. Once she was in the throes of violent dance, even the zoolipt would know that stopping the dance would kill her more quickly and surely than any veil energy could.

She braced herself with feet wide apart, hands together and cupped around black stones. She knew it was pointless to try to find an easy passage to the Stones' presence. Their illusions had the force of reality; they could fool her endlessly. She would have to call down fire and walk toward them on feet that scorched glass tiles, fire dancer burning alive.

She reached for the veil's pouring energies, calling them to her in a soundless cataract of demand and response. She burst into flame, streamers of gold and orange and white writhing as she fought to shape energies she had not been meant to touch. Dissonance ripped through her, shaking her to her core.

The fragile cages on the worry stones thinned almost to nonexistence as her energies were disrupted by contact with the veil. A gout of black gushed up her arms, akhenet lines swallowed in a freezing instant, her energy and life pouring into the black stones in her hands.

Her scream could not be heard above the mindless roar of fire. Energy ripped through her and sank into the stones. She was a living conduit, a flesh-and-bone connection burning between unliving veil and unknowable crystals. For an instant she writhed with the passage of energies that would have consumed anyone but a Senyas dancer; and if it lasted more than an instant, it would kill her, too.

She grabbed on to the tatters of her control, took the incoherent energies and hammered them into cages once again. The onslaught of absolute cold stopped immediately. In a reflex as old as her earliest dancer lessons, she threw away all the energy she did not need for caging the worry stones. She had just enough control left to aim the fire at the wall in front of her.

The wall vaporized. Through the gaping, smoking hole she saw the huge room where dazed worshipers stared at a crystal universe that grew more alien and more powerful with each moment.

Lights in the building blinked and died, though she was barely touching the veil now, only a tangential hold, enough to sustain a controlled dance. But the veil was like a living thing, slippery and changing, never the same twice. It cost nearly as much energy to use the veil carefully as it gave her for her dance.

The floor beneath her feet burned with each step, leaving smoking footprints behind her. She did not notice. Nor did she notice the wisps of ash that were the remains of her clothes drifting in her wake. She only sensed a vague relief as her akhenet lines burned bright and free, unfettered by irritating cloth.

The veil calmed, but she did not trust it. Its energies were as treacherous as the Ecstasy Stones waiting ahead. She used the veil only lightly, only when and as she must.

Coolness nudged behind her eyes, urging her attention and her body forward, to the place where the Stones waited, a bright island in a pale sea of faces. With each forward step, moans came from the worshipers, a sound so low it was more like wind than voices.

She turned aside, not for the moans but because she had seen her Bre'n towering over the worshipers to her left. The instant her path turned away from the Stones, the Ghost clawed at her eyes and whispered frantic negatives.

With a twitch of akhenet lines, she pulled a Ghost shield around her and went to Kirtn. She wanted to hold him, to flow against his hard body and match him flesh for flesh; but she saw the swirl of energy between her Bre'n and the Ecstasy Stones and knew that her touch would kill him.

Dancer fire licked out, tracing the bonds between Bre'n and Ecstasy. Fire raced like a whip uncoiling and snapped around a Stone. There was a high, crystal cry, cut off as she made a familiar cage around the Stone.

The Stones struck back, sucking energy out of their worshipers like a dancer taking power from a core. But cores were not alive. They could not scream and writhe and fall forward on dead faces.

She sent out another streamer of fire, surrounding a second Stone, cutting it off from the blinding brightness of the others. The worshipers groaned as the Stones demanded more. People crumbled to the floor like sand sculptures caught by a rising tide.

Kirtn staggered, torn between two kinds of fire. His raw agony was another kind of fire raging through her, tearing apart her mind and her dance. She knew there was no time left to sift cautiously through alien energies and trap Stones one at a time. Too slow. There were too many Stones and they were getting more powerful even as she danced.

They were killing her Bre'n.

(dark stones)

She looked at the entropy pooled blackly in her hands.

(bright stones)

She looked at the blinding crystal island built on the faces of the dead, Kirtn dying—

(now)

All her choices were gone.

She hurled the caged stones toward the glittering island. She had no hope of their going that far, but they flew from her hands as though called. In the instant before the stones fell on the island, she peeled off each golden cage, loosing the compressed blackness inside.

An endless downward spiral of ice and darkness sucked at her fire, at her mind, at her life. She reached for the chaotic veil energies with every bit of her dancer power. The veil came to her in one blazing instant. She burned savagely, screaming and twisting, consumed. With the last of her control she built a bridge of fire between herself and the alien island. Then she let hell rage through her, a blazing violence of veil energies that forced a melding of black and bright crystals.

Screams beat on her, human and crystalline alike; but she held, ignoring the fire consuming her, refusing to smell her own flesh burning, terrified that the zoolipt would not understand. It was her last gamble, her hope that the zoolipt would know that if she hesitated or turned aside now, she and everyone in the room would die as her parents had died, burned to ash and gone by savage fire.

The universe narrowed to a single arch of fire shaped by dancer imperative. Flesh smoldered between akhenet lines gone wild. Blood ran molten over hot bones. Too much heat, too much power, too much fire for a lone dancer to hold, but there was no choice, no other way but violence and the hot cinders of hope.

Blackness came, an endless rolling thunder, hot not cold. Black fire consuming her. She could not hold any longer but she must hold. She must. Hold.

Let it go, dancer. It's over. Let the fire go.

Kirtn's voice in her mind was a sweet, living river pouring

through her, ecstasy that created rather than destroyed. She
let go of everything, let her dance slide like time racing
through cool fingers. . . .

He caught her as she fell to the burning floor.

XXIV

Fssa's head, incandescent with the wild energies he had absorbed, hovered over Rheba. Her akhenet lines were hot. Lightning raced over them, echoing her speeding, erratic pulse. Her hair seethed and whipped, riding the violent currents of force that still roiled throughout the room. Her half-opened eyes were molten gold. She was barely conscious, still shuddering in the grip of the flames she had called.

"Is she all right?" asked Fssa, concern bright in his whistle.

Kirtn could not answer for a moment. He was holding her, letting the dissonant energies she had gathered drain through him. His flesh convulsed with alien currents. He braced himself and endured as Bre'ns had always endured, lightning rods for dancer energies. By the time most of her excess was spent, he was both appalled and humbled by the unruly forces she had called into herself.

When her akhenet lines no longer surged violently, he let out his breath in relief. The worst was over. Yet it would never really be over, not for him. Now he had one more nightmare to break his sleep; he would never forget the moment he woke from killing Ecstasy and saw his dancer burning out of control. He had tasted her death then, ice and ashes in his mouth. Even now he was afraid to believe she was alive. No dancer had ever burned as she had burned and survived.

"Is she all right?" demanded the snake again in shrill ascending notes.

"I think so," whistled Kirtn, doubt, disbelief and hope rippling in his reply. His fingertips traced her akhenet lines. He was amazed by their number and complexity, the places new lines had ripped through hot flesh and old lines had thickened, deepened, branched and branched again, channeling fire in elegant arcs and whorls. There was no darkness in her new or old lines, no clotted convolutions where energy

183

could pool murderously. She burned clean and bright beneath his hands.

But he kept smelling scorched fur, though she was no longer hot enough to burn him.

He muttered and ran his hands over his body, wondering where he was burning. He grabbed the Fssireeme coiled beneath his chin. He snatched back his fingers and sought a more gentle hold on the snake. If it were not for the zoolipt's tireless presence, his neck would be cooked. "You're too hot, snake," said Kirtn, gingerly unwrapping Fssa and flipping him into the nearest patch of Rheba's chaotic hair.

The snake made an embarrassed sound and slipped between the hot, silky strands. Balanced on energies only he understood, he slowly brought his body down to a temperature more compatible with his Fourth People friends.

Rheba's head turned restlessly. Her eyes opened blind gold. She called Kirtn's name as she had called it when she thought he was dead, when too much fire poured through her, consuming her. Then she felt his presence surrounding her. Despite the pain tearing her body, she wrapped her arms around him and buried her face in the warm hollow between his chin and shoulder.

"I thought—I thought—" Her arms tightened convulsively. She could not finish, but they were touching, their thoughts clear in each other's mind.

She thought she had killed him with her uncontrolled fire, a dancer's most terrible nightmare come true.

"The zoolipt," she sighed, seeing his neck heal with each breath he took. And her own skin and bones, less painful every second. "It nearly killed me to take the veil all at once," she said finally, explaining the currents of pain that still washed through her. "But I was afraid the zoolipt would stop me if I did it slowly. I outsmarted the Zoolipt," she said, smiling through lips that cracked and bled.

Zoolipt laughter, smug and warm, a taste like turquoise on her tongue. Instantly her lips felt better.

Kirt smiled. "Did you? Or did you just teach it the dancer version of cooperation?"

"What's that?" she said, licking her lips with a tender, tentative tongue.

"When all else fails," he said dryly, "burn it to ash and gone."

A flash of turquoise in her mouth, then the zoolipt curled back upon itself and sank into the tasty pool of her body, leaving behind a healing benediction. She groaned at the pure pleasure of breathing painlessly. At the moment she could forgive the zoolipt anything—even its inability to cure her of Itch.

"Are you happy now, Ghost?" she murmured.

Nothing answered, neither coolness nor itching, not even the sense of anticipation behind her eyes.

"Ghost?" said Kirtn, bending even closer. Her eyes were cinnamon and gold now, more beautiful than he had ever seen them.

She laughed softly, then coughed because her throat was not yet fully healed. "My mind isn't burned out," she said in a husky voice. "Itch is a Ghost."

Kirtn's slanted eyes narrowed. "A Ghost? A Fifth People?"

"Yes."

"How do you know?"

"K'Masei told me. He's not what we thought he was." Her lips trembled. "I hope I didn't kill him when I burned my way in here."

"Tell me about your Ghost," he said quickly, pulling her mind away from the man she might or might not have killed with her dance.

"It had some connection with the Ecstasy Stones, but I don't know what it was." She frowned. "Itch isn't in my mind anymore. I must have done what it wanted." She sighed and smiled, relieved that the Ghost's histamine presence was gone. "Thank the Inmost Fire."

The sound of familiar voices approached. "I told you," said i'sNara. She leaned heavily against f'lTiri, but she was smiling. "Where there's smoke there's Rheba."

"Are you all right?" asked Rheba slowly. "There was so much fire. . . ."

F'lTiri smiled and managed an illusion of strength. "We're fine. Whatever you did to the Stones gave back most of what they had taken from us."

Rheba pulled herself up in Kirtn's lap and looked over his shoulder. Everywhere around the room, illusionists were slowly getting to their feet, helping their friends carry out the weak and the dead. There were fewer of the latter than she had expected—and more than she wanted to live with. As the Yhelles worked their way around the room, they avoided the scorched mirror table where Ecstasy Stones had been heaped in all their alien brilliance.

"I'm sorry . . ." she murmured, counting motionless bodies with lips that had been peeled raw by fire. Ecstasy had slain most of the dead illusionists, yet she feared she had killed some of them with her violent dance. She had not meant to, but they had died just the same.

I'sNara followed Rheba's glance, understanding all that the fire dancer had not said. "They aren't counting the dead," said i'sNara, pointing to the illusionists who worked to put their world back in order. "They know they had Daemen's own Luck just to survive the Stones."

Two illusionists approached, followed by several children. Kirtn recognized Ara. She was holding hands with a man who had i'sNara's lips and f'lTiri's knowing eyes. Koro. The younger children ran forward and wrapped themselves around their parents.

Rheba was relieved to see that the children were alive—gaunt, scorched and grubby, but whole. After a few moments they crowded forward eagerly to peer at the furred, muscular man and the strange woman dressed only in radiant akhenet lines.

"Careful," warned f'lTiri as his youngest reached toward Rheba's bright hair. "You'll burn yourself. She's not an illusion."

The child, a young girl, looked frankly skeptical. "Maybe. But then what's that strange-looking thing in her hair?"

Fssa's sensors wheeled at the child's blunt question. He was used to Fourth People thinking of him as ugly. It still hurt, though. He retreated behind a curtain of flying hair, concealing himself from childish curiosity.

"Is Fssa all right?" asked Rheba, searching through her hair for the shy Fssireeme. "My dance didn't hurt him?"

"He's fine," said Kirtn. "It would take a nova to light up his thick hide."

Her fingers found Fssa's supple body. "You're beautiful, snake," she whispered, knowing his vanity had been scraped by the girl's question. "Even more beautiful than Rainbow," she added when the snake still did not surface out of the depths of her hair.

Fssa's head poked out as though to check her words against Rainbow's multicolored reality. "It's gone!" whistled Fssa shrilly.

Rheba stared at Kirtn's chest. The Zaarain construct was no longer hanging around his neck. She felt Fssa begin the transformation that would let him probe the electromagnetic spectrum until he found his odd friend. She gritted her teeth in anticipation of the headache the snake's search would cause.

"Where's Rainbow?" she asked Kirtn quickly.

Kirtn looked down at his chest. Nothing decorated it but random patches of burned fur.

At the same instant, a terrible suspicion came to Kirtn and Rheba. As one, they looked toward the mirrored table where Ecstasy had held sway over a race of illusionists. The table was canted to one side. Some Stones were scattered randomly across the floor. Others had somehow managed to form a loose pile. In the center of that pile lay a double-stranded crystal necklace that flashed with every color Fourth People could see.

She shook Fssa out of his mushroom shape and pointed toward the pile of Ecstasy Stones.

"How did Rainbow get over there?" asked Fssa.

"I don't know," said Kirtn, pulling Rheba to her feet. He looked at her. "Do you want to know badly enough to have Fssa ask?"

"No," she said curtly. "Even the thought of Fssireeme-Zaarain communication makes my skull shrink."

Fssa twisted in silent protest, an act of astonishing restraint for the endlessly verbal snake.

Rheba walked up to the fallen Ecstasy Stones more confidently than Kirtn or the illusionists who followed her. Unlike them, she knew what the crystals had been and what they no longer were. Entropy had balanced ecstatic creation. The crystals were no longer dangerous—as long as the illusionists had the sense to keep them separated.

She and Kirtn stood quietly, staring down at the pile of crystals. Minor good wishes emanated from the Stones, wan reflections of former Ecstasy. For the moment, the Stones were as drained as the humans. It was not the crystals, however, that worried Rheba.

"It's bigger," she said, her voice as grim as her flattened lips.

"What?" said Kirtn.

"Rainbow is bigger. That rapacious Zaarain construct has swiped some Ecstasy Stones."

Kirtn frowned and wished he could deny it, but he could not. There was no doubt that Rainbow was bigger than it had been. There was also no doubt where the increase had come from.

"That's the end," said Rheba flatly. "It might have been a Zaarain library once, but all that's left of it is a thief and ripping headaches for me. Rainbow doesn't go back on board the *Devalon*."

Fssa made a distressed sound. He whistled urgently from his hiding place in her hair. "A few Ecstasy Stones won't hurt you. Rainbow has them fully tuned and integrated into itself. Nothing bad will happen. You only need to worry if you get too many Ecstasy Stones together. If we take some away, we're doing the Yhelles a favor."

Before she could speak, more arguments tumbled out of the Fssireeme's many-mouthed body. "Rainbow doesn't mean to hurt you. It's just rebuilding itself, trying to remember its past. It gets so lonely with no one to talk to. I'm the only one who understands it. Please, dancer, please . . .?"

Fssa's chorus of emotion-drenched Bre'n whistles defeated her. She groaned and gave in as she always had given in to the snake's musical pleas for his odd friend. At least the silly Fssireeme had not fallen in love with a histamine Ghost.

She snatched up Rainbow and yanked it over Kirtn's head. With small, musical sounds, the Zaarain construct settled itself on Kirtn's chest.

"What about the rest of them?" said Kirtn, looking distrustfully at the remaining Stones. "They're exhausted now, but—"

"Exactly," said a voice from behind them.

Rheba spun around. "K'Masei! You're alive!"

The illusionist bowed wryly. "Scorched, blistered and frightened out of the few illusions I had left, but alive—thanks to your advice and the inexhaustible Redis plumbing." His smile faded as he looked down at the Ecstasy Stones glowing with innocent goodwill. "I'm dividing them into six piles, one for each island city. Serriolia's Stones will be divided equally among the surviving clans."

He waited, but no one disagreed. He bent over and began methodically sorting Stones. One by one, other illusionists came to help.

Rheba watched for a moment, then turned away. She had seen enough Ecstasy Stones for this or any other Cycle. Besides, she suspected that where there were Stones, there were Ghosts. She did not want to stand around and accidentally inhale one of the itchy devils.

She looked around quickly but saw nothing more she could

do. The Ecstasy Stones were quiescent. The illusionists were home again, as safe as anyone in Serriolia. At the spaceport the *Devalon* waited, bulging with hopeful slaves. It was time to hold another lottery, redeem another promise, deliver more former slaves to their unique and uncertain futures .

And it was time to get on with her own future, time to find other survivors of Deva, time to find a new planet where Bre'ns and Senyasi could build a new life from the ashes of the old. She looked at the tall man beside her. Her fingertips savored the unique textures of his arm.

"Ready?" she asked softly.

He bent over and drank his dancer's sweet-hot fire. "Yes."

As they turned to leave, f'lTiri approached. I'sNara clung to his arm. Their youngest children trailed behind. He bowed formally to her and covered himself with his most obsequious illusion.

"We would like to go with you. Our clan is dead. There's nothing but illusions for us in Serriolia now. And," f'lTiri smiled faintly, "as you might have noticed, we were born with more than our share of illusions."

Surprise flickered in Rheba's akhenet lines.

"If there isn't enough room for all of us," said i'sNara quickly, "we'll wait until the lottery brings you back this way." She watched Rheba intently, trying but failing to conceal her eagerness beneath an illusion of indifference.

Rheba looked at the three children. All wore the same expression of burnished innocence. She tried to imagine what life on board the *Devalon* would be like with three little illusionists popping in and out of reality. She sighed and smiled crookedly. At least her Ghost no longer haunted her. "I already have a zoolipt, a Zaarain construct and a Fssireeme—who am I to choke on three small illusions?"

"Welcome home," said Kirtn, smiling at the Yhelles. Then he added with a poet's pragmatism, "Where we're going, a few illusions might come in handy."

"Where are we going?" asked the smallest illusion.

"I don't know," admitted the Bre'n.

"Then getting there will be very difficult."

Rheba leaned against Kirtn and laughed weakly. Getting there was never the problem for dancer and Bre'n. Getting out alive was.

"Doesn't anybody know where we're going?" asked the child plaintively.

"Nobody knows," began Rheba, then groaned and rubbed her eyes.

"What's wrong?" asked Kirtn, pulling her close to him.

"My Ghost is back. It knows where we're going."

"Wonder if we'll be safe there," whistled the Bre'n, a sardonic twist to the notes.

Rheba's eyes itched furiously, telling her more than she wanted to know.

ANN MAXWELL lives in Southern California with her husband, Evan, and their two children. She is the author of a number of excellent science fiction novels and has coauthored many books with her husband on subjects ranging from historical fiction to thrillers to nonfiction. Some of her earlier works have been recommended for the Nebula Award and nominated for the TABA Award. Also available in Signet editions are Ann's fine science fiction novels, *The Jaws of Menx*, *Fire Dancer*, and *Dancer's Luck*.

Ø

Science Fiction from SIGNET

(0451)

*Prices slightly higher in Canada.